High Stakes

Books by John McEvoy

The Jack Doyle Mysteries
Riders Down
Close Call
The Significant Seven
Photo Finish
High Stakes

High Stakes

A Jack Doyle Mystery

John McEvoy

Poisoned Pen Press

Copyright © 2014 by John McEvoy

First Edition 2014

10 9 8 7 6 5 4 3 2 1

Library of Congress Catalog Card Number: 2014938595

ISBN: 9781464202742   Hardcover
       9781464202766   Trade Paperback

Poisoned Pen Press
6962 E. First Ave., Ste. 103
Scottsdale, AZ 85251
www.poisonedpenpress.com
info@poisonedpenpress.com

Printed in the United States of America

Like all the others before,
this is dedicated to my family.

Acknowledgments

My thanks to faithful sources of encouragement Frier C. McCollister, Kirk Borland, the Tilton family, Joe Hoy, and Gwen Macsai; to William M. Sheridan and Eoin Purcell for valuable advice; and to editor Barbara Peters and the dedicated staff at Poisoned Pen Press for their continued expertise.

"I have an agreement with Father Time.
I don't mess with him, and he don't mess with me."
—Bernard Hopkins, age 49,
world light-heavyweight boxing champion

"Life's not the breaths you take but the moments
that take your breath away."
—George Strait

"Something, like nothing, happens anywhere."
—Phillip Larkin

Chapter One

The March half-moon played hide-and-seek behind a screen of huge clouds that scudded across the midnight sky. After moving silently up the concrete walkway to the Large Animal Barn at Croft College, she bent down a few feet behind the dark blue campus police car and peered through its rear window. A young officer was in the driver's seat, hat tilted over his eyes and his earplugs in as he dozed to the low volume country western song twanging out of his iPad mini.

At the back entrance to the long, white barn she crouched at the door, quickly used her tension wrench and steel pick on the simple lock, and slid inside the long, dimly lit, one-story wooden building. The corridor ran between stalls housing a couple of Black Angus heifers and a Holstein cow. She softly walked forward. Her masked face momentarily split in a smile as she inhaled the familiar smell of hay and horse.

The lock had been easier to pick than Secretariat in a Fantasy League Race. That was a relief, she thought, as she brushed a trickle of sweat from her forehead, took a deep breath. No noise from the wide metal door either opening or closing, very little from the dark bay mare looking out from her stall at the north end of the barn. So far, so good. The inquisitive mare twitched her ears in a tentative greeting as the dark-clad figure slowly approached. She watched the visitor with luminous brown eyes above her long face with its large crooked white star. Her racetrack days, when regular attention was paid her by attentive humans, were long behind her.

As her soft muzzle was being stroked, the mare heard a gentle voice saying, "You've been probed, prodded, perhaps bred to a lesser representative of your species. You are not an object of well-earned affection, but of experimentation. No more, babe, no more."

The needle sank deep into the broad bay neck delivering the large dose of phenobarbital. The mare twisted her head away but quickly stopped as the drug took effect. With a shudder, she collapsed on the stall's floor.

The woman put the needle and syringe into her right jacket pocket. From the left one, she took out a printed card and quickly entered the stall. She placed the white placard on the dead horse's neck. In large dark letters, it read:

NO MORE EXPLOITATION OF
THIS ONE OF GOD'S CREATURES

It was the second time she had left such a message. After a final pat on the mare's neck, the woman exited the stall and moved rapidly, silently, to the south barn door and slipped out into the dark night. The heifers and the Holstein swiveled their heads to watch her go.

Chapter Two

Jack Doyle slid into the driver's seat of his gray Accord, feeling, as his good friend Moe Kellman would put it, "top notch." He turned on his windshield wipers as he pulled out of the Fit City Health Club parking lot in Chicago's Loop and drove up Dearborn Street. Not even this wet, chilly, dreary, unpleasant early spring morning could dim his mood as he looked forward to his breakfast meeting at Petros' Restaurant, two blocks from his north side condo.

He had joined Kellman, Chicago's reputed furrier-to-the-Mob, at Fit City at six thirty for their regular workout in the small boxing room with its ring, light and heavy bags, free weights, and space for jumping rope. The two had met and bonded there several years before, both eschewing the other exercise areas of what they considered this yuppie-infested club. Their friendship during the previous two years had featured ownership of a talented colt named Plotkin. This fifty thousand-dollar purchase had wound up winning more than three hundred thousand dollars on the track and was now churning out more profits for the pair. Plotkin was serving his first season as a popular young stallion, with a stud fee of ten thousand dollars, and a book of fifty mares he would be bred to this spring.

For Doyle, these workouts gave him a chance to replicate old moves he'd employed as an amateur boxer twenty-five years earlier when, at age eighteen, he'd won a Golden Gloves title at one hundred sixty pounds. The diminutive, seventy-something Kellman, as a boy growing up on Chicago's tough West Side, had fared well in many a fracas. His brief amateur career as a lightweight boxer had been aborted by service with the U.S. Marine Corps during the Korean War.

After Doyle's first set of seventy-five push-ups and then three minutes of rapid jump-roping, and Kellman's fifty sit-ups and push-ups, they both paused and the little man said, "What do you hear from the breeding farm? How's Plotkin doing?"

Doyle took a towel to his head of sandy-colored hair now darkened with sweat. "I called the farm manager, nice guy named Paul Mann, yesterday afternoon. He said Plotkin has 'serviced' eighteen mares so far. That's what they call it in their business, 'serviced.' He's got another thirty-two scheduled in the next few weeks. If a mare doesn't get pregnant on the first try, she gets another attempt free of charge. So far, that hasn't been necessary, Mann told me."

"Great news," Moe said, picking up his jump rope and placing it on the bench beside him.

"Absolutely. I went out to the farm, Hill and Dale, one morning last week. Watched Plotkin being bred to a couple of mares. I must say that our stud approached his assignment with considerable enthusiasm. Probably has a libido much like that of his younger owner, if I may say so myself."

"You just did," Moe laughed.

"Mann at Hill and Dale gave me a little tutorial on breeding horses and famous breeders. One of the latter group, he said, was an Italian named Federico Tesio. He bred a bunch of good runners. According to Mann, Tesio's famous quote about his success was that he had 'learned to listen to the stars and talk to the horses.'"

Moe reached for a towel and began drying himself off. "Yeah? Well, I remember reading somewhere that breeding thoroughbreds is like playing chess with nature."

As he pulled on his gloves before heading for the heavy bag, Doyle noticed Moe taking a pair of cross-trainers out of his gym bag and pulling the crumpled paper from within them.

"New kicks today, Moesy?"

"Right." Kellman held one of the shoes up to his face. "Which is the best smell in the world? Newly mown grass? The inside of a new car? Or brand new shoes?"

Doyle grinned. "I'd vote for the smell of a new woman."

"Good luck to you there," Kellman replied before they began their forty-five minute workout routines.

Doyle's decision to make this post-workout breakfast appointment resulted from a phone call he'd received the previous evening. Picking up his cell at the programmed sound of the first bars of jazz standard "Take the A Train," Doyle heard a gruff voice he recognized say, "This is Damon Tirabassi. I presume you haven't forgotten me, Jack."

"I've tried mightily," Doyle said, "but to no avail. What's on your bureaucratic mind? I guess it's not worth asking how you got my unlisted cell number." Doyle had first met Tirabassi and his FBI agent partner, Karen Engel, six years earlier when he had aided them in bringing to justice a sadistic media tycoon who was killing his own thoroughbred stallions for their insurance values.

"Don't bother about how we got your phone number. I'm calling because we could use your help, Jack. Karen and I want to meet with you."

"Help for what? Don't tell me that stallion killer wangled an early parole."

Tirabassi said, "No, no. What we're dealing with now is another horse killer, or horse killers."

"You're jivin' me!"

"If only," Tirabassi said. "How about meeting at that greasy spoon in your neighborhood that you like? Tomorrow at nine?"

"Agreed. Breakfast will be on you."

Chapter Three

Doyle slid the Accord into his slot in the basement garage of his condo building, locked it, and briskly walked the four blocks to Petros' Restaurant, determined, as usual, to be on time. The FBI agents always were.

Petros', which Doyle had frequented for several years, was one of the numerous Greek-owned Chicago restaurants that provided decent food at reasonable prices. Owner Petros, a voluble immigrant from an Athens slum, had long been under the impression that he looked very much like the late Telly Savalas and loved to be referred to by the actor's first name. Doyle never obliged him.

"Mornin', Smelly," Doyle said as he walked past the cash register Petros was manning. Petros, using a wet thumb as he counted a wad of paper currency, looked up and barked, "Have a seat, Jeck. We'll start your breakfast. Raw bacon, eggs under hard, hash blacks, and burnt toast, eh?" He smiled widely under his bushy mustache.

Doyle paused. "Are you using growth hormone salve on that item under your big ugly nose? That 'stache looks like it could strain stew, much less soup. And, yeah, give me the usual," Doyle said, walking to the back booth of the long room. He saw Karen Engel smile at him before she took a bite of toasted bagel. Her colleague, Damon Tirabassi, put down his coffee cup and nodded. "Thanks for coming, Jack," Karen said.

Doyle looked at her appreciatively. "You never change, Karen," he said to this tall, attractive woman who, now in her late thirties, retained the fresh look and athletic physique of the varsity volleyball captain she had been at the University of Wisconsin-Madison. "Damon," Jack added, "you're starting to show a little wear and tear, if I do say so."

The middle-aged Tirabassi's once-black head of hair had noticeably grayed as it simultaneously thinned. His bright white shirt showed the start of a midriff bulge over his belt. He winced as Doyle continued, "Hey, no offense, Damon. You know my middle name is candor."

"I thought it was Smartass," Tirabassi growled.

"Is that Bureauspeak now?" Doyle asked. "Let's get down to business here, folks. What's this about more horse killings"?

Tirabassi took the lead after reaching into his suit coat pocket for a well-worn notebook. "March eighteenth this year was the second one we've been assigned to investigate. The first was in February at the University of Racine veterinary school in southeastern Wisconsin. The recent one was at another Midwest vet school, this one at Croft College in south central Illinois. A twelve-year-old thoroughbred mare found dead in its stall. An autopsy..."

"You mean necropsy," Karen politely interjected. "That's an autopsy for horses."

"Yes, the necropsy determined the Croft College cause of death was a massive dose of phenobarbitol. Same as with the first one at Racine."

Doyle leaned forward. "What the hell? Why would somebody knock off an old mare living at a college?"

Karen opened her briefcase and extracted a five-by-eight note card. She waited until waitress Darla refilled Doyle's coffee cup before handing it across the table. In large, bold face, printed letters, it read:

NO MORE EXPLOITATION FOR
THIS ONE OF GOD'S CREATURES

"This was it? No signature? Nobody taking credit? Not some religious nut?" Doyle said.

"Look at the back of the card," Damon said. "We don't have any idea what it means. Could be from some deranged horse-hater. Or somebody who doesn't like horses used for testing. You know, a so-called ethical humanist. Or humane ethicist. Whatever."

Doyle saw one line of type:

RIP FROM ALWD

"Rest in peace from who? What's ALWD?"

"It is some previously little-known, evidently very radical imitator of People for the Ethical Treatment of Animals. PETA for short. That organization, a self-described 'animal rights advocate,' claims to have more than three million members and supporters around the world. ALWD stands for Animal Life With Dignity.

"All we know about this outfit," Tirabassi continued, "are the cards, identical to this one, that were attached to the two horses that were killed this way. We questioned the national president of this ALWD, a man named Randolph Stumph. Lives in Urbana, Illinois. He wouldn't say how many people belonged to ALWD. And he swears he knows nothing about any horse killings. All Stumph would tell us is that ALWD 'campaigns vigorously for the abolition of all animal experiments.'"

Doyle signaled Darla for a coffee refill. "I'm not sure I understand why these horses were sent to college."

Karen said, "Racine and Croft both have research centers dealing with horses. They study breeding, reproduction, parasite problems, foal diseases, all kinds of equine issues. Parasites have become a particular concern recently, they tell us. So, people at these vet schools work to develop preventive measures. Like vaccines to combat infectious diseases. Or new diagnostic tests."

"Retired horses," Damon said, "are donated to the vet schools for these research purposes. The donors are assured their horses will get absolutely top, humane, painless care. But I guess these ALWD kooks don't believe that to be the case."

"How was anybody able to get to these horses to kill them?"

"Jack, university or college vet school barns have not been on high security alert. Until now," Damon said. "Whoever, if it is just one person, got into the University of Racine building by opening a side window and climbing through. This last one, down at Croft College, entrance was gained by picking the lock on the front door. With, evidently, a so-called security guard snoozing in his car only a few yards away," Damon said disgustedly. "Both of these killings came late at night or in early morning, and the horses killed were retired thoroughbred runners. ALWD's Stumph explained that it was 'perhaps some overzealous activist.' How I hate that word! Along with gadfly, which also means loudmouth," Damon added.

Doyle gave Tirabassi a long look. "Yeah, I know you FBI people have a hard-on for activists. The Occupy protestors. Dr. King. Hell, probably Paul Revere, if you would have had the chance. All enemies of treasured complacency."

"Jack, we didn't come here to argue with you or your views," Karen said sharply.

"It wouldn't be any argument you'd win," Doyle shot back. He drained his coffee cup, took a deep breath. "As to the matter at hand, is there any money involved in these killings? Like warnings to pay for protection against this shit?"

"Nothing," Karen said. "These killings seem to be the work of some fanatic, some animal-lover who evidently opposes the horses being used for any experimental purposes, no matter how benign and well-monitored the treatments."

"Lover of animals," Doyle corrected. "The only animal-lover can be another animal. Unless, of course, you count some shepherds of sheep flocks." Darla arrived with the check. Doyle, with a practiced motion, slid it under Tirabassi's coffee cup. "You ever hear of an attorney named Art Engehardt?" Doyle said. "A friend of mine?"

Karen smiled. "I think so. He represents a lot of racetrack people, right?"

"Correct. But years ago, right after he got out of law school, he worked as a prosecutor for a county down in southern Illinois farm country. One of his first cases involved a sheep herder who had been caught having intercourse with a female member of his flock. A Humane Society member had provided a photograph of this bestial incident. It showed the ewe, or whatever they call them, turning her head around and licking the hand of the herder. Art went into court thinking he had slam-dunk conviction. That changed when the jury had seen the photo and Art overheard one of the elderly bib-overall-wearing jurors say to another, 'You know, Seth, some of 'em will do that.'"

Tirabassi glowered. "Can we get down to business here? Are you going to take this situation seriously or not?"

"Why the hell should I? I don't owe you people anything. And why, may I ask, is this on the Bureau's front burner? Haven't you got enough to busy yourself with dopers, illegals, terrorists, Occupiers, etcetera?"

The agents exchanged a glance. Then Karen said, "I'm almost embarrassed to tell you this, Jack. But our Chicago supervisor is a longtime, uh, admirer of horses. He was a show ring competitor in his youth. He's got two daughters who are currently avid equestrians. Believe me, he's fired up and on this case."

Doyle drained his coffee cup. "Why me?"

"Frankly," Tirabassi replied, "we don't have the time or manpower to devote to this matter. Even if we did have them, we don't have an agent with the background to deal with horse problems. *That's* where you come into it. You know racing, the people in it, you know and like horses. Your success with Plotkin proves that. And I understand you're currently not wanting for money. Besides, you're not busy now, are you?"

"I'm between assignments," Doyle said. He hadn't worked since his client, young jockey Mickey Sheehan, had returned to her native Ireland the previous year after her very successful campaign at Heartland Downs Racetrack outside Chicago. As her agent, Doyle had done very well financially with his twenty percent of her considerable earnings gleaned aboard horses he had selected for her to ride. Now, the profits from Plotkin's stud career were being added to an investment account the size of which Doyle had never in his dreams envisaged.

A few years earlier, Kellman had advised Doyle to turn his investment portfolio over to a man named Marcus Dehnert. Moe, like so many clever Chicagoans, always had "a guy," a go-to specialist in important fields of endeavor. His "guy" for financial advice was Dehnert. "He's called 'The Man With the Golden Grasp,'" Kellman had said. "He's made money for me for years, Jack. Last year he bought gold for me at eight hundred dollars an ounce and sold it at twelve hundred. Yeah, it went up after that. But Marcus goes along with Bernard Baruch's theory. Baruch, a famous financier years ago. You ever hear of him?"

"Before my time."

"Baruch was huge. Advisor to presidents, so on. He said, 'Nobody ever went broke taking a profit.' Sound advice, believe me."

Doyle sat back in the booth. "Damon, you say you think I'm not 'wanting for money?' Has somebody at the IRS filled you in?"

"Where we got our information doesn't matter."

"It matters to me," Doyle said. "Although I know there's nothing I can do about it. As for my situation, yeah, I've got a nice cushion. I'm not threatening to join the One Percenters. But I'm in good shape. I am not like some poor bastards I know who probably wake up every morning with creditors next to their beds, testing their breaths with a hand mirror to make sure they're still alive. But I don't see how I can help you deal with these horse killings."

Karen said, "With all your contacts in racing, you could start asking around. Are people aware of what's going on? If they are, I'm sure they're concerned. Do any of them have an idea about who could be doing this? Look, Jack, we're desperate for any information you could garner, *any* possible leads. This killing campaign, and it looks just like that, a campaign, has got to stop."

Chapter Four

Karen winced at the sound emanating from Damon's breast pocket. Doyle said, "What the hell is that? Sounded like a baby burping."

Tirabassi took his cell phone out of his sport coat jacket pocket. Frowning, he said, "There's something wrong with this ringing thing." He left the booth and walked outside to start his conversation. When he returned minutes later, he said to Karen, "You-know-who. The Boss. Wanted to see how we were coming along here."

Karen said, "That will give you an idea, Jack, how seriously our supervisor is taking this case. He calls one of us three or four times a day for a progress report."

Doyle couldn't resist. "If I was him, I'd be concerned, too. Your organization's record of dealing with horse racing isn't exactly stellar."

Tirabassi banged his coffee cup down on the table. "What's that supposed to mean? Didn't we nail Harvey Rexroth? That s.o.b. who was killing his own stallions to collect insurance claims?"

"Well, yeah. But remember, Damon, you managed that *primarily* as a result of my excellent, undercover efforts working the case on your behalf. Admit it. Without me, who knows how long Rexroth would have continued on his illegal way?"

Karen said, "Oh, come on, Jack. It wasn't a question of you single-handedly saving the day. As much as you'd like to think so. Pass the cream, would you please?" she said with a smile.

Her partner glared at Jack. "Don't forget that the Bureau helped convict that big-time race-fixer on the East Coast a few years back."

"Yeah, a *lot* of years back," Doyle shot back. "And let's not forget one of the Bureau's comic racetrack capers." He paused to retrieve the salt shaker and apply a liberal portion to what remained of his eggs. "I refer, of course, to the famous FBI Owner Case."

The agents glanced at each other, obviously puzzled. Damon barked, "What the hell are you talking about?"

Doyle kept them waiting while he chewed his last piece of bacon. After a sip of his coffee, he said, "I guess they haven't featured this case in *Highlights of FBI History*. It happened at a little upstate New York track. Two of your really enterprising agents, suspecting that races were being fixed, got the okay to buy and run a horse of their own at the track in question. They purchased an inexpensive gelding, using a go-between to handle the deal. This allowed these two go-getters easy access to the backstretch. Posing as owners, they said they were area used-car dealers who had 'always wanted to own a racehorse.' Naturally, they used fake names. By hanging around the track they evidently hoped to gain information enabling them to break what some informant had claimed was a race fixing ring. They carried out this ruse for almost two months. Started 'their' horse four or five times. You want more coffee?" He paused to signal Darla that he did.

Damon leaned forward. "Get to the damn point, Jack."

"Calm down, my man," Doyle said. "I'll give you the good news first. While that was going on, the horse they acquired, The Zackster, or some name like that, actually won a race and placed in two others. So, he paid for his purchase price and his training bills. As a result, this unique exercise of law enforcement didn't cost the U.S. taxpayer anything."

"Glad to hear that," Karen smiled. Damon maintained his frown, saying, "I know there's a kicker to this story."

Doyle said, "Of course there is. While thriving in the horse ownership business, your agents failed to discover any race-fixing.

Anything illegal. Didn't unearth any suspected criminal action. Just wasted their damn time.

"Maybe the informant had pulled their legs. Or maybe your guys were inept. The irony of this situation is the fact that, by using phony names on their state racing licenses, they violated the law that prohibits hidden ownership. Which happens to be a felony. But I guess that falls into the means-justify-the-ends theory you folks ascribe to, right?"

"All right, Jack, you've had your fun with us," Damon said. "Bottom line time here. Are you going to help us or not?"

Doyle slid out of the booth and got to his feet. "Let me think about this. I'll call you in a day or two. You still have the same cell phone numbers?" They nodded yes.

Chapter Five

A surge of unseasonably warm weather had turned this part of early spring in Chicago into a bonanza of unusual but very welcome beauty. On his route from his condo to Heartland Downs Racetrack, Doyle drove past tentatively budding trees, early green grass, and beds of small bright tulips waving bravely in the strong breeze from the west. "No global warming, eh?" he said to himself. "And I guess the Flat Earth Society must still be holding meetings."

Doyle parked his Accord in the lot outside the track kitchen. Walking through the Heartland Downs barn area, he was greeted vocally or with a nod by almost everyone he encountered: grooms, hot walkers, trainers, exercise riders, jockeys, jockeys' agents, veterinarians. This was routine at racetracks, Doyle had learned, but certainly not among the frequently dour-looking citizens he passed on his city runs and walks, the majority of them earplug-equipped or talking on cell phones. As a kid, Doyle had been trained by his parents to always say hello to people he met on the street, a practice he'd carried forward, only to be ignored or rebuffed most of the time in adulthood. The few urban exceptions he knew were people walking their dogs.

Maybe the civility he admired was a product of racetrackers being so dependent on each other for work in their various capacities. Things could change in a hurry, a stable suddenly taken out of business by a disgruntled owner, its employees becoming flotsam on the backstretch job market. Jobs were lost, and sought. Options had to be kept open. Maybe that was the grease that morphed into politeness. Or, maybe these folks were just happier about where they were, what they were doing in life.

Doyle was looking for his friend Ingrid McGuire, the bright, young, and very pretty veterinarian he'd met when he was working as a jockey's agent. Ingrid had developed a large racetrack practice, one of the features of which was her striking ability to communicate with horses via what was, for Doyle, a mysterious sort of telepathy. Yet he knew it worked, had observed the results, her equine patients silently imparting to Ingrid what proved to be their wants, dislikes, and, sometimes, fears. The numerous naysayers, including Jack, who had initially scoffed at Ingrid's claims, had for the most part become converts. Having watched her in action, Doyle was impressed by her very obvious respect and affection for her four-footed clients. "They're all individuals, Jack," she had emphasized to him. "They are remarkable creatures to be treasured."

Rounding the north corner of trainer Ralph Tenuta's barn, he saw Ingrid in Stall 1, running what looked to him like some sort of power tool over the long back and hind quarters of a black gelding whose nameplate read Pick the Packers. Above the noise of the machine Ingrid said, "Hey there, Jack Doyle. Good morning." She briefly shut off the machine, took out a handkerchief and wiped the perspiration from her tanned face. Her long blond ponytail extended through the back of the ball cap she was wearing with its "Save Old Friends" logo, the motto of a national organization dedicated to preventing retired racehorses from being sent to slaughterhouses and therefore winding up on foreign dinner tables. Then she resumed sliding the noisy tool back and forth as the gelding's whole body gently vibrated.

"Morning, Jack," said Tenuta from the doorway of his nearby office. "You waiting to talk to Ingrid?"

"Yes. Good to see you Ralph. What the hell is she doing to that horse with that machine?"

Tenuta laughed. "Another step forward in Ingrid's horse helping. Look at old Pick the Packers. Loves it. Last week, Ingrid went through this routine with him and he went to sleep right afterwards. Was snoring like a human. Next day, he won here, running the best race of his life."

They watched as Ingrid turned off the machine and packed it in a large leather carrying case. She gave Pick the Packers a final pat on his neck and came out of the stall. "I've got one more of Ralph's horses to work on, Jack. Want to come with me?"

"Sure." He and Tenuta followed her down the shed row to where a red chestnut filly looked at them expectantly. As Ingrid opened the stall door, the filly whinnied a welcome. Tenuta said, "She'll be doing some of her chiropractic work on this one. Name is Mady Martin. Ingrid has helped her a lot."

Ingrid proceeded to pick up, bend, then rock back and forth each of Mady Martin's legs before fully extending the left fore and swinging it side to side. "So, Jack," she said as she worked, "what's up?"

"Something maybe you can help me with," Doyle said. "Ingrid, you've heard about those horses being secretly killed at university vet schools?"

She turned her attention to Mady Martin's left fore, yanking it backwards and stretching it, then did the same thing to the right fore. "Yes, I heard about that. Weird, huh?" Ingrid began to crank the appreciative filly's neck from side to side, grunting softly with that exertion. "What's your interest in these killings, Jack?"

"I've been asked to try and find whoever is responsible by some people I know. Couple of FBI agents. These are criminal acts they're dealing with. Have you heard any scuttlebutt about who might be doing this? I know you stay in contact with a lot of your fellow vets."

Ingrid nodded as she prepared to finish Mady Martin's treatment. "Naturally, there's been some talk about it. But nobody I know seems to know what's going on. They figure it's some nutcase from some loony animal rights outfit. Who knows?"

Tenuta poked Jack in the arm. "Watch this windup she'll do. I've never seen anything like it."

Ingrid plucked a carrot out of her carrying bag and waved it in front of Mady Martin's eager nose. Leaning against the filly's side, she held the carrot to the back of her head. Mady Martin craned her neck back to nearly touch the carrot. Ingrid did the same thing on the horse's other side as the filly nickered impatiently. Then Ingrid held the carrot under the horse's belly. This stretching exercise concluded with Ingrid feeding Mady Martin that carrot plus two others.

As Ingrid hooked the stall webbing shut behind her, Tenuta said, "Couple of guys were talking in the track kitchen this morning about the horse killings you mentioned. Buck Norman brought up the name of that kook that used to date Pat Caldwell. Esther Ness. I worked for her for about ten minutes. Among other things, she was a shouter for what she called 'horses rights.' Didn't you know her, Ingrid?"

Ingrid shrugged. "Just to say 'hi' to. I used to see her around."

Doyle said, "Who is Pat Caldwell?"

"He's the fella that's the chart caller here for *Racing Daily.* Pretty colorful guy," Tenuta answered. "But he does a great job, right Ingrid?"

Ingrid said, "As far as I know he does. You watch the races and read his descriptions of them more than I do." She looked at her watch. "Gotta hustle on, guys. Buck Norman's got a new two-year-old filly in his barn that won't settle down. Wants me to find out what the troubled youngster is thinking. If I hear anything about the horse killings, I'll give you a call, Jack."

The men watched appreciatively as the tall, assured, attractive woman walked toward her truck. "She going out with anybody now?" Doyle said.

"I hear she's been dating Bobby Bork, that assistant racing secretary here. What," Tenuta smiled, "you interested?"

"Naw. Just curious. We're just friends. I know Ingrid had a tough stretch of life with that alcoholic vet partner of hers before he died driving into a moving train last year. I just felt sorry for her, the trouble he'd been giving her."

Tenuta said, "Same with me. She deserved better than that bastard."

They walked up the shed row. Tenuta paused to pat an inquisitive two-year-old colt named Mr. Rhinelander who had poked his head out above his stall webbing. "This one's going to make his first start pretty soon, Jack. I think he's going to be damn good."

Doyle didn't answer immediately. He was thinking about what Tenuta had just said about Ingrid McGuire's new romantic interest. "This Bobby Bork," he said disgustedly, "I had a lot of dealing with him when I was entering your horses for you a couple of years ago. You know what they call him over at the racing secretary's office? 'BM Bork.' Which stands for Big Mouth. He's evidently a smart enough guy, but he's not too high up on anyone's list of favorite people. Especially my list.

"Weird, isn't it," Doyle continued, "that Ingrid would link up with another asshole following in the sorry wake of the late vet? I mean, this is an intelligent, likeable woman. Hard to figure that she should be so stupid on the social side of her life."

At Tenuta's office door, Doyle said, "You hear anything about these horse killings, you'll let me know, right?"

"Sure. You're in a kind of a hurry on this, aren't you Jack?"

"Why wouldn't I be? It's a damn shame what's been going on."

Chapter Six

Minutes after Doyle had tipped the Fab Rib Guys delivery man and deposited the brown bag with its aromatically enticing contents on his kitchen table, his phone rang.

"Jack, sorry to call this late," said Karen Engel. "But we were wondering if you'd discovered anything about those deaths?"

"By 'we' you mean dour Damon and your demanding boss, right?"

"Please, Jack. Cut the sarcasm for a change. I wouldn't be bothering you like this if it wasn't a pressing matter."

Doyle started to open the large Styrofoam container. He looked down appreciatively at the sauce-dripping slab of baby back ribs that was surrounded by a bag of French fries and containers of collard greens and sweet potato pie. He relented.

"Karen, nothing's come up yet. I only went out to the track today to start inquiring." He paused to extract a couple of fries from their package. "Tell you what I'll do. I'll set up a meeting with Ingrid McGuire. You remember her?"

Karen said, "Sure. Your pal the horse whisperer."

"Horse communicator," he corrected. "I'll phone her in a few minutes. After I have my dinner. Okay?"

"We'd all appreciate that, Jack."

He turned on jazz station WDCB to hear announcer Barry Winograd introduce "the title cut from the Kelly Brand Quintet's great new CD 'Afternoon in June.'" Doyle set about relishing two of his favorite things in life, great food and great music.

>>>

Two mornings later, shortly before noon, Doyle waited for Ingrid at the entrance to the noisy, crowded Heartland Downs track kitchen. Salsa music blared from the sound system inside, causing conversational voices to be raised. Her red pickup truck sped into the nearby parking lot a minute later. "Sorry I'm late," she said. "I've been up all night with a horse of Bud Bauder's that was threatening to colic. Got him straightened out, though. Sorry I'm dirty, too," she said as she slapped the dust off her jeans.

"I see you're limping a bit. What happened?"

"A frisky colt kicked me in the knee yesterday. Still hurts."

Entering the large building with its rows of tables and lengthy aisle of cafeteria-style breakfast offerings. Doyle said, "I'm not really hungry. All I want is coffee. How about you?"

"Same."

"Okay, let me grab a couple of containers and we can sit outside in relative peace and quiet."

They walked to one of the old wood picnic tables that sat beneath a huge weeping willow tree. The early morning sun had erased the dawn air's haze and its light lay gently on the scarred surface of the table. Doyle said, "Thanks again for meeting me, Ingrid. You must know the reason why, right? Have you had a chance to ask around about a possible horse killer?"

"All business, as always. Right?" Ingrid sipped her coffee before continuing. "I've talked to everybody I know who I think might have an idea as to who's responsible for these so-called mercy killings. The only name that ever comes up is that girlfriend, or I guess ex-girlfriend, of Pat Caldwell's. You know, the guy who calls the charts here for *Racing Daily*? Esther Ness."

Doyle waved hello at Steve Holland, a horse owner he knew who was headed for the track kitchen, *Racing Daily* in hand. "What do you know about Caldwell?" he asked Ingrid. "I know what he does here, but I've never met him."

"Pretty friendly kind of guy. I've talked to him a couple of times at the monthly cookouts the track sponsors for all the backstretch people and racing office personnel. "She smiled.

"That's also where I first got to know Bobby Bork. Guy I'm going with now."

Doyle said, "How long has Caldwell been calling the charts here?"

"Oh, several years. He worked other tracks before getting this plum job. He's a tall, skinny guy, must be six foot four or five. Always wears a coat and tie at work. People say he's real easygoing when he's not doing his job. At work, he's all business. I once heard a woman horse owner ask him at one of the cookouts, 'Mr. Caldwell, how do you ever manage to tell where every member of a twelve-horse field that's speeding down the backstretch a quarter-mile away from you is at? How do you figure out *who* all those horses are in all that rushing? And *where* they are then?" Caldwell just smiled at her. He told her, "I've got a great memory for what horses look like, and the colors their jockeys wear. Besides, everybody's gotta be someplace."

Their conversation was interrupted by the screech of pickup truck brakes on the nearby roadway. They heard a horn blast and a shouted oath from the halted tan truck.

"What's that?" Doyle said.

Ingrid said, "That's that crabby old trainer Sid Morris. He braked to avoid hitting a squirrel that was hopping across the road."

Doyle said, "Hopping? Don't they run, the quick little creatures?"

Ingrid smiled. "Take a good look some time. They run up trees. But squirrels don't synchronize all four feet like horses do, or dogs, when they move on the ground. They hop. Both front feet hit the ground, then both back, and so on. Like rabbits. Kangeroos, too."

"Very educational," Doyle said. "You've taught me about horse communication, now the ambulatory methods of small rodents." He looked at his watch. "You think Caldwell is around now?"

"I think he's usually started his workday in his office, that's up in the press box, by now. I understand he comes in before the day's races to review tapes of the previous day. Like I said, he's supposed to be very dedicated, one of *Racing Daily's* best callers. He does the Kentucky Derby every year as well as the Breeders' Cup.

"Word is," Ingrid continued, "that Caldwell is a big bettor and quite good at it, too. And," she laughed, "his hobby is shopping for antiques. They say he's put together a very extensive collection that he keeps at his unmarried sister's house someplace in upstate New York. He's never been married, either. I know he buys a new Caddy every two years. Another rumor is that Pat doesn't trust banks. That he keeps rolls of cash in tomato cans buried under the light posts on his sister's property. Like I said, he's a lifelong bachelor. But he's always in a relationship with some woman or another, including that Esther Ness."

Ingrid crumpled her empty coffee cup and flicked it into the nearby trash can.

"Let's take my car," Doyle said. When they reached the Accord, he stepped ahead of her and opened the passenger door. Ingrid smiled. "So gentlemanly."

"And debonair. Cavalier. Modest…" Doyle replied with a laugh.

This mood of congeniality was suddenly interrupted by the sound of a woman's scream. "Oh, no," Ingrid said, turning back. "I know that girl."

She was looking toward the south side of the track kitchen building where a small Hispanic girl, wearing a groom's regular garb of tee-shirt and jeans, had her back pressed against the wall, face in her hands, weeping. Confronting her was a burly Mexican-American man. He was cursing her loudly in Spanish, stopping only to slap her with an open right hand every few oaths.

Ingrid ran toward them, calling, "Rita, Rita. What's wrong? What's happening here?" She pointed a finger as she ran. "You, mister, stop that. *Stop* that."

The man turned his broad back and administered another ringing slap to the small, tear-tracked brown face in front of him. Triumphantly, he turned back to face them. "You, beetch, you keep out of this." Rita tried to slip away. But he caught her arm and again jammed her back against the wall. "*Puta*." There were other snarled words in Spanish aimed at Rita. Another slap and anguished cry rang out before Doyle ran forward and plowed his right shoulder into the man's back and thrust him forward, banging his head into the kitchen wall. Rita scurried around them toward Ingrid.

The man recovered his balance. Shook his head. Bunched his large fists and stepped toward Doyle, eyes wild, forehead bleeding from its meeting with the wall.

Doyle used one of his best old boxing moves. Started a long, lazy, looping right hand intended to miss and create confidence. The man ducked it easily and began to say something in Spanish. He crouched, reached into a back pocket, brought out and opened a switchblade. It flashed in the morning sun as he lunged.

Doyle sidestepped, easily evading the thrust. He pretended to start the same right-hand looping punch. The man ducked again, sneering with confident recognition. The sneer had a short shelf life. Doyle stepped quickly to his left, planted his back foot, and pistoned three powerful left hooks deep into the man's right side. Under the rib cage. Right on the liver. With a nearly breathless squeal of pain, gasping for air, the man fell onto his back, and began to moan. Doyle picked the knife off the ground, walked slowly to a nearby refuse corner, and deposited it in the recycle bin.

Ingrid's suntanned face, for the past few seconds flushed with worry, creased in a slight smile aimed at Jack. She had an arm around the terrified Rita and began to walk her into the track kitchen. Looking back over her shoulder, she said, "I'll call Security, Jack."

Doyle's adrenalin flow slowed. He looked down at the bulky Mexican-American man, who was now struggling to sit up, wheezing softly, clutching his right side. Doyle pushed him back down. He grabbed the man's belt and flipped him sideways, then reached into the man's back pocket, took out a worn wallet containing an Illinois Racing Commission's groom's license. Photo, name, D.O.B., undoubtedly a spurious home address and Social Security number. If United States racetrack backstretches were checked for accurate numbers such as these, Doyle knew, they would soon be seriously emptied.

Doyle gave the man a light kick in the leg. Anger flared from the prostate man's eyes. "Hey, Rodrigo. Take a look at me. You try any more beating up women, *amigo*, I'll be back to see you. Day. Night. Or some surprise time in between. *Comprende?*"

A half-hour later, after escorting the shaken Rita to her dormitory room, Ingrid and Jack went to the Heartland press box to see Pat Caldwell. But when they got there, Caldwell's assistant and call taker, the person who wrote down his description of horses' positions in their races, Sheryl Stefanski, informed them that Caldwell had made an emergency visit to the dentist that morning. "Just as well he wasn't here for you. An abscessed tooth, he figured. He was grouchier than a fat man starting Weight Watchers. I know. I'm married to one that just has. Anyway, come on back between races this afternoon."

Chapter Seven

They met at the clubhouse entrance just before the fourth race. Ingrid pressed number six on the elevator panel, and they got off at the press box level. They heard track announcer John Toomey say, "They're in the gate. We're ready for a start. And they're off." Ingrid preceded Jack onto the porch where Caldwell was poised, binoculars aimed at the track below, his call taker, Sheryl, ready to record his report of the race about to get under way.

The event for filly and mare claimers took a minute and twelve seconds for the winner to complete six furlongs. Jack and Ingrid listened, rapt, as Caldwell rattled off the position of each horse in the event four times. His account was much more detailed than that of announcer Dooley, which they could hear in the background.

"Mitt the Flip still on top as they turn for home but about to give way like the faint-hearted phony he is…Kansas Mama a length back and a length before Horace Nealy. Favored Tricky Travis still fifth and five lengths back, doesn't look interested today. But shifting to the outside now and moving like a bat out of hell and going to make me a rich man is old Ready Roger. He's gonna win off all by himself!"

Doyle knew that none of Caldwell's colorful editorializing would make it into the straightforward reportage eventually comprising the *Racing Daily* chart footnotes of this race. But he smiled in appreciation as he listened to Caldwell.

After the horses had crossed the finish line, Caldwell kept his binoculars on them until they'd been pulled up, turned around, and began jogging back. Sheryl picked up her clipboard. She said, "Pat, these folks want to talk to you. This is Ingrid, and that's Jack."

Caldwell smiled and shook their hands, saying, "Ingrid McGuire. The famed veterinarian and horse communicator? And Jack Doyle, former jock's agent? Come on into my office. I want to take a quick look at the tape of this race before Sheryl sends her chart on the computer. Then we can talk."

They waited as Caldwell reviewed the just-completed race, rewinding the shot of the final turn to watch it three times. "That's what I thought," he muttered, "old Mitt the Flip came out two paths when he started to quit, bothered Horace Nealy." He made a note on the yellow legal pad next to the television before turning to them. "What can I do for you folks?"

Doyle summarized the recent horse killings, Caldwell acknowledging that he'd heard about them. Ingrid recounted her efforts to discover possible suspects. "I haven't had much luck, Pat. The only name I kept hearing was Esther Ness."

Caldwell groaned and sat back in his chair. "Aw, crap."

"You know her, right, Pat?" Doyle said.

"Yeah, sorry to say I do. We had a thing going for a month or so back in the winter. It ended. Pretty badly."

Ingrid said, "What can you tell us about Esther?"

"You got a day and a half?" Caldwell said with a grimace. "No, here's the short version. We met at a horsemen's association dinner a year ago. She helped sponsor it. She's an heiress. To a dog food fortune. Very intriguing woman. Very, very smart. But, as became evident to me after a while, she's got some loose screws."

Doyle said, "What do you mean?"

"Esther has a lot of interests, and a lot of money. She travels around the country, sometimes around the world, on whatever whim hits her. Unpredictable? Oh, yeah. When she had her own racing stable, she went through trainers like an allergy-sufferer through Kleenex. Generous with her money? Sure, but only if you agree with her. She's spoiled, pampered, eccentric, good but not great looking, but interesting as hell."

Caldwell paused and went to the window to aim his binoculars at the field of horses walking out of the paddock tunnel for the next race. They heard him saying quietly to himself, "Chris Kotulek's gelding in the white and blue, all red on the two horse, three horse only one with blinkers,"etc. After a minute, he turned back to them. He was smiling now. "That must sound kind of outdated, right? Most of the announcers today call the race using the color-coded saddle cloths to identify by numbers. I was brought up as a chart caller by men who prided themselves on memorizing jockey silks for each race. Pretty impressive skills. You finish one race, erase memory of those colors, and insert another bunch into your head in the next twenty minutes. I've never been able to give up that old-fashioned way of doing it. Matter of pride, I guess. Or stubbornness."

Doyle said, "Anything else you can tell us about Esther Ness?"

"You've got to understand, Esther did things you'd never forget, some of them good things. About a year ago, she taught herself to play the guitar. In only about three weeks, she was pretty decent at it! She started appearing at the Heartland Downs Chapel Sunday mornings. Reverend Dave, he's in charge of the backstretch ministry, welcomed her. She did what she called 'A Sunday Sermon Through Song.' I went to one of these. Hey, the woman was something to hear and watch. The congregation loved her, especially after she threw in a couple of Hispanic-sounding numbers.

"I didn't attend the next week's service. At that one, according to Reverend Dave, she was handing out business cards. Wait a minute." Caldwell walked to his desk, opened the middle drawer. He gave an embossed, laminated business card to Doyle who leaned over to allow Ingrid to see it. In addition to the color photograph of a thirtyish, dark-haired woman who was smiling confidently at the camera, there was a list of the services she offered:

- *A Musical Ministry. Concerts, Workshops, and
  Private Performances Upon Request.*
- *Trans-Denominational Minister/Wedding Officiant*
- *Certified Passion Workshop Facilitator*

Doyle said, "Wow." He handed the card back to Caldwell who returned it to his desk drawer. "Anything else?" Doyle said.

"Probably too much to tell. And I probably don't know the half of it. What I *do* know is that Esther is obsessed with the belief that animals, especially thoroughbred horses, are too often being mistreated. She loves just about every non-human creature that walks. Or flies, for that matter. One night when I picked her up—she lives with her mother in a mansion out in Barrington Hills—she was wearing a tee-shirt that said 'Adopt a Canadian Goose.' She seemed to me to kind of get nuttier the more we went out. I finally quit her."

Doyle frowned. "What do you mean, 'kind of'? I hate that expression. Last week I read about a football lineman who beat up his girlfriend and said things 'kind of got out of control,' that he 'kind of' messed her up. The woman was hospitalized. Then there's that fourth-rate celebrity actress who comes out of rehab every few months always saying she 'kind of' lost control of her life. They'd probably say the *Titanic* 'kind of' sank. I hate that."

Ingrid and Caldwell listened to this brief diatribe in stunned silence. Doyle blushed. "Forgive me. Sometimes I get worked up about things that rile me. So Pat, when you said Ms. Ness 'kind of' got nuttier, it set me off. Sorry. Go on."

"I shouldn't have used those words, Jack. You're right. There's nothing halfway about Esther's eccentricities. She's a nutcase."

Ingrid said, "So much so you think she'd kill horses to, quote, 'put them out of their misery,' unquote, like the notes left behind suggest?"

Caldwell considered this. Finally, he said, "Tell you the truth, I wouldn't put it past her. Esther's basically a good gal, believe me. But she's a fanatic on this subject. But she's also one very, very bright woman. Not one used to getting her hands soiled in any kind of dirty work. But, with all her money, I guess she could afford to hire out jobs she doesn't want to do." He paused to look out over the racetrack. "And," he said slowly, "get her going about retired horses being used for experiments, or whatever, and she loses all cool. Hell, when she came to the track she wouldn't even *watch* races. Couldn't stand to see jocks using their whips."

Riding down in the elevator, Doyle said, "I'm glad you asked Caldwell for Esther's phone number."

"Odd that she doesn't have a cell phone. That he contacted her by calling her home."

They sat on a bench outside the clubhouse entrance. Doyle pulled his phone from his pocket.

"Wait. What are you going to say to Esther?"

Doyle said, "Just that I'd like to talk to her. About her charitable work for animal safety. That I'm interested in becoming involved. How's that sound?"

Ingrid shrugged. "Okay, I guess."

The phone at the Ness home rang seven times before it was picked up. Doyle asked to speak to Ms. Ness. After he gave his name, he was told by a woman identifying herself as Esther's mother that Esther "continues to be traveling out of the country." Was there a way to reach her? "Oh, no," the woman laughed, "our daughter is a very independent spirit, Mr. Doyle. I have no idea where she is or when she's coming back. But, she always does. I'll tell her you called and leave her your number. Let me get a pen…"

Chapter Eight

Doyle returned from his early morning run along Chicago's beautiful lakefront, feeling, as usual, both pleasantly tired and thoroughly invigorated. Five miles in forty-five minutes without pulling a hamstring or popping a quad. A good feeling on a soft and sunny early summer morning.

As the door to his condo foyer closed behind him, he noticed that his mail had already arrived. It included a couple of bills, that week's *The New Yorker* and *Sports Illustrated,* and the usual collection of unwanted catalogs plus a few requests for charitable donations. Standing out was a beige envelope bearing several Irish stamps. He waited until he had toweled off and downed a bottle of cold water before opening it.

The enclosed invitation was from the Irish Sportswomen's Association, an organization he had never heard of. It summoned him to a dinner in Dublin honoring the Association's Person of the Year, Mickey Sheehan. As delighted as he was surprised, Doyle grinned while uttering "Yesssss! All riiiight!" His one-time jockey client had obviously made her successful mark in her native country after returning from her stint in the States at Heartland Downs.

Thanks to e-mailed updates from Mickey's older sister, free-lance journalist Nora Sheehan, Doyle was aware that Mickey's first full year of riding back on home turf had been notably successful. Mickey had finished fourth in Ireland's very competitive jockey standings, the only woman in the top twenty, with ninety-seven victories. An impressive eight of those triumphs had come in stakes races. As was the case at Heartland Downs when Doyle was selecting horses for her to ride, little Mickey had become a big name.

In addition to the invitation, there was a handwritten note in the envelope:

> *Dear Jack, I know this is short notice, but Mickey and I surely hope you can come over for this dinner. It would be great to see you again. If you wish, you could stay with me in the little house I recently rented in Bray. Let us know soonest, please. All the best, Nora*

During the Sheehan sisters' previous summer spent in the U.S., when Nora served as companion and chaperone for her jockey sister, Doyle had become close with both. Especially the beautiful, witty, and adventurous Nora, an ambitious freelance journalist. Doyle booked mounts for Mickey and, on several mutually pleasing occasions, bedded her sister. Like Doyle, Nora was an ardent believer in lovemaking between eagerly consenting adults without, as she once put it, "any bit of string attached." He couldn't have agreed more.

Nora, never married and some ten years younger than Doyle, had asked him about his marital status, having assumed, she said, "that you are single."

"Twice married," he told her. "Two painful disasters. Never again. As far as women go, I live my life *a la carte.*"

Doyle placed the envelope on the coffee table, walked over to look at his desk calendar and saw nothing but white space for the Irish weekend in question. Certainly he could take at least a few days away from his sleuthing in pursuit of the mysterious horse killer, which had thus far been an exercise in futility. Then he got out his credit card and linked to the Aer Lingus website on his laptop.

Two afternoons later Doyle took his window seat on the about-to-be-filled airplane destined for Dublin. He nodded to his seat partners, an elderly couple both quietly friendly and disposed to keeping to themselves. Fine with Doyle. He'd suffered in-flight boors during previous flying days. There was very little chatter, he noticed, as most of the younger people on board were engrossed with texting or already leaning back, eyes closed and earplugs in, listening to music they'd brought.

He accepted a copy of *USA Today* provided by the flight attendant offering reading matter up and down the aisle. After a quick perusal of the sports section, he was about to place the paper in the seat pocket in front of him when he noticed a bold-faced story on the business page.

"Internet Phenom Reaps Fortune" read the headline above the photo of the large, gloating face of a young man named Wendell Pilling. According to the article, Pilling, now in his late twenties, "created and developed the latest sensational entry in the lucrative field of Internet social media. Only three years after its introduction, his company was sold to a giant American hedge fund for an estimated half-billion dollars.

"What next for this young genius?" the story continued. "'I'm not one to brag,' Pilling said. 'I'll just be looking around for new worlds to conquer. Isn't that what Alexander the Great did when he was about my age?'"

Doyle crumpled up the paper. "Christ, another Gen X asshole," he muttered as he shoved the paper into the seat pocket. The elderly lady beside him gave him a startled and inquiring look. He sat back in his seat. "Not to worry," he smiled. "It's just something I read in the paper." He turned away and looked out the window as the plane headed east, away from the starting-to-set sun.

Chapter Nine

Waiting in the Customs line at Dublin Airport, Doyle looked ahead of the crowd in front of him and grinned as he spotted the same effusive official he had seen on his only previous visit to his ancestral homeland. He well remembered the tall, lanky, friendly, middle-aged man energetically greeting both first-time visitors and returnees. Doyle didn't need to see the man's nametag to know it said F. Flynn.

"Doyle, now. From the U.S. of A.," Flynn said as he opened the passport. "Ah, now, a second trip here, eh? Well, Mr. Doyle, welcome home. Are you back to see relatives?"

"No, just friends."

Flynn waved him forward. "I'm sure you'll be seeing old ones and making new ones, yeah."

When he'd phoned Nora the previous afternoon to tell her his arrival time, she'd said, "Sorry I can't meet you, Jack. I've got an assignment to finish for my new Internet employer, World Irish. I'll be busy all day."

"No problem," said Doyle, disappointed though he was.

Nora said, "Just take a taxi to the dinner and I'll see you there. You can park your luggage in the cloakroom until we go to my place after the event. Cocktails at six, dinner at seven. Travel safely. Mickey and I are very much looking forward to seeing you."

Doyle told the driver, "the Mansion House," then settled into the backseat of the taxi. Traffic was heavy this late Saturday afternoon. Driver Tim Carey could be heard muttering in frustration as they were forced to lag for blocks behind a slow-moving bus.

A copy of that day's *Irish Times*, the nation's leading daily newspaper, lay on the seat. Doyle picked it up. His eyebrows elevated when he saw a headline at the bottom of the front page "Reptile Sanctuary Opens."

"I'll be damned," he said.

"What's that, sir?" Carey said.

"Story here about a reptile sanctuary. I thought your island was famously free of snakes, thanks to St. Patrick."

Carey laughed. "For the most part we still certainly are. Are you reading now about the man who has been saving snakes?"

"Yes."

"Well," Carey said, "those creatures are not native to our island. Back in the boom days, owning a snake became kind of a status symbol for, thank God, a small segment of our new rich folk. They were paying, oh, six hundred or seven hundred Euros for these imported creatures. Said they used them for conversation starters, if you can imagine that now. But it happened. Then, when the boom went bust, many snake owners discarded their so-called trophy pets. Feckin' amazing."

Doyle said, "I'd agree with that." He opened the paper to where the story continued. "Says here the fellow who opened a reptile sanctuary is housing a couple of pythons. And a California king snake, whatever that is. Even a six-foot boa constrictor. I'll be damned," Doyle repeated as he put the paper back on the seat next to him.

Ten minutes into the ride, as Carey waited at a traffic light, Doyle saw a large, noisy group of protestors marching up and down outside six-story building that appeared to be abandoned "What's that all about?" he said.

"Ya see the weeds in the sidewalk there?" Carey answered. "Inside that dingy brick facade you'd find ripped up floors and holes punched into walls. What you're looking at is one of what we call our 'ghost developments.' Apartment buildings thrown up when the Celtic Tiger was roaring." He lowered his window and spat into the street. "Now, of course, the Tiger has turned feckin' tabby. Some folks call it the 'Celtic Carcass.' I don't know if I'd term it that meself. What you're seeing is a bunch of furious folks who bought apartments in a building that was never completely finished before the economy tanked and the value of the building went down the drain with it. They're stuck. They're still supposed to keep up mortgage payments on those failed properties. And they're furious mad. Can't blame 'em, yeah. There's a protest there every weekend."

The light changed. Carey took a sharp right. "Let me show you another bunch," he said. "Won't take but a minute, it's on our way."

Five blocks later, Doyle could begin to hear the bullhorns. This was an even more vociferous collection of citizens, both sexes, many ages and sizes.

"See those protest signs?" Carey said. "This group is on about the one-hundred Euro tax on all households by our government. Thieves and ijits sank the feckin' economy and now regular folk are supposed to do the rescuing. Well, that's a non-starter for these folks. Or me either." He rolled down his window for another emphatic expectoration before finally pulling up to the entrance of Mansion House on Dawson street, site of the dinner.

"Well," Jack said, handing in the fare and a sizeable tip, "that was an educational trip."

Doyle had done his Google research regarding this famous edifice. It had been the official residence of the Lord Mayor of Dublin since 1715. Tonight's event would be held in Mansion House's Round Room, built in 1821 in preparation for a visit by England's King George IV. The Round Room accommodated as many as five hundred diners, Nora had e-mailed him, adding, "The place reeks of history. There'll probably also be layers of whiskey and ale fumes in the mix during cocktail time."

Before he'd reached the top of the steps, he saw Nora Sheehan waving a greeting. They embraced. "My God," Doyle said, "this damp climate surely agrees with you. You look terrific." He took a step back for assessment. "Great green dress that matches your eyes," he said, "and a certain flush of excitement highlighting those classic cheekbones. Must be my presence."

Nora laughed as she took his arm. "Same old Jack Doyle. Thank heavens for that."

He shifted his traveling bag to his left hand and circled her small waist with the other arm as they walked through the entrance.

"The coat room folks will take your bag now," Nora said. "I'll have room at my little house for it tonight." She gave his arm a squeeze.

Nora led him to a table in the front row and introduced him to the six people already seated there, all friends of hers from Dublin's journalism world. A hulking man named Seamus O'Sullivan gave Doyle a hearty handshake while thanking him for "coming to us across the pond. I know Mickey is delighted you're here."

Doyle shook hands with the other men and smiled at the ladies before sitting down and looking up at the head table that stretched across a raised stage. Little Mickey Sheehan, beaming, waved enthusiastically down at him. More used to seeing her either in jockey silks or morning work clothes for exercising horses, he looked appreciatively at her petite figure in a stylish light blue dress with white collar and cuffs. He waved back before walking to the bar for cocktails for Nora and himself.

Dinner was buffet style. Following Nora in the line, Doyle opted for the green pea and ham hock soup, char-grilled Hereford sirloin steak ("It's not Gibson's back home, but it's pretty damn good," he told Nora), white chocolate raspberry truffle. Her salad and salmon *pave*, Nora said, "was surprisingly excellent for catered food of this sort." Nora nudged Doyle when they looked over from their table to see Mickey go through the food line for the second time. "The girl still measures five feet and weighs just over seven stone," Nora said. "A marvelous metabolism for that lucky person."

Before the speeches began, Doyle said, "Nora, what about your brother Kieran? I see he's not here. Are he and Mickey still back on good terms?" The riding siblings, estranged for years, had reestablished a relationship the previous summer when Mickey rode against, and defeated, her older brother in a rich race at Heartland Downs. That was headline news in the racing world, the young female apprentice besting her older brother, the man who had for several seasons been Ireland's leading jockey.

Nora said, "Oh, Jack, you know Kieran. An iconoclast of the first order. He has little time for racing's press, or its fans. Good public relations has never been one of Kieran's strengths."

Seamus O'Sullivan leaned forward across the table toward Jack. "Kieran pulls no punches along those lines. I covered probably the last dinner at which he spoke publicly. Kieran was very definite, the scowling little man. Said most turf writers don't know shite, that they just write what they want to write, not knowing what they'd seen. Somebody asked him if he felt any obligation to communicate with the bettors. Hah! Kieran's response was, and I remember it well, 'My first obligation is to the horse. Then the owner and trainer. You can have all the bettors. They're like coat holders. If you get in a fight, they're happy to hold your coat. If you win, they're with a winner. If you lose, they keep your coat.'" Doyle joined in the laughter at that statement. "That's our brother," Nora said quietly.

"Have Mickey and Kieran ridden against each other here recently?" Doyle said.

Nora said, "Not recently, and not ever over here. They rode against each other a couple of times in France, once in Germany. Kieran won them both. Mickey got a third and a fourth.

"It's not like it is in the States. Here in Ireland, direct competition between blood relatives is prohibited under the rules of racing. Of course, they've ridden on the same racing program, but never against each other. That's so there can never be any possibility of collusion. Not that Kieran or Mickey would ever agree to anything like that."

"You must be a very suspicious people," Doyle smiled.

"Perhaps rightfully so," Nora said.

Chapter Ten

As tea, coffee, and after-dinner drinks were being served, mistress of ceremonies Bernadette Ann Trainor tapped the microphone for attention and the program proceeded. First up was a five-minute video of Mickey Sheehan riding highlights from races both at Irish tracks and Heartland Downs. The topper, of course, was Mickey's thrilling photo-finish victory aboard Plotkin in the Heartland Downs Futurity in which she beat her famous brother Kieran. The video elicited hearty applause, as did Ms. Trainor's introduction of the honoree.

Watching his former client approach the microphone, Doyle thought, *She is a marvel.* He vividly recalled the horrible racing accident in which Mickey had been involved when he served as her agent at Heartland Downs during her lone Chicago summer. The anguished trip to the hospital that followed, the fearful hours before it was determined she had suffered no critical injuries when she'd plummeted to the turf, her protective helmet leaving a large divot, "only" a badly bruised face and tendon damage in her right wrist and hand. He remembered Nora's yelp of relief when the emergency room physician delivered that report and Nora's assurance. "My sister will fight back from this, Jack," she'd said. Embracing the trembling Nora that evening, Doyle had his doubts. He shouldn't have.

During the weeks after the spill, Doyle watched Mickey almost immediately begin physical therapy. Her rehab regimen included swimming and jogging to maintain aerobic levels and she resumed her yoga that she said helped her with flexibility and balance. All of it led to her being back in the saddle in less than a month, this to everyone's amazement accept Mickey's.

As Mickey waited for her injuries to heal, Doyle remembered her telling him, "Thoroughbreds use rein tension to keep their balance. That leads to a constant downward pull on a jockey's hands and arms. We have to have extremely good hand, forearm, and core strength."

Mickey laughed, "People don't realize that riders even have to have very strong *neck* muscles. Try putting on a helmet that weighs a pound and a half or so when you're not real fit, then try keeping your head up for a couple of minutes so that you can see where you're going. Doesn't sound hard, Jack. But it is. Especially when you're on top of a horse going forty miles an hour."

Jack had come to learn plenty about racing. But not until booking mounts for Mickey had he come to fully appreciate what it took to be a professional athlete in a sport so dangerous that an ambulance followed the contestants around during every race "just in case."

Jack felt a surge of pride as little Mickey moved purposefully to the podium. She grasped the microphone but had to lower it slightly before beginning a brief and well received acceptance speech in which she thanked the Sports Association, her parents, "my sister Nora, who is here tonight. And Jack Doyle, my American agent who is sitting with Nora and was gracious enough to fly over and attend tonight. This award is more than I could ever have dreamed of winning. I thank you all so much." After a wave of cheers and clapping, Mickey said, "And now, I'll answer a few questions. If you have any," she grinned.

A large, well-fed man at a front table raised his hand. "Do you get 'up' for the bigger races?"

"No, not at all. I get 'up' for all of them. I remember reading something that the great American jockey Bill Hartack said many years ago. He said he rode 'every race like it was the Kentucky Derby.' I can identify with that, all right. To my mind, the man who owns the cheap horse deserves the same treatment as the man with a good horse. I would consider it dishonest to try harder on one man's horse than on another's." She paused before saying, "I believe my famous brother Kieran feels exactly the same way. You could call it The Sheehan Way."

That answer drew enthusiastic applause. Mickey grinned before concluding, "I've always believed that, whether it's a small race or a big race, there's no honor in riding and losing. There's only honor in winning."

Nora and Doyle looked on proudly as they joined in the audience's rousing standing ovation for the now blushing little jockey. Ms. Trainor announced that the program was over and thanked everyone for coming. Mickey remained near the podium, signing autographs for several of the admiring attendees.

"The kid did great," Jack said.

Nora nodded. "That she did, indeed."

Walking with Nora toward the exit, Doyle felt a tug on his sleeve. He looked down at the friendly face of Niall Hanratty's wife, Sheila. "Hello," he said. "Didn't know you were here, Sheila. Where's the Prince of Irish Bookmakers?"

Sheila frowned. "He's over in London on business. Jack, have you got a wee minute? I need to speak to you about something."

Doyle introduced Sheila to Nora, told Nora he'd meet her at the front door "in a couple of minutes." Sheila led him to a now vacant nearby table. They waited for a busboy to clear it before pulling out chairs.

"It's always a pleasure to see you, Sheila. Did you come up by yourself from Kinsale?"

She gestured toward a small group of women near the door, one of whom waved as the others looked expectantly at her. "No, I came up with the friends you see over there. I don't want to delay them, so I'll get right to the point, Jack. I am very worried about Niall. There have been some things happening, some recent incidents that scare the bejesus out of me. And he pays them no mind."

Doyle frowned. "What kind of incidents? What do you mean?"

She leaned forward to say quietly, "I think someone, or some people, intend to do him harm." She took a deep breath. "First, there was the morning in Kinsale when he was nearly run over by a hurtling van that didn't stop. He just barely dodged out of the way. He never even told me about that. His man Barry Hoy mentioned it to me a few days later.

"About two weeks after that, when Niall was driving home from work one night, somebody roared up from behind and banged into him on the coast road just miles from our house. He fought to keep his car off the side leading to the edge of the cliff. Managed to pull up short just in time. Again, it was a van, and it sped away. No, he did not get the license number. This, he at least *did* tell me about when he finally got home. I'd never seen him shaken like that. That's why I pressed him about what had happened before this second incident. I had to administer a large cognac and some heartfelt pleading before he would talk about it. But the next morning, it was as if he'd erased these incidents from his mind and expected me to do the same. I can't do that, Jack. My dear husband can be a very stubborn, self-confident person. You might call him bullheaded. And, as a matter of fact, I have."

Doyle smiled. "I have observed certain bullheaded traits in your husband. But did Niall report these things to the police? Your Garda?"

"Only after I kept after him and after him for a whole day and night to do so! But nothing came of that. Without anyone witnessing these events, there was really nothing for the Garda to go on. And now, Niall has gone back to just playing down the whole situation. He refuses to discuss it with me. Says there's nothing to be worried about. You know how obstinate he can be! He's always been on about the virtues of self reliance. And I admire that attitude, up to a point. But this has me worried sick."

One of the women near the door called out, "Sheila," and pointed to her watch. Sheila nodded. Getting to her feet, she said, "Niall greatly respects you, Jack, after all your dealings with him over that Chicago racetrack. So, here comes me asking you a big favor. Could you come down and talk to Niall? Find out what he thinks might really be going on? God knows he won't tell me. He's made a career out of protecting me from any worrisome news. But I can't sleep until I'm assured he's safe. The business he's in, as you well know, is not entirely populated by role model citizens." She picked up her purse and dinner program. "He'll be back from England and in the Kinsale office tomorrow."

Doyle thought of the much-needed assistance he'd received from the bookmaker and his bodyguard, Hoy, two years before in that backstretch barn at Monee Park, his life on the line.

"My flight home is Tuesday morning, Sheila. Please tell your husband I'll see him in his Kinsale office tomorrow. Tell him I'll buy him lunch."

Sheila gripped his hand and kissed him on the cheek. "God bless you, Jack, and thank you." She stood up and walked away.

Nora took Doyle's arm as they left Mansion House. "What was that all about with Sheila Hanratty?"

"The Inquiring Reporter wants to know, eh? I'll tell you on the drive to your house."

Chapter Eleven

Doyle awakened to the inviting odor of frying bacon. For a brief, pleasant moment, he thought he was back in his childhood home on an early Saturday morning, awaiting his mother's call to breakfast. He rolled over in the rumpled queen-size bed to see that Nora was not there.

He found her in her kitchen, scrambling eggs. "Turn on the toaster now, will you Jack?" She looked over her shoulder to smile at him. She was already dressed in sweater and jeans. "I thought after your estimable efforts of last night, you'd need some caloric fortification."

Doyle, wearing only his boxer shorts, nuzzled her neck as he stood behind her, laughed. "Caloric fortification? The striving journalist in you comes out early this morning."

Their romp in the bed the night before had left them pleasured and ready for sleep. He had never been with a woman he found so sexually compatible. Their lovemaking the summer Nora had spent in the U.S. with Mickey had been great but never as enjoyable as last night, and Doyle told her so. "Ah, but now I'm operating on my home turf," Nora said. She turned to kiss him. "Tend to your eggs and rashers, now."

He'd always had trouble taking orders, especially from women. Sister Mary Margaret, his eighth grade teacher at St. James Parochial School, was one exception, being young, bright, and blessed with a sense of humor. Nora was another, but her commands were usually issued while naked in bed with him.

Doyle mopped the egg remnants on his plate with his final piece of brown bread. She looked at him admiringly. "I've never known a person to eat so rapidly and with such relish."

"It's what keeps me energetic. Like, right now, I am completely revived and restored." With a leering nod toward the nearby bedroom, he said, "I've got some time now before I have to leave."

Nora said, "So you may. But you'll not be enticing me to share it with you in there. Not this morning, at least." She began to gather and wash the dishes. Doyle went to get dressed.

"Is there anything I should know about your car?" he said when he emerged from the bedroom. Before finally going to sleep the night before, they had planned this day. Nora said she would be working from home, so Jack could borrow her five-year-old Peugeot to drive down to Kinsale. "It gets a bit temperamental sometimes," Nora said, "especially when you do your shifting. Like me, it's not always an eager starter in the morning. Just be patient. And the steering sort of pulls to the right, I haven't had a chance to get that corrected. It uses regular petrol. Don't be afraid to top it up before you return tonight." They kissed at her doorway before he walked down the block to the red two-door car. It was a 2007 model, the original gloss lost in the sixty or so rainy Irish months preceding this one, but still looking good.

The interior of this vehicle, like that of many busy journalists the world over, was a slum. Newspapers and folders were scattered over all the seats but the driver's. An assortment of used coffee containers and fast food wrappings littered the floors front and back. "How could a woman who's such a careful housekeeper live with this mess?" he muttered.

"GPS?" Nora had laughed the night before. "Not on this working girl's salary. You'll have to depend on that now-archaic traveler's aid, the map."

Doyle reviewed the map he'd placed on the steering wheel before he turned on the ignition. The route looked fairly straightforward. "If I can remember to stay on the left side of the road, I'll be all right," he said to himself.

This summer morning was a bright one and traffic moved steadily on M7-M8 toward Cork. Doyle broke up the three-hour journey by stopping for petrol before the turnoff onto N27 for Kinsale and his meeting with Hanratty. As he filled the Peugeot's tank, he watched with amusement as a young, red-haired woman, dressed in a midriff-revealing tee-shirt and tight shorts, stretched to clean the top of the back window of her dusty blue Golf. Like many of her sex and age, she was evidently either a regular patron of tanning bed salons or a user of the popular spray-on version of skin coloring. Probably the latter, Doyle thought, noticing white patches she'd obviously missed on the backs of her knees. She'd be noticeable in this country's predominantly pale-skinned populace.

Before returning to the highway, Doyle rummaged in Nora's music CDs in the left door pocket amidst used tissues and a variety of receipts. He smiled as he found one of his favorite Van Morrison song collections, *Irish Heartbeat*. He skipped ahead to track four, "The Star of the County Down."

Listening appreciatively, Doyle thought of one of his college roommates, a budding musicologist named Billy Munger, who frequently declared at late night drinking sessions that "George Ivan Morrison is by far, *by far,* the best bad-voiced singer ever."

He turned the CD off when the song ended. "Mr. Morrison," he said to himself, "your voice is a long way removed from golden, but you sure as hell have got some Hall of Fame chops."

Doyle switched to the radio and listened to a woman author described by the interviewer as "a great authority on the iconic Irish writer Brendan Behan." The next few minutes were taken up by the guest's description of the late novelist/playwright's father, "...a wily but extremely lazy man. His wife was always after him to dig up their backyard so she could have a garden there. He never would. But after she had long hounded him, one day he dialed the local Garda station to report that he'd received a 'disturbing phone message from an anonymous caller.' The message warned that some 'IRA members had secretly planted explosives for use in bomb-making' on that part of the Behan property. The Garda sprang into action. They dug up the whole yard but of course did not find anything. That night, when Mrs. Behan returned home, her husband told her the garden was now ready for planting."

>>>

Approaching Kinsale on N27, Doyle looked forward to again seeing Niall Hanratty, even though this meeting was sparked by Sheila Hanratty's concerns for her husband's safety. Doyle and the Irish bookmaker had become friends during an afternoon a few years before when they shared a box at the Curragh races. That friendship had solidified one night several weeks after that when Hanratty helped thwart a man intent on murder in a horse stall at Monee Park Racetrack south of Chicago.

During their initial meeting, the bookmaker had taken some pains to explain his first name. "Not a common name here, Jack. There was an Irish king named Niall centuries ago. He was called 'Niall of the Nine Hostages' because he was in the business of ransoming people. A most industrious sort of fella back around 400 A.D. His best known captive was none other than St. Patrick. King Niall was said to have let him go free for nothing. And Patrick, of course, went on to become the patron saint of Ireland."

Doyle smiled. "Wasn't St. Patrick supposed to have driven all the snakes out of Ireland?"

"Have you ever seen one here, Jack?"

Not wanting to rile his friend, Doyle answered, "Not in person, no."

"And I doubt that you will," Hanratty laughed.

Doyle said, "I assume the bookmaking business has been enough to keep you out of your predecessor's ransoming trade?"

"Indeed it has. Evidently, King Niall and I have only one thing in common. Now, this is Sheila's view, understand."

"What's that?"

"The woman has long considered me to be a control freak, which I admit is somewhat the case. But not to the extent of old King Niall. Legend has it that, as he lay on his deathbed, he insisted his family and friends rehearse their planned spoken memorials to him. He was said to have done quite a bit of editing of these statements before he passed on."

Chapter Twelve

Kinsale hadn't changed since Doyle's only previous visit more than two years earlier. Nor had it changed in the many years before that. This popular resort town, some twenty miles south of Cork City on the Celtic Sea, would see its small population of less than three thousand swell throughout the summer with tourists on holiday. Its harbor, from which thousands of Irish citizens had fled the Great Famine of the nineteenth century, featured a yacht marina that today was replete with expensive craft. Very visible in the harbor was the statue commemorating the dozens of survivors and hundreds of corpses brought to Kinsale in the spring of 1915, victims of the *Lusitania*'s sinking.

He drove slowly down heavily trafficked Market Street, Kinsale's major thoroughfare, before spotting an open space. "Rarity of rarities," he muttered as he quickly backed into it, barely beating a big, blue SUV whose driver reacted with a horn blast and fist shaken out of his window. Doyle waved cheerily to the man and locked Nora's car. He was only a block from the Shamrock Off-Course Wagering Shop.

Minutes earlier, seated at his desk in the second-floor office of his shop, Niall Hanratty had looked at the wall clock. He'd expected Doyle a half-hour before and was growing impatient. He said loudly, "Tony, bring in the prelim reports will you? I've got time to look at them."

From the much smaller, adjacent office, Anthony X. Rourke, Hanratty's longtime genius number cruncher, corporation secretary, and minority owner if not close friend, came through the doorway. Rourke was a short, thin, middle-aged man who, as long as Niall had known him, and despite having had his salary steadily advanced over the years, still dressed like modern-day version of a Dickensian clerk. Rourke had recently developed a slight stoop to accentuate his already poor posture. In his quiet voice, he reported, "It's lookin' like a grand day for us so far, Niall."

Niall nodded appreciatively as he quickly perused the columns of computer printout figures. "This should put a bit of a smile even on your serious visage," he said to Rourke. "The favorite players have gone huge, and got stuffed so far. And the longshot punters, with rare exceptions, failed just as badly."

He got to his feet, stretched his tall, physically fit frame, and reached for his suit jacket. "Remember Jack Doyle? The wild American boyo? He's due here soon to have lunch. Would you join us? These figures you've compiled, Tony," he said, tapping the stack of printouts, "warrant a celebratory pint, yeah."

Hanratty's jovial mood, as usually the case in the course of their long association, was not contagious. The soft-spoken Rourke shrugged and shook his head no. "You go on, then, Boss. I'll have the junior lads finish up for me and get a good early start for home."

"Safe home, then, Tony," smiled Hanratty. Rourke lived in his native town of Cork City, a place from which he'd never moved. "Tony, on your way out tell Barry he can have the rest of the day, too." Hoy, a one-time heavyweight boxing champion of Ireland, worked as Hanratty's driver, bodyguard, retriever of debts overdue, and, as Hanratty put it, "representative-in-waiting to some of our society's potentially disturbing elements." Like Rourke, he had been with Shamrock from Hanratty's launch of the company fifteen years earlier, an enterprise that began in one modest Kinsale storefront and now extended to ten counties in the Republic and parts of the North. Hanratty often remarked to his wife, Sheila, "I've had two main men with me all the way.

Tony looks like a barely nourished librarian. Hoy reminds me of Victor McLaughlin in that old John Wayne movie about Ireland. I've been lucky to have 'em."

At the door, Rourke turned to say, "I'll tell Barry on my way out then."

Doyle began to push open the Shamrock door just as it was jerked from the inside. He almost fell against the emerging Barry Hoy who laughed and said, "Heard you were coming, Jack." They shook hands. Hoy said, "The Boss is waiting. Take those stairs to the right of the betting windows."

At the top of the stairs, Doyle nearly bumped into the descending Rourke, who nodded a polite but unenthusiastic hello. The surprised accountant stumbled forward as his precariously perched bifocals fell off his nose. Doyle snatched them midway of their fall toward the stairs. "Och, Mr. Doyle, I didn't see you coming up. Those are some quick hands you've come equipped with. Thank you," he added as Doyle handed him the eyeglasses. "You know the way to Niall's office? Good. Welcome back and good-bye to you for now." He continued his careful descent, right hand tight on the banister.

Doyle gave a quick rap on Hanratty's door and entered. Niall, grinning, quickly came around the wide, paper-filled desk to reach for Doyle's hand saying, "Bless you, Jack, for coming down. You surely didn't have to. But you've pleased my dear Sheila by doing so. She's worried about me. She shouldn't be, of course, but she is. So I didn't put up too much of a protest when she told me she'd asked you to meet with me. Glad to see you again, my friend."

Hanratty snatched his suit coat off the back of his chair and shrugged it on. "Because of our success together in the States, Sheila has enormous confidence in your assorted abilities that I described to her, probably with some degree of exaggeration. She's come, poor woman, to envision you as a master of not only deduction but arbitration and confrontation."

He picked up a large thick brown envelope, moved to the door, and waved Jack through. "But let's talk from behind a pint or two and over a lovely little lunch. Are you with me?"

Chapter Thirteen

They slowly made their way the two blocks on tourist-crowded sidewalks to Hanratty's favorite Kinsale restaurant, McCann's Oyster House, a venerable local institution that overlooked the harbor. After they were seated at Hanratty's customary table near the wide front window, he introduced Jack to their smiling waitress. "Katie, meet Jack Doyle. He's come all the way from the States, Chicago exactly, to dine at Kinsale's most deservedly famous restaurant." A few minutes later, Katie delivered pints of Smithwick's. "*Slainte,*" Hanratty said, and touched his glass to Doyle's. "Half-dozen fried oysters to start, then the grilled sole," Hanratty said to Katie. "Double that, please," said Doyle.

Hanratty took a long pull on his lager before opening the envelope he'd brought. "Now, I know Sheila's concerns about my safety have extended to you. She talked to you about it at the dinner last night, which is why you're here. Yes, there were a couple of minor traffic incidents. I wish to God I had never mentioned them to her, for she's magnified them way out of proportion."

He paused to attend to the lager before saying, "But I want to show you some things that should flush your fears, Jack. You must understand that you can't be in a business like mine without making people unhappy, causing complaints. Not surprisingly, over the years I've gotten obscene phone calls and a drawer full of nasty, semi-literate letters from disappointed punters blaming me for their ineptitude."

"Complaints about what?"

"Imagined harm that's been done them. They've lost money and they blame me. My odds were 'off.' Or my clerks short-changed them. Or the particular shop of mine they frequent wasn't open early enough for them to get a winning bet down before they went to work. *Always* a supposed winning wager, of course, never a loser. Or, the shop wasn't open *late* enough. The lines were too long. There weren't enough bet takers behind the wickets. Oh, numerous are the grievances abounding in the lives of these losers. Most of my customers, God love them, are quite aware I run an absolutely honest business. Always have. Always will. That's why they keep patronizing Shamrock Off-Course Wagering. Why my business has thrived and grown. But there's always an element of nutters roiling the shallow waters.

"It's the same old self-deceiving bullshit, year after year," Hanratty continued. "There's a stream of it that pours through the bloodstreams of bad bettors everywhere. You probably know many of them back home that are eager to announce their big scores, right? Whether it's betting horses, dogs, football, baseball, or the stock markets. But how many ever report their far more numerous losing days?"

Doyle said, "Hardly any that I know. I guess it's the same all over."

"Wherever men risk their money," Hanratty said. He paused to fork up one of the plump oysters, gently dipped it in the cocktail sauce, chewed with evident satisfaction. Then his frown returned. He opened the eleven by thirteen brown envelope he'd brought and extracted several sheets of paper as well as a standard sized envelope. "This is just a sampling from my collection of loony letters I've received over the years. Please note the address on this one," he said, handing a small envelope to Jack.

Hanratty's name and home address were centered in the proper place. In the upper left corner, however, where the return address should have been, was written in large, vivid purple letters:

HERPES TEST RESULTS
(Personal and Confidential)

"Oh, sure, you can laugh, Jack. So humorous, yeah? Well, maybe not so much the first time one of these envelopes arrives at my house to be retrieved from the mailbox by Sheila. With all three of our young sons looking on, only the older one hiding a grin, the rascal, his brothers horrified. And maybe not so humorous when such items started coming to my office here and the other offices around the country. After a while, it gets real damn old. I've heard the area postal workers find these mailings to be sources of considerable laughter. Well, they are not so to me."

Doyle said, "I suppose you've no idea who sends these."

"You're wrong there. Under the purple 'Sincerely' at the bottom of each bitter letter there is indeed a signature in a bold hand. From some gobshite calling himself 'Tim of Tipperary.' He's been lavish with his postage the last few months."

"What is his message? Or messages?"

Hanratty said, "It's always some claim about how one of my shops has deprived him of some bonanza he had coming. His repeated charge is that when he wins a bet, the odds I've provided are, as he writes, 'disgracefully feckin' low, you cheatin' bastard.' It's a sentence he tends to repeat. He's an expert at irritation."

Doyle was puzzled. "I don't get it. Don't your bettors set the odds with their wagers?"

"No, no, not at all, Jack. In our betting shops over here, *we* determine the odds. We can raise or lower them to reflect supply and demand. I think your Las Vegas casinos do the same thing with bets on football and basketball games, maybe boxing, too, I don't know. The Vegas fellas, they employ—and so do we over here—a fluid process. Now, horse racing in the States is different. Your punters are betting *against each other*. That's your pari-mutuel system. There's not as much of that here as you have. And none in my shops."

Doyle said, "I never knew that. Just as, I guess, many American racing bettors don't realize they are actually in direct competition with each other. I've often heard some satisfied guy say after a winning bet, 'Well, I'm betting with "house money" from here on today.' He obviously was not aware that there *is* no such thing as 'house money' at racetracks. Casinos, sure. But our U.S. tracks don't give a damn what a bettor does as long as he *bets*. They're taking out their percentage of every bet made, and so are the states in their taxes. Doesn't matter to the people who own Heartland Downs or Belmont Park or Santa Anita *who* wins or loses. What matters to them is the volume of bets placed, what they call the churn."

Doyle paused as Katie deposited another pair of Smithwick's pints on their table. "Loonch will be right up," she said. "The sole is grand today, Niall, I've tried it."

Hanratty thanked Katie and turned to Jack. "Your pari-mutuel system, Jack, I don't see the joy in that," he said. "I prefer our way. It's a contest. It takes brain work on our part, and on that of our customers. We can shift the odds lower if we have a great exposure. Bettors can shop the odds looking for what they think is their best advantage. Kind of an interesting, like, game, you know. A competition. Not just sitting back and slicing off a piece of every Euro passing through."

Considering Hanratty's expanding empire of obviously profitable betting shops, Doyle could certainly understand his host's thinking. "Niall, what about competitors? Would any of them try to harm you?"

Hanratty smiled. "I seriously doubt it. True, we had some lively little turf wars, pardon the expression, some years back, when my business was just getting off the ground. But for the most part, things worked out peacefully. Especially after Barry Hoy and a couple of his similarly large cousins had serious talks with a few potential rivals that threatened to show up on the disruptive side. Barry and his lads brought them to their senses, if you know what I mean. It's rumored one of the real obstreperous fellas, up in Limerick, earned a trip to a hospital emergency room. I know nothing of the details of that, of course. Peace has been reigning for a long time now, I am happy to say."

An hour later, they parted with a handshake outside the restaurant. Doyle walked to Nora's car for his drive back to Dublin. He'd have one more night at her place before his next day's return flight to Chicago. After his talk with Niall, he decided would phone the worried Sheila and reassure her that her worries were needless, that her husband was, as usual, in control of things.

He had another satisfying listen to the Van Morrison CD as he headed back up the N27, toward dinner with Nora, he hoped, if she wasn't working late.

Chapter Fourteen

Sheets of rain pounded her windshield making the driving, what with the auto's lights off, very difficult late this spring night. The whirring wipers almost obscured the Swine Research Center sign as she passed it. She cautiously turned into the long drive from the county highway and headed toward the parking behind the Large Animal Building.

The previous night, she'd used the Google search engine to access and examine the layout of Indiana's Carmel College School of Veterinary Medicine. Her destination was well removed from the college's main campus.

At the far end of the parking lot, she spotted a large truck that was piled high with bales of now sodden hay, and pulled in on the far side of it. The downpour began to diminish. The only other vehicles in the lot were two empty pickup trucks, one with a small horse trailer attached. She quickly reviewed the plan of action she had laid out using the precise information confidentially supplied by a sympathetic Carmel College staff member, one of her fellow ALWD members and a longtime "animal activist."

Waiting for the rain to subside, she sat back in her driver's seat and closed her eyes, remembering a watershed moment in her life. She had just turned thirteen when she accompanied her favorite aunt on a mission for the Equine Rescue Society. It was a cold, gray December morning when they and several other volunteers arrived at the rundown farm outside of Pekin, Illinois. Her Aunt Julia, vice-president of the organization's area chapter, had been tipped off by an anonymous phone call the night before. According to the caller, "Horace Beasley, that sorry, cheap son of a bitch, is starving his poor horses. He's abandoned them and moved away. You will never see that bastard. But you better hurry and see them horses."

Aunt Julia led the way past the small, weather-beaten house toward the paddock fence behind it. Then she halted, hand going to her mouth as she gasped, "Oh, my God."

In front of them were four horses, two browns and a black and a gray. They were in appalling condition, their ribs showing, sores festering on their legs. They hardly had the strength to raise their heads to look at the visitors.

Aunt Julia opened the gate and entered the paddock, hands extended. She chirped and called out and, finally, one of the old brown horses struggled to make its way to her. It stopped and glanced at the water trough, which was frozen solid. Then it raised its head and looked at the visitors with filmed eyes and an expression of puzzlement and pain that would never be forgotten by the visitors.

The Rescue Society's horse van arrived an hour later. By then, the gray mare had laid down and died in the frost-rimmed grass, despite all their efforts to keep her on her feet.

The three survivors were helped gently into the horse van headed for the Rescue Society farm nineteen miles away. The little, emaciated black gelding died en route. The other two horses survived and eventually were restored to good health and given good homes.

Late that memorable afternoon, walking back to Aunt Julia's truck, the sun suddenly slashed through the winter cloud cover. But it did nothing to raise their spirits. She could even tonight hear Aunt Julia's impassioned voice saying, "No animal should ever be mistreated like that. They depend on us for almost everything. They deserve our love. Most of all, they deserve our respect."

The rain suddenly stopped and she sat forward in her seat. She put on her gloves, pulled down the black raincoat hood over her head. Ready. Set. She ran across the parking lot to the door her fellow ALWD member had promised her would be left unlocked. She closed it quietly. The interior of this building was lit by ceiling *lights set at a dimmed level. No problem. She knew where she had to be. Third stall from the left. Poking her head out of it, watching intently, was a two-year-old filly named Fullerton Avenue, who had been just recently donated to the Carmel vet school by her Chicago owner after being injured in training, an injury that would prevent her from ever competing on the racetrack. Thus, her retirement and donation to the school.*

She paused for several moments to speak softly to the wide awake, nervous Fullerton Avenue, who was eyeing her apprehensively until she finally settled, accepting the presence of this stranger. Perhaps happy for the unexpected late-night company.

"At least they've fed you well while they've demeaned you," she whispered, stroking the horse's long brown face.

Then she reached into the pocket of her rain jacket for the loaded syringe.

Chapter Fifteen

Feeling not a bit jet-lagged as he settled in the backseat of the taxi taking him into Chicago, Doyle dialed his home message machine. He trolled through robo-call offerings of reduced mortgage rates (he didn't have a mortgage), "virtually free" electricity billing, offerings of life insurance rates so absurdly low that he laughed aloud. Ahmad, his driver, looked back over his right shoulder. "What you call good news, then, sir?"

"Hardly. Just nonsense news," Doyle said before continuing.

Next came a series of eight messages from the FBI, each of the last seven more urgent than its predecessor. Tirabassi and Engel alternated in asking, then pleading, then ordering Doyle to return their call ASAP. He decided he'd wait until he was home before doing so.

Ahmed drove directly to Jack's northside Chicago condo without further comment or question. Doyle was impressed.

"Ahmed, how do you know so much about the city? Where to go? According to that license pinned up on the dashboard, you've only been driving a cab six months."

A wide grin appeared under Ahmed's impressive mustache.

"I study…I am what you call a slick study, since I got here."

"Quick study," Doyle said, immediately wanting to retrieve his automatic reaction in correcting his driver.

Ahmed, unfazed, turned the final corner toward Doyle's address, slowed, and pulled carefully into the No Parking space in front of the condominium building.

Jack paid the fare and added a sizeable tip.

◇◇◇

After unpacking his suitcase, Doyle went to the refrigerator, grabbed a bottle of Guinness, and sat down at his desk before reaching for the phone. He quickly reviewed the FBI messages. Then he called Karen's number. She picked up on the first ring.

"Jack. Where are you? We've been trying to contact you. We've got bad news. Another horse killing."

"Aw, damn," he said. "I was in Ireland for a few days. Sorry to hear this. Where and when did this killing happen?"

"Two nights ago at Carmel College over in north central Indiana. Same MO, same result. And same kind of ALWD message left behind. This creep not only has a murderous bent, but he seems to enjoy rubbing our faces in it."

Tirabassi came on Karen's speaker phone. "Where the hell were you, Jack? I thought you promised us you'd concentrate on this case. And you went, where, to Ireland?"

"You know damn well I went to Ireland. Your vast organization could easily figure out my travel schedule. Damon, I had some business over there. Took a couple of days. I didn't think I need your permission to use my passport. Remember, I'm a volunteer here." He slammed the Guinness bottle down on the desk.

Karen came back on. "Sorry to be so critical, Jack. It's just that we've got to get to the bottom of this posthaste. Our Super is seriously on our backs."

"Karen, that I understand. But look at it from my standpoint. All I can do is use my racetrack contacts, keep my ears open, hope to get lucky. What you've got here is some lunatic driving Midwestern highways at night going about what is obviously undetectable criminal business. I don't know how you expect to stop this jerk. You can't station twenty-four-hour surveillance at every veterinary school in the country."

It was Damon on the line now. "Of course we know that, Jack. Our only chance is to get a tip. Find an informant. With your racetrack contacts, you are apparently our best bet."

Doyle laughed. "Well, our government is in deep shit if Jack Doyle falls into its 'best bet' category." He paused to polish off the Guinness. "Okay, folks. I'll keep asking questions. Keep my eyes open, etcetera, etcetera. I have no intention of ducking out of the country on you. I'll stay on it. Okay?"

He could hear Damon's obviously relieved exhalation of air in the background before Karen said, "Fair enough, Jack. Do your absolute best. *Please.*"

He went to his couch, turned on the television. Too early for the Chicago Cubs' night game. MSNBC was on, but Doyle was in no mood to listen to the bright, effusive host of this particular talk program, a man so determined to dominate the proceedings that he would ask his well-chosen guests a good question, then mainly answer it before allowing them a chance to do so.

Still restless, he checked his watch. Early evening, maybe not too late to get in touch with Ingrid. He knew she usually went to sleep early because of her dawn appointments at the racetrack. She picked up on the first ring.

"Hi, Jack. I assume you heard the latest."

Doyle said, "Oh, yes. Bunch of messages from my pals, the distraught FBI agents. They're getting heavy heat from above to find this killer. Anything new on your end? Rumors, scuttlebutt?"

"No, afraid not. Just wild speculation. Some people think it's an embittered racetrack worker who was fired and is seeking revenge. Another theory holds that it's a disbarred vet, also taking revenge. A third school of thought, if you can call it that, is that these ALWD people, it may be several of them involved, are dedicated to raising their profile by continuing the killings. From that standpoint, they've enjoyed success. Every news report on the dead horses mentions ALWD, although their leadership continues to deny any involvement."

She sighed and Doyle could envision her yawning. He knew she was at Heartland Downs every morning by five. "I won't keep you," he said. "If you hear anything, or anything comes to mind, call me on my cell. Any time."

"Will do. Will I see you at the track this week?"

"Probably. 'Night, Ingrid."

Chapter Sixteen

Doyle finished his five-mile run along the lakefront shortly before eight o'clock. He felt great after shaking out the effects of air travel and his few exercise-free days in Ireland. Inside the vestibule, he picked up his copy of the *New York Times*, as well as the *Wall Street Journal* of his across-the-hall neighbor, an elderly crab named Hannah Hansen. The bane of his early existence in the condominium building, she had complained to the condo board about the "raucous terrible music coming from that Doyle's place across the hall." In response, he increased the volume on his CD player for a couple of nights before relenting and using earphones when he wanted to hear Dizzy Gillespie's band roar. She never thanked him. The few times they met in the hallway, Hannah scowled while Doyle silently bowed in her direction. He still brought her paper up to her door whenever he saw it downstairs.

One message on his answering machine. "Call Mr. Kellman, please." He did. Kellman's secretary Joanie Saltzman answered with a "Good morning, Jack," and put him through.

Moe said, "How about lunch today? We haven't talked for a while. I want to hear about your foray to Ireland. The FBI case. So on. How about it?"

Doyle said, "Fine with me. Where?"

"Al Fresca's would be good."

"I think it's supposed to rain today. I don't know about eating outside. Anyway, where do you want to go?"

Moe said, "Jack, sometimes you exasperate the hell out of me. I'm not talking about having lunch *outside*. I mean the new restaurant just opened on North Clark by Al Fresca. He's the nephew of Sal Fresca, an old friend of mine from the west side."

Doyle groaned. "Al Fresca. Not al fresco. Sal Fresca. Is this a version of Abbot and Costello's Who's on First routine?"

"You want to have lunch there or not?" Kellman barked.

Doyle couldn't resist. "Is your old friend Al Dente going to join us?"

Moe hung up.

The rain predicted by Chicago television's panel of highly paid weather prognosticators did not eventuate. Moe and Jack sat at one of the half-dozen sidewalk tables outside the bustling new restaurant. Doyle had enjoyed a tasty *bruschetta* and was content to relax as Moe worked his way through a large bowl of thick, aromatic, garlic-laced pasta and bean soup. The early afternoon sun warmed the steady stream of pedestrians on Clark Street.

Doyle drank from his bottle of Moretti Beer, an import from Italy that he had begun to favor. "Know what my Uncle Colin Doyle used to say?" he asked, sitting back in his comfortable wicker chair, contented.

"Tell me."

Doyle said "Colin's mantra, if an old Mick can have a mantra, was 'Pray Irish. Eat Italian.'"

Bowl empty and removed, Kellman drained his Negroni and signaled for another. "So, Jack. You had a good trip to Ireland?"

"Yes. Saw Mickey. Went to a dinner where she won a big award. Spent some time with Nora. Both girls said to say hello to you. And I visited Niall Hanratty down in Kinsale."

Kellman frowned. "Why? You're not exactly the roaming tourist type."

"His wife, Sheila, asked me to talk to Niall. She's concerned about some threats he's received. I spent a couple of hours with him. He brushes off the threats. Probably needless concern on the part of a loving wife according to Niall. Sheila is really a sweet, sweet person."

The entrees arrived, sausage and rigatoni for Doyle, a "chef's specialty" pasta presentation for Moe with shrimp, pecorino, and plenty of garlic over linguini.

Moe took a piece of the warm Italian bread, passed the basket to Jack. "What about here, what's going on here? The horse killer thing?"

"No progress, Moe. Another strike a couple of nights ago in another Midwest university facility. No clues, no traces. Damned if I can come up with any way to solve this nonsense, no matter how much the Feebs pressure me. I've put out feelers, asked around, tried to put myself into the mind of the kind of person who would be doing this. Sneaking into silent buildings full of animals in the middle of night and going up to one, some unsuspecting horse, and lowering the boom. I can picture it happening. But I can't picture who the hell is doing it."

He plunked down his empty bottle of Moretti. "You tell me how to find a way through this mess."

"I don't think I can do that, Jack. But I can counsel you to be patient. Sooner or later, whoever you're after will screw up. They usually do. Prisons are full of front-runners who didn't look back to see what was gaining on them until it was too late."

Their conversation was interrupted by a cry of, "Hey, Moesy," and the arrival at their table of a heavyset, sixtyish man wearing a broad smile, a rakishly crumpled gray fedora, a rumpled seersucker suit. "Oh, shit," Moe muttered, before standing up to reluctantly shake hands and say, "How are you, Marty? Jack Doyle, meet Marty Farley, an old friend of mine."

Farley nodded at Doyle before turning to smile again at Kellman. Farley reached to pull out a chair from the table, but Moe laid a hand firmly on his arm. "Marty, sorry, no schmoozing today. Jack and I are going over some serious business. Know what I mean?"

Farley backed up a pace, smile erased. "Well, sure, Moesy. I'll just go inside and wait for my companion." With a resentful nod toward Doyle, he walked away.

Doyle said, "Why the brush off? Who's Marty Farley?"

Kellman sighed. "Known him for years. Former newspaper reporter, then started his own little public relations firm, always around, a full-time hustler. Before he got lucky in love, I used to wonder how this pain in the ass could make a living. He came up with some of the goofiest ideas you could imagine. One year, he was going around trying to raise capital for what he described as a 'Luxury Retirement Home at an Affordable Price.' He was going to call it The Last Stop—for, quote, 'Seniors with Senses of Humor,' unquote. Needless to say, this didn't fly. Besides a source of goofy ideas, he's a major league motormouth."

"Verbally incontinent?"

"Exactly," Moe said. "Never shuts up. Probably talks all night in his sleep. But as a perfect example of 'You Never Know in Life,' Marty a few years back meets a rich divorcee and they fall in love. He marries into a scrap-metal fortune. Lives up on the North Shore with his little, homely wife who must have been desperate to corral a husband. Highland Park, I think Marty got into Democratic politics up there. Even with all that money he married into, Marty's still the biggest freeloader I've ever known And that, my friend, is saying something." He drained his Negroni. "Marty is also a dedicated boozer. One of your people, so no surprise there. Irishers."

Doyle said, "Don't try to get a rise out of me with another of your ethnic slurs. You're awfully insensitive for an elderly Yid."

Kellman said, "May I continue?"

"Go ahead. I've got the Anti-Defamation League on speed dial."

Their waiter carefully placed the bill in the middle of the table, where it was ignored.

"Couple of years ago," Kellman continued, "I was invited to a very select Democratic Party fund-raising cocktail party at the Drake Hotel. Major league party donors. Couldn't go, I was going to be out of town. I ran into Marty in the Loop the day before and, for some goddamned reason, I don't know what came over me, told him about this party and asked him if he wanted to go in my place, said that he could use my invitation.

Well, sure. This was a freeloader's wet dream. Free booze, free food, rubbing elbows with the inner circle.

"The next morning I get a call at the office from a friend of mine, John Doherty, who was at the party. He lives north, too, Lake Forest I think. Anyway, John gets on Amtrak to go home from a dinner meeting after work, starts walking down the aisle of the Metra car until he comes to a guy passed out in the middle of the aisle, guy he recognizes. Lying on his back. Snoring. Emitting alcohol fumes. People are stepping over and around him. It's obvious the guy's not sick, just passed out from sloshing down drinks. Doherty recognizes the guy. It's Marty Farley. But the prostrate Marty on his suitcoat chest is wearing a large identification badge from the party that says in capital letters MOE KELLMAN on it. Doherty thought this was very funny. I did not."

"Did you call Marty on this?"

Moe shook his head no. "Wouldn't do any good. He'd just apologize for something he could barely remember doing and go ahead with his wealthy wife in his wavering life. What can I tell you?"

Conversation halted as a Clark Street bus stopped, disgorging passengers and exhaust fumes across the street. "I don't know how good Al Fresca's going to do being so near this kind of traffic crap," Moe said, sneezing."Let's get out of here. Hear me, Jack?"

Doyle looked away from the street and back at his friend. "Sorry, Moe, I can't help thinking about this horse killer deal. He or she will strike again, of that I am sure."

"What makes you so sure?"

"Percentages. Somebody gets going on a success streak like that, they don't stop. They start feeling stronger as they go on. Percentages say this villain or villainess or kill team, or whatever the hell it is, won't stop until they *are* stopped."

Kellman said, "You and your percentages. I'm not so sure about that stuff. That guy with baseball, James, and the kid with politics, Silver—yes they impress me. Love you, Jack," Moe smiled, "but I'm not quite sold on you along those lines."

"Oh, yeah?" Doyle put on his sunglasses, leaned back in his chair. "I'm pretty good at that. Give me a couple of minutes. I'll show you."

"Show me what?"

Doyle leaned forward, elbows now on the table. "Moe, I'm going to tell you right now that, in the next fifteen, twenty minutes, we'll see at least ten women hurrying by here on that sidewalk in front of us pushing baby buggies, infant carriages, whatever they call them. I'll order dessert while we wait. You want some cannoli?"

Kellman said, "Why should I sit here watching matrons or their hired help pushing babies past me? What are you talking about, Jack?"

"At least sixty percent of these women will be, watch for it, pushing with one hand and talking on their cell phone with the other. Bet on it."

"I'll take that bet. You and your generalizations. I'll go for a double sawbuck. Order the cannoli. I'll have a grappa while I wait here to collect."

It didn't take as long as Doyle had predicted. Sixteen minutes later, ten carriage-pushing young women had gone past them down the nearby sidewalk. As Doyle gleefully point, "Not six but *seven* of the ten yapping on their phones."

Kellman pulled a bill out of his thick rubber-banded roll of currency. The only other item buried in this stack, Doyle knew, was Kellman's driver's license. The little man hadn't used a wallet since he'd had his pocket picked one furlough night in Seoul while on leave from the Marines during what he still bitterly referred to as the "Korean so-called fuckin' conflict."

Doyle put the money next to his coffee cup. "Moesy, I'll buy lunch. I feel bad taking advantage of you like that."

"Yeah, yeah, yeah."

Doyle said, "You've got to start giving me a little more credit for my theories. Remember that time last year? We were driving to Heartland Downs and we bet on the landscape companies? I said at least seventy-five percent of the trucks we'd see that day would have Mexican-American names on them. Garcia Gardening. Martinez Landscaping. Jose Hidalgo and Sons. You scoffed. Then we saw a dozen of those trucks. Nine of them had Mexican names on the side of them. You paid up, but I should have bet you more."

They got up from the table. Moe said, "Thanks for lunch, you sneaky bastard. I've got to get back to work."

Chapter Seventeen

Six hours away in Ireland, as Jack and Moe were waving goodbye to the effusively grateful Al Fresca on North Clark Street in Chicago, Niall Hanratty walked out of the Kinsale headquarters of his Shamrock Off-Course Wagering firm and took a deep breath of the early evening air. Sleeves still rolled up, suit jacket carried over his shoulder, a bounce in his step even after the twelve-hour stint he'd just put in. It had been a huge winning day, one of the best in the fifteen-year history of Shamrock and its forty-four-year-old founder and owner. Hanratty had suspected as much. His hopes were confirmed by Tony Rourke's final tally of the day. Business had boomed at nearly every one of the Shamrock shops scattered about Ireland, making prospects look bright for the establishment of two new ones in England. As usual, the famous race meeting at Royal Ascot across the Irish Sea stimulated bettors' plans and hopes and, today with a flourish, Shamrock's bottom line.

Even now, going on nine, the streets and sidewalks of this small, picturesque town were crowded. Hanratty paused at the entrance to his parking lot to inhale the familiar smell of the nearby harbor. He speed-dialed his home. "Sheila, we've had a brilliant day," he told his wife. "Tell the boys to wash up and get ready. We'll go out for dinner tonight, right?"

"Grand idea, Niall. I'll have them ready. Dermot is due back just now from hurling practice. Pat and Liam are out in the pool.

We'll be quick. I'm eager to hear about your day. Will you be along soon, now?"

"Ten minutes, tops. Then I'll shower quick, change clothes, and we'll be off. Do you mind going back into town to Moran's? If not, call ahead, ask for our regular table on the patio." Hanratty smiled as he heard her enthusiastic reply.

Four and a half miles up the coast road, as he listened to his new CD of The Chieftains, the descending sun was layering light on the blue-green waves of the sea. Niall shaded his eyes and lowered the driver's seat visor as he made the turn leading to his home two miles away. He slowed the BMW at the spot where the road narrowed next to a cliff overlooking the churning waters.

The Chieftains' music suddenly blared, then just as suddenly stopped, as the BMW seemed to hit a snag and veer violently. Niall fought the pulling steering wheel. He heard a thumping sound as first the right rear tire blew apart, then the right front. The vehicle violently veered toward the cliff edge.

Niall pumped the brake. Wrenched the steering wheel to the left as he neared the drop-off. The knuckles of his large hands on the steering wheel were bone white. "Aw, Jaysus," he muttered as he exerted every ounce of his panicked strength.

Two seconds later, the BMW came to a tottering halt on the cliff's edge. Hanratty sat still. Breathing heavily, he was careful to keep himself centered in his seat. The BMW's right front tilted precariously. He carefully detached his seat belt and opened his door. He leaned out and placed his left hand on the graveled roadside. He slowly shifted his body toward the door and began to ease out.

Niall was nearly free when his right foot caught on the slowly receding lower edge of the driver's side door. He felt himself being pulled back with the now moving auto. Both hands gripping at the roadway gravel, he kicked as hard as he could. His foot came free. He fell facedown before turning up and onto his side in time to see his BMW tilt and began its end-over-end descent to the boulder-strewn border of the beach three hundred meters down.

He got to his feet and looked down at the debris of his auto. "Thank God there was no one on that strand when that happened," he said to himself. He wiped the sweat off his forehead with a slightly trembling right hand. Wiped the smear of blood off his forehead which he'd scraped on the roadway. "And thank you, Lord, that I wasn't down there for that landing."

After retrieving the cell phone that had fallen from his shirt pocket, he began walking up the side road to the highway. He took several deep breaths before Sheila picked up and he told her he'd "be a bit late. I'll tell you why when I get there." He cut off the connection before she could launch a question.

Walking down the gravel-bordered coast road toward home, Hanratty thought, *This was no feckin' accident. Not with two blown tires.*" Striding more quickly now, his jaw set, he called the cell phone of an old friend, Kinsale Garda Captain Dion Fryer. Filled him in on what Niall said were "recent happenings out here, my friend. When you dig my auto out of the rocks and sand, you'll see what caused that mess. Call me when you know anything."

Only a few yards after Niall had turned onto the main road leading to his home, his neighbor Emma Morrissey pulled up beside him in her station wagon. "A lift, then, Niall?" she said, leaning across the passenger seat toward the door she'd opened. Emma took a long look at Hanratty's scraped face and dusty clothes. He said, "Had an accident, Emma. Thanks for stopping."

When Niall walked in his door, Sheila looked up and frowned. "What happened to you? Was that Emma dropping you off?"

Niall took off his jacket with its newly torn sleeves, put his cell phone on one of the front hall tables. "Tell you what. I'll give you the whole story after I use the shower and change. Tell Moran's we'll be a bit late. We'll have to take your SUV." He gave her quick kiss and trotted up the stairs.

Garda Captain Fryer called Hanratty just as he and his family were finishing their desserts at Moran's. Neil excused himself and walked out onto the patio. "What is it, Dion?"

"Niall, both your right tires were punctured. Not so that you'd feel it when you first started driving, but soon enough. Must have been done right before you got in the car. Actually, I'm surprised you drove as far as you did before those tires fully gave way. Obviously, the cuts were not from the tumble down the cliff, Niall. This was some mischief purposely done, and malicious mischief at that. You're lucky you got out of the car in time."

Hanratty's jaw tightened as he heard Fryer ask, "Any idea, now, Niall, who'd be doing something like this to you?"

"No, Dion. There were a couple of other little incidents before this that I didn't take too seriously. I see now that was a mistake. Some *gombeen* has surely got it in for me. I've got to find out who."

Chapter Eighteen

Anyone bothering to watch as they took their slow paced morning laps around the Lexford Federal Prison exercise yard would have considered them to be an unlikely pairing. The older, shorter, heavyset man was continually voluble, hands active as he slashed the air, emphasizing his talking points. Next to him, the somewhat younger, much taller, much slimmer man was mainly silent, bent forward to listen to his companion. He occasionally stopped to adjust the new hearing aid he'd received two days before.

It was an overcast, unusually cool summer day in northwestern Wisconsin. Other prisoners perambulating inside the double-fenced perimeters wore windbreakers and caps. The Odd Couple strolled along unconcerned by matters farenheit, wearing their government-issued garb of khaki shirts tucked into khaki trousers, brown work boots. Harvey Rexroth was a large shirt, forty-inch waist, size nine footwear. Aldo Caveretta was medium shirt, thirty-three-inch waist, an eleven D.

Rexroth had been born into wealth and raised and pampered from childhood. Caveretta was a middle-class product of a small Kansas City suburb populated by third-generation Italian-Americans, most of them upright and law-abiding citizens. He had been recruited by the minority as a bright teenager, his college and law school educations surreptitiously financed by it. On their prison yard strolls, the stocky, completely bald Rexroth, referred to as Daddy Warbucks by some of the inmates, had to look up at his lanky, composed companion.

The Lexford Prison wardrobe was a continual irritant to Rexroth, a man previously accustomed to five thousand-dollar suits, imported handmade shirts, and custom-made ties, the cost of any one of which would feed an extended family in a Red Lobster Restaurant on any given night. Besides the expensive clothes, he missed the absence of servants, the expensive and nubile young women he retained for various entertainment purposes, the cadre of fawning order-takers that had surrounded him in each of his four luxurious U.S. residences and at his Bahamian estate, during his glorious dominating period when he headed his inherited media conglomerate. Though it had wound up putting him in Lexford, Rexroth even somewhat missed the less-than-successful thoroughbred racehorse operation he'd launched. That was it. He had no immediate family. His closest business cohort was tucked away in a different federal prison. But far outweighing all of this was Rexroth's molten hatred for the man who helped the FBI put him in Lexford on charges of insurance fraud and racketeering.

Caveretta was in residence as a result of a multi-charge racketeering conviction. It stemmed from his longtime role as legal advisor to Marco Scaravilli, Jr., veteran head of the Kansas City Outfit. Neither the attorney nor the media mogul ever mentioned the chain of events that had landed them in Lexford, though each man was well aware of the other's background.

The regular morning exercise the chunky media baron and the lanky lawyer engaged in was mandatory at Lexford, one of the so-called country club prisons in the federal penal chain. It featured minimum-security, healthy and not unappetizing menus, psychological counseling, tennis and *bocce* courts (in deference to high-ranking Outfit members, primarily from Chicago and Cleveland), horseshoe pits, convenient phone access, and a softball diamond that was seldom used since most of the potential players were middle-aged or older, well past even sixteen-inch slow pitch days.

Behind Lexford's double-fenced boundaries there lived in modest, but quite comfortable, cubicle housing some five hundred convicted white collar criminals who had dirtied their pinkies in physically non-violent ways. Among them were two ex-governors of a Midwestern state notable for producing such offenders, two former U.S. Congressmen, a scattering of various states' legislators. The majority of the population was comprised of felonious investment experts and banking executives, thieving businessmen, and corrupted attorneys. Among the latter was Rexroth's companion, Caveretta, on enforced sabbatical from his post as *consigliorie* for the Scaravilli Family.

This was at least the fifth time that the persistent Rexroth had questioned Caveretta about the progress, or lack of it, of their current project, which was arranging for someone to murder Rexroth's nemesis, Jack Doyle. It was Doyle, posing as a veteran horseman and working at Rexroth's huge Kentucky breeding farm, who had come up with the evidence of the cold-blooded killings of heavily insured stallions that eventually led to Rexroth's conviction.

Toward the end of their first year at Lexford, Rexroth and Caveretta found themselves sharing the same psychiatric counselor, Dr. Patricia Hough. Even this practiced practitioner marveled at the two men's shared ignorance of, or outright contempt for, morality. Rexroth enthusiastically regaled the stunned doctor with tales of his lifelong ethical duplicity. Caveretta was far less forthcoming, but the similarities between his life views regarding people who for some reason "owed," and those of Rexroth, stunned Dr. Hough. She considered it not surprising that these two men bonded while waiting for their appointments in their uneasy counselor's outer office.

So, when Rexroth asked his new friend during one of their spring morning walks if he could arrange to have someone killed, the response was a simple "Who?"

"A sneaky bastard named Jack Doyle. A Chicago guy."

Caveretta stopped. "Not, I presume, mobbed up in any way."

Rexroth said, "Of course not. The man is a tool of our repressive federal government." He took a couple of steps and deep breaths. No time to engage in another right-wing rant. "I don't know any Mafia people."

Caveretta smiled as he walked forward. "You must think you do *now*. Or you wouldn't be bringing this up, Harvey."

A tennis ball flew over the nearby court fence toward them, its propellant cursing at its flight. Caveretta reached up a big hand and snatched it out of the air. Tossed it back over the fence.

Caveretta said, "I'm not going to ask you why you want this guy killed. My question, Harvey, is this. How much will you pay? You want it done soon, it'll cost you. I'd put it at fifty grand before I even talk to my people. That would be wired to a bank routing number. *All* in advance. *Capice?*"

Rexroth shrugged. "Piffle."

Caveretta stopped walking. "Did you say cripple? You want a crippled hit man?"

"I said, 'piffle.' You know, a mere bagatelle."

Caveretta leaned toward Rexroth, puzzlement evident on his long, sallow face. "A dear rag and bell? What the hell are you talking about?" Irritated, he fiddled with his hearing aide, muttering, "Fuckin' government-issue."

Rexroth, trying to tamp down the level of his irritation, said, louder, "Never mind. Can you get this done, Aldo? Every day that conniving bastard keeps breathing makes me seethe. I need him gone." Another right-handed chopping of the air for emphasis.

Caveretta glanced behind him before saying, "Look, Harvey, this kind of project cannot be carried out in days. I have to talk to people. Not just over the phones here with the fed ears stuck to the line. I have to use other methods of communication. It'll take some time."

They walked to the northwest corner of the fence before turning back. Rexroth was trying to contain his exuberance as they passed under a guard tower, ignoring one of the resident Prairie State ex-governors also walking beneath it who strode past, smiling and waving at them.

"Stupid bastard must think he's running for office," Rexroth snorted. "To think I shoveled major money to that nitwit's campaign. I thought he was a cleverer crook than he turned out to be." Rexroth shook his head in disgust. "You just can't count on a lot of those thieving bastards."

They turned left at the southern barrier, heading back toward the entrance, before Rexroth suddenly stopped and grabbed Aldo's elbow. "My friend, who do you think would carry out this, uh, assignment? I've heard about guys like Slicer Sam, Golf Bag, Stan Hunt, Jimmy Nibbles. Will you get somebody like that for this?" Rexroth said eagerly. He frowned before adding, "Especially for this kind of money?"

"Jimmy What?" Caveretta said. Agitated, he took another try at properly adjusting the beige item in his right ear. "Harvey, those are all bullshit names. People see them in movies, TV, and think that's what our guys are called. Our people have regular names. None of which," he said, opening the door for Rexroth, "you will ever know."

Chapter Nineteen

One of the names that would never be given to Rexroth was that of W.D. Wiems of Lawrence, Kansas, a graduate student in computer science at the state university where he had met the well-known campus figure Marco Scaravilli the Third, the youngest son of Kansas City Outfit boss Marco Scaravilli, Jr. Young Scaravilli was in his first year of graduate school in business. A gun nut from boyhood when he would join his cousins to blast away at targets on the back acreage of his grandfather's secluded rural estate, Marco Three, as he was known to his relatives, maintained that interest at Cartridge Central Shooting Range on the southwest edge of his university city. He did it for pleasure, not vocational preparation. Like most fourth- or fifth-generation descendants of this country's Mafia pioneers, he had been guided from youth to be far away from the family business and into the legitimate side of American commerce. Marco Three was on track for an MBA and eventual management of his father's extremely private hedge fund. His only brother, Dario, had been steered by his shrewd, demanding parent into the study of law, not breaking it. Several other professional people were leaves on the now nearly legitimatized Scaravilli family tree.

One late Friday night, Benny LaPier, owner of Cartridge Central Range, accepted Marco Three's Remington .44 and state-of-the-art stereo earmuffs, for placement in the building's locker section. "Hey, Marco," he said. "Take a look at that skinny redheaded kid at the end station on the right. He can shoot the lights, and everything else, out." They watched a ten-minute display of gold medal quality shooting from this unlikely look-ing marksman. With his tall, slim frame, long pale face, head of unkempt bright, orange-red hair, he looked completely out of place in this locale. As the bull's-eyed targets were returned on the wire to the shooter, LaPier said, "Damn! How about that kind of shooting!"

Marco Three said, "Fucking amazing. And he's left-handed."

"So what? So was Billy the Kid."

The redhead approached the counter with his weapon and gear. Marco Three stepped toward him, saying, "Hey, some fantastic shooting, dude." He extended his hand. "My name is Marco. Can I buy you a beer across the street at Shorty and Lammy's? I'd like to learn who taught you to shoot like that."

Awkward silence before the redhead muttered, "W.D. Wiems." He quickly looked Marco Three up and down, glanced at the range owner, then shrugged and said, "See you over there."

Marco Three had never considered himself a talent scout, per se. But he knew that his father's reduced, though still potent, organization had for several years been without what for many previous decades was a farm system of eager brutes. There was a late night when Marco Three and his father had shared *grappas* in the mansion's kitchen, Marco Jr. as serious as his favorite son had ever seen him. Marco Jr. leaned forward, his hairy, bowling pin-sized forearms on the oak table, pensive look on his lined face. "See, it's a problem we'd never thought we'd see. Guys my age, guys who came up like me, Feef in Chicago, Bruno in Jersey, other top guys, we all steered our sons away from Our Thing. Then, one day, we look around and we got nobody coming up we can trust to do things. Our made guys, *merde,* they're about down to handfuls. Old, fat, and lazy. Pass the biscotti."

Marco Three said, "Papa, how many of these, like, experts, lethal-wise, do you need?"

His father emptied his glass of *grappa* and re-filled it. "Not that many. It's all changed. The hitters we used to need, we don't need that many anymore. Some muscle still for bookmaker clients, loan sharking, although that's way down what with all those fucking Cash Caller Quickest Money or whatever they call them shylock stores, not so much anymore. But, every now and then, you need somebody who can take care of business in the old way of taking care of business." He stopped to dip an almond biscotti into his glass of *grappa*. "My problem is the, you know, what do you call it?"

"Scarcity," Marco Third said. "Lack of talent."

Marco Three had that conversation in mind as he bought W.D. Wiems his second Miller Lite, himself another Crown Royal rocks to nurse. He'd tried to talk a little sports with Wiems. Asked him about school, how he liked being a KU grad. Was he getting "any pussy here in Lawrencetown?" Wiems showed no interest in any of these subjects. Then Marco said, "Hey, dude, I never saw anybody shoot like you did over there tonight. Where'd you learn how to do that?"

Wiems slowly shifted his eyes from the TV screen with its Ultimate Fighting Championship match that was entrancing most of the bar patrons. "My step-father taught me. He was a Marine sniper in 'Nam, he said. I believed him. Saw him shoot like a laser beam on our farm property. That's when he wasn't falling down drunk, or taking swipes at me and my Mama, who kept putting up with it. And him."

Wiems took a swig of beer. He turned away from the television screen to look directly at Marco Three, eyes bright behind his tinted, nerdy, black-framed glasses. "I had to finally get around to stopping that shit, you know? Both of them died 'accidental deaths.' They had to if I was going to get my life going. So, I inherited some money. Step-daddy's life insurance policy was a good one. The old bastard aimed it down at Mama, that stupid bitch, then down to their only child. Me." A hint of what Marco Three thought might be a rare visible expression flickered across Wiems' narrow, normally impassive face. Wiems smiled before adding, "Dude," and turning to look back up at the television screen.

Marco Three winced as he processed that matter-of-fact statement. He distractedly waved away the bartender's offer of "Another round for you fellas?"

"Guy runs the range told me you're majoring in what, computer science?"

Silence. Marco Three took a deep breath, tried again. "You from around here?" he said, lightly touching Wiems' arm for an answer. Mistake.

Wiems pivoted to shake off Marco Three's hand. Eyes a cold blue, color of an Arctic sea, unwavering. boring into his inquisitor. The answer was so quietly said it might have been "Topeka" or "Tupelo."

Marco Three said, "Hey, I was only asking. You know?"

He backed off as they both listened to calls coming from a newly arrived set of customers now seated down the bar, loud drunken demands for a television switch to an NHL hockey retrospective of the Stanley Cup Finals. The bartender obliged, ignoring protests from the now out-ranked UFC faction, figuring more spending would be coming from this freshly arrived and thirsty-looking group. He summoned a waitress to help him fill the newcomers' loud orders. The hockey contest was halted by a mid-ice scrum involving a half-dozen enthusiastic combatants all of whom had wisely removed their upper dental plates before the game's start.

Wiems ignored this. Started to slide off his stool. Marco Three quickly got up, saying, "I have to go. I'll walk out with you. Let me pay." He made sure Wiems saw him lay a fifty-dollar bill down on the damp bar.

In the drizzling rain of that Kansas night, he paused, buying a little time as he lit a Marlboro. Offered the package to Wiems, who shook his head. "I need to ask you something, Wiems. I heard what you said tonight. But I got to know, just between you and me, and just to get this straight, does the idea of killing bother you? People, that is."

Wiems moved slowly toward his big, all black Harley-David-son Harley Iron 883, parked five yards away, Marco Three trailing him, thinking *maybe I pushed this too far. Shit.* Wiems rested his skinny backside on the side of the bike, preparing to put on his helmet. "Between you and me," Wiems said, accurately imitating Marco Three's voice, "I've done some of that. Some for fun. Last few years, some for money. I don't need to do any for fun anymore." He paused. "And, *dude,*" he said mockingly, "I know who you are."

Wiems threw his right leg over the Harley and sat, helmet still in hand. "Mr. Marco. Three, Two, Four, whatever. And your family. Tell you the truth, I wouldn't mind doing some off-the-books business for you folks." A pause, Wiems looking off into the night, Marco Three struggling not to look surprised or impatient with this obviously psychotic, malicious, but very prime prospect.

Wiems said, "That means I deal only with you, none of your *groombuds* or whatever you call them."

Marco Three refrained from uttering a correctional *goombahs.* "Only with me? No problem. That can happen." He paused to wipe moisture from his forehead. Rain drizzle? Nervous sweat? Didn't know or care. "What about money? Pricing?"

Wiems turned on the ignition and the big cycle coughed briefly before smoothing. "All depends on the assignment. I change cell phones regularly. Don't give me your e-mail," he said, hint of a smile along with the words. "I'll find it. That's another thing I'm good at. You come up with some work for me, leave a message to yourself on your e-mail about where and when you want to see TK. And we'll meet." Wiems straightened the cycle front wheel and got ready to leave.

Marco Three, excited now, thought, *Topeka Kid? Tupelo Killer? Holy shit, who cares? This could be our guy.* He took two quick steps toward the Harley.

"*Wait.* Wait." He grabbed Wiems' left arm. "I've got a question, W.D." After a deep breath, and a look around the parking lot, Marco said, "What's your range? Like, how far would you go, for one of these, uh, assignments? Well paid assignments," he quickly added.

Wiems tugged his tinted, visor helmet onto his head, booted the kick stand into place.

"The known world," Marco Three heard Wiems say. Then the big Harley jumped forward, spraying gravel behind it, some of it across Marco Three's ankles and feet. He watched Wiems roar off into the night. Smiled as he looked ahead to reporting these promising findings to his father.

Chapter Twenty

Shortly after one o'clock the next afternoon, Marco Jr. looked up from the desk in his backroom office at Primo Pizza, one of seven such Scaravilli family food outlets scattered about the Kansas City area, to see Marco Three coming through the doorway. With his father busy on the phone, Marco Three reached into the little office refrigerator and extracted a Mountain Dew. He flopped down on the worn, brown, leather couch and waited while Marco Jr. continued his phone call. Marco Three realized the conversation did not involve any other of his family's numerous business enterprises, the two floral shops, a large construction company, five car washes, the limousine rental service, all located here or in other Midwest cities. What his father was dealing with here had to do with more traditional Scaravilli concerns.

"Bruno, you got a real problem with Mr. No Name over there. You tell me he again won't pay what he owes. That he's getting nuts, threatening to go to the cops. Well, here is my advice to you. Here is what I recommend. *Trunk* the fucker. Let me know how it goes." He slammed the phone down.

Marco Three sat forward. He was about to say, "I never heard trunk used as a verb before" in a piece of advice involving murder, but he decided not to when he saw the dour look on his father's face. The older man said harshly, "What the hell happened to you? You look like you got run over by a booze truck. You weren't due to come down from school until next weekend. What's going on?"

His son, pale, shaky, but grinning, leaned forward—"Pop, I had a terrific night. Celebrating. Probably too much. And I didn't get much sleep before I drove down here. Covered the thirty-three miles in about twenty minutes. My new MG drives like a dream. But, Pop, I had to hurry here and tell you in person. What I've got lined up is…"

His father held up a hand to interrupt. Clicked on the intercom. Ordered "two espressos, a slice of pepperoni and cheese, and a big glass of milk, Angela." Marco Jr. had for years recommended pizza and milk as a hangover antidote to be followed by strong coffee. "What celebrating?"

"Celebrating a big find I made. Pop, remember when we were discussing the, uh, shortage of guys to carry out, uh, certain kinds of business?"

"Yeah. So what?"

Marco Three said, "Have I got a guy for you. Hungry. Terrific with guns. Low-profile, high-quality in the brains department."

His father nodded appreciatively. "Interesting. Very interesting. I'd like to look this guy over before we talk any business." He waited until waitress Angela had entered with the tray and placed it on the couch next to Marco Three, who nodded this thanks as she left the room.

"Tell you what. Bring him to me. Make it next Sunday, here, after I get back from eight o'clock Mass." He made a mental note to also update Aldo Caveretta on the progress of this talent search the imprisoned attorney had put in motion.

Chapter Twenty-one

Carlos Hidalgo carefully pulled into the VIP parking area in front of Event, the ultra-popular nightclub on Chicago's near north side. He waited as an attendant rushed forward to open the right rear door of the white stretch limousine for Wendell Pilling, who grunted as he slid his jumbo-sized body outward. Emerging right behind him was diminutive Donny Bruno, the lone vice-president of the revolutionary Internet company Pilling had devised, developed, and sold for a half-billion dollars.

Hidalgo waved at the attendant, who motioned him to turn into the nearby alley where he could wait, as usual. Hidalgo nodded a thank you.

Engine off, his seat back now, Hidalgo lowered his chauffeur's cap over his eyes. Also as usual, he had no idea how long he would be on duty this night. Pilling, now Hidalgo's sole employer, had proven very unpredictable during the six months Hidalgo had worked for him. These had included some trying times, especially at the start. What Pilling considered good-natured bandinage, Hidalgo not surprisingly recognized as abuse. Pilling frequently addressed his driver saying, "Hey, beaner." And "you slick spick." And Pilling's favorite: "WB" for wetback.

Carlos Hidalgo, fifty-two years old and an undocumented immigrant with a family of five, quietly suffered these indignities because his wealthy employer had him on a retainer for five times the normal rate in the city of Chicago.

⟩⟩⟩

Once ushered past the lengthy line of people waiting to be admitted to Event, Pilling folded a fifty-dollar bill into the hand of the obsequious shift manager who said, "The usual, Mister P?" An affirmative nod was the answer. Donny Bruno, as usual close at the side of his friend and employer, commented, "Looks like a cool collection here tonight."

Pilling ignored him and went up the carpeted stairs to the club's Premier Suite, a large room with five black leather couches, a lengthy glass coffee table in front of each, on which had been placed silver buckets containing magnums of Dom Perignon. Pilling walked to the wide glass window overlooking the huge, packed, dance floor with its dozens of denizens gyrating to a DJ-produced beat that was audible even up here. Strobe lights bounced off the silver chandeliers and the dancers—couples, racially-mixed couples, singles concentrating on their moves—formed what Bruno said, "Looks like another real wave of humanity, right, Wendell?"

Pilling didn't answer. Bruno was used to such treatment from the hulking genius beside him. Ever since they had shared a dorm room at Cal-Tech twelve years earlier, the diminutive, talkative Bruno had stayed paired with the student referred to as "Weird Wendell" by classmates who, years later, deeply regretted such denigration of the man who would become one of the richest of America's under-thirty moguls.

The opportunistic Donny Bruno had a good eye for the main chance. Bruno attached himself to his brilliant roommate to such a degree that caused other students to call him "The Human Barnacle." That university association developed into a bonanza for Bruno, who rode the coattails of Pilling's extraordinary success in the Internet world. They were a genuine odd couple in many ways, yet brothers under the skin in other ways. Bachelors, neither physically attractive, but as Bruno happily put it, "Smart as hell and rich as Croesus. Especially my man Wendell."

To Pilling it looked like another boring as hell night in Chicago, his hometown. He moved away from the window that overlooked the frenzied dance floor. Shrugging off his size fifty, two thousand-dollar beige cashmere sport coat, he sat down heavily on the nearest couch. A nod, and Bruno quickly reached for the nearest bottle and poured champagne into an out-sized goblet before handing it to his boss.

Bruno poured a half-portion for himself. He said, "Wendell, why so glum? Looks like a lively scene here. I'll bet things will pick up once word spreads that you're here."

"I doubt that," Pilling said. But then his face brightened. "Those girls we had up here last week—did you spot any of them downstairs?"

"No."

A waitress in an outfit skimpy enough to make a Hooters girl look overdressed opened the suite door to ask, "Mr. Pilling? Anything you need? As always," she added with an inviting smile. He ignored her.

Bruno said, "We saw her last time here. That's Destinee. Knockout-looking broad. Am I right?"

Pilling drained his goblet and motioned for a refill before saying, "Yes, I remember Destinee. That night she was wearing a short skirt slit to her clit. So what? I don't like over-advertised pussy."

"Jesus," Bruno muttered to himself. "Another long night of dissatisfaction from Wendell." Bruno had a hard time fathoming Pilling's discontent. Social misfit that he was, Pilling ironically had made his fortune in the world of social media. He sold his company at the peak of an Internet boom. But scooping up his millions had not satisfied this brilliant eccentric. Pilling had rushed to purchase expensive homes in three cities, several overpriced artworks, and a half-dozen valuable antique autos. None held much interest for him. As for romance, Pilling's chances were compromised by the fact that he looked like an adult version of the Gerber baby with slightly more hair. Bruno was no George Clooney either, but he had little trouble connecting with women, especially those he made sure knew of his economic worth and connection to Pilling.

The double doors of the suite banged open, startling both men. In strode a party of seven, led by a man Pilling and Bruno immediately recognized—the famous TV chef Robby Maye. Two men and four gorgeous women trailed after Maye, who was talking excitedly.

Donny Bruno jumped up to protest this noisy intrusion. But he was stopped in his tracks by Robby Maye's outstretched hand and huge smile. "Hey, sorry, if we're kind of loud. Won a big race out at Heartland Downs this afternoon with a horse I own." He gestured to the group behind him. "The winner's circle celebration continues."

Maye clapped his hands and turned to face his group. "Everybody who made money today betting on my winner give me a kiss."

At first appalled by this noisy group, Pilling watched intently as they settled in on the several nearby couches to share the champagne that Desiree hurried to pour. Even Bruno kept quiet and looked on.

Ten minutes later, waiters came in bearing platters of jumbo shrimp, expensive cheeses, and two lavish vegetable trays. Robby Maye tasted one of the shrimp, then nodded his approval to the lead waiter before pressing a bill into his hand. "Good work, my man," Maye said. "Have a Benjamin on me."

Maye turned and said, "Hey, Pilling. The manager downstairs said you were up here. I've heard a lot about you. You and Shorty there want to join our party? We're having a bigger-than-big night."

To the insulted Bruno's amazement, Pilling agreed. Bruno watched his boss amble over to sit down next to the florid-faced celebrity chef. The two talked earnestly, ignoring the rest of the party. Leaning forward, Bruno heard Maye say, "Wendell, no matter all the success I've had—a top cable show, chain of restaurants, best-selling books, all great stuff—I've never had the kind of kick like I did when my horse Here's Cookin at U won this afternoon. You just can't beat that, man. Sure, plenty can go wrong owning racehorses. But the highs, man, let me tell you they are *very* high."

A few minutes later the conversations in the suite decreased when Maye grabbed a remote control and turned up the sound coming from one of the fifty-two-inch color television sets on the back wall. "Check this out, gang," he shouted.

There on the giant screen was a shot of the winner's circle scene from that afternoon. Maye, standing a bit uneasily near his colt, was being interviewed by a nationally known sportscaster whose network had that afternoon televised the big race. Here's Cookin' at U pranced about before the smiling jockey dismounted and a groom led him away. Maye and his group high-fived each other, the trainer, and the jockey.

The sportscaster finally managed to interrupt the jubilant hooting and hollering and collar the famous chef once more. Pilling leaned forward, peering at the screen. He listened as the hyped-up Maye said his colt would, "Now be aimed at the Heartland Downs Futurity. We're gonna kick ass again that day!"

The parking attendant knocked gently on Carlos Hidalgo's driver's side limo window. Carlos grunted, shook himself fully awake, and slowly motored from the alley to the front of Event. He waited as his employer and his employer's often irritating companion were settled in the backseat.

Leaving Rush Street and heading toward the Outer Drive and Pilling's penthouse residence, Carlos was surprised to hear the usually morose Pilling's enthusiastic cascade of talk. "I've got to get a great horse, Danny! Shit, I've got all this money and nobody knows about me but the other one-percenters in this country. You saw how much fun Robby Maye is having? His face on national television? Why not me?"

They rode the elevator to the fourth floor where Bruno got off. He lived in an expensive but comparatively modest condo purchased with the windfall from his association with Pilling.

On the ninety-fourth floor of this premium downtown Chicago condominium building, Pilling entered his penthouse and walked directly to his office. His prized mastiff he called Big Boy struggled to his feet, accepted a pat on his huge head, and wagged his tail before lying back down to again sleep. Pilling sat down in front of one of the six computers on the large table in mid-room. He logged on to begin a search for information.

Three hours later, the dark sky over nearby Lake Michigan now creased with the start of dawn, Pilling sat back in his chair, tired but satisfied. He had zipped through a thorough search of the thoroughbred horse business, a task that pre-Internet would have involved weeks if not months.

He had no interest in breeding racehorses, or in waiting for one of the major sales at which to bid on one. He wanted action now. A ready-made runner of ability and promise, locally based, available for him to buy *right away.*

Wendell Pilling sat back in his twenty-four hundred dollar black leather desk chair and smiled as the printer spewed forth the information he was after. He had been in need of a new challenge, and here one was. If Robby Maye, that "former fry cook" as Pilling thought of him, could achieve national renown beyond his original field with horses, then so goddamned well could Wendell Pilling.

Chapter Twenty-two

"Okay, Marcus. Thanks."

Doyle turned off his cell phone, having concluded a short conversation with his crack economic advisor, Marcus Dehnert. Careful man that he was, Dehnert always contacted Doyle directly before making any major move in asset management. Half the time, Doyle hardly knew what Dehnert was talking about in the areas of bonds management, hedge fund positions, or soybean futures. He just went comfortably along with what Dehnert came up with. The result had been a nice, steady growth in his portfolio.

He was heading out his condo door when the cell phone buzzed again. Seeing it was from Karen Engel, he re-entered his den/office and sat at his desk. "Doyle Investigations at your service."

"Hah. We'd sure like to see some proof of that claim," Karen said. "Which is why I'm calling. Are you busy tomorrow? I could use your help."

Doyle said, "I lead an active life, my dear. But I could probably clear my schedule. What have you got in mind?"

"Our boss, the man with the intense interest in this matter, points out that none of our people have visited the scenes of these horse-killing crimes. The Agency has just relied on reports from the locals on the scenes, which in all cases thus far have been college campus versions of security. Kind of weak, in our view. So, I am requested to personally visit one of the scenes. I'm going to Carmel College in Indiana starting tomorrow morning. It's about one hundred forty miles down there so I'd like beat the early rush hour traffic out of Chicago. I'd like you to go with me. Different set of eyes, and all that."

"Wait a minute. You want me to spend several traveling hours in the chilling, less-than-thrilling presence of Damon Tirabassi? He can't be any more excited at that possibility than I am. As you surely have become aware, your crabby colleague doesn't much care for me."

Karen said, "I've noticed that. And he's really only crabby when he's around you. But there's no need for you to worry. Damon can't go with us. He's been called to D.C. for his semi-annual review by our superiors." She giggled. "He calls it a 'professional proctology.'"

"I didn't know Damon had that much of a sense of humor."

Karen said, "Jack, let's face it. He's not the only person you know who doesn't, well, 'much care for you,' as you put it. You tend to be abrasive a lot of the times. Acerbic. You know what I mean."

Doyle, starting to get pissed off, was about to prove her right when he sat back in his chair, took a deep breath. "And often an asshole. Does that sum it up? Is that what you're saying?" He thought he could hear her draw a deep breath, too. Karen said, "Could we get back to business here? What I called about?"

"I looked around the room and found my composure," Doyle said. "Proceed."

"Shall I pick you up at Petros' at about six-thirty. Is that good? Are they open then?"

Doyle said, "That Greek starts heating the grease at six. Want to join me for an early breakfast? I'll buy."

"Frankly, watching you devour another one of your cho-lesterol-packed platters does not appeal to me. Bring me out a Danish and a large decaf, black, okay? I'll be in front of the restaurant."

"In one of the usual, unmarked, extremely recognizable government-issue cars?"

"Of course."

Doyle laughed. "If I supplied you with one of Petros' Greek-baked leaden Danishes, you wouldn't be able to steer the car. I'll grab you a raisin bagel from the Brooklyn Boys shop down the street. They've got decent coffee, too. See you in the a.m."

Karen was an excellent driver, smoothly zipping down the Dan Ryan before taking the Chicago Skyway to the Indiana Tollway and heading east. Wearing a dark blue pants suit and white blouse, black hair cut short, practical shoes, she looked to Doyle like her usual model of efficiency. Maybe a couple of worry lines had been added to her pretty face since he'd first known her, perhaps a pound or two to the athletic frame that had earned her a scholarship and women's volleyball honors at the University of Wisconsin-Madison a decade earlier. He sat back in his seat, ready to enjoy again the company of this attractive woman. He said, "I've been to Carmel in California. Never to the Hoosier version. How long do you figure it'll take?"

"We should be there by ten. That's when we're scheduled to meet with the head of the college vet school. A Dr. Hank Oettinger. He's still pretty shaken up over the death of their horse. Eager to help me. Us," she amended, smiling.

Doyle said, "I guess these fed mobiles don't allow for music CDs. Anything frivolous of that sort."

"'Course not."

He looked out the window at the gray industrial face of Gary, Indiana. and briefly recalled a song of that name from some movie musical soundtrack his folks played. "What about polite conversation during these taxpayer-financed ventures? That okay?" Karen smiled in agreement, keeping her eyes on the string of long distance haulers she was about to pass. He'd finished his coffee now. The sun was struggling to supersede the glowering Gary skyline. Doyle was beginning to feel perky.

Karen tucked into the right lane. "Talk about what?"

"What did you do before the Bureau? I know you were a UW athlete, then a lawyer. Mind me asking?"

She laughed. "Like it would bother you if I did? We've got a couple of hours to go. Hand me half of that bagel, will you?" The next sixty minutes went quickly as they chatted. After Karen turned off Highway 94 onto Interstate 65 heading south for Indianapolis, the cloud cover lifted. Tall wind turbines dotted the green fields in some areas near the highway.

"I think you know I come from Kenosha, right, Jack? Southeastern Wisconsin town, not far north of the Illinois border, right on Lake Michigan."

"I remember you, or Damon, telling me that. Didn't a bunch of actors come from there?"

Karen said, "Yes. Quite a few. Don Ameche, Jim Ameche, Charles Siebert, Harry Bellaver, Daniel J. Travanty, Mark Ruffalo, Al Molinaro, some others I can't recall. Except, of course, Orson Welles."

"Wait a minute. I think I read somewhere that Welles was born there. But that he didn't live there long."

Karen turned to Doyle to grin, "Orson probably lived there just enough to get his genius going."

She adjusted the air conditioner. "That okay?"

"Fine."

"The reason that I was thinking about my hometown this morning is that this is the date of the annual Taste of Kenosha held there at a place called the Brat Stop. Food, drinks, music all day and most of the night." She laughed. "There's going to be a music group appearing that I'd not heard of. According to the e-mailed notice of the event I received, a female accordion group called The Squeezettes will be providing, I am quoting now, German power-polkas."

"Hmm," Doyle said. "That's a musical concept new to me. But, back to famed Kenoshans, what about Don Ameche's cousin Alan Ameche? Great football player at your alma mater. Heisman Trophy winner, later All Pro with the Baltimore Colts, right?"

"Better believe Alan was from Keno. My dad, when he was in Bradford High School, was a lineman on Alan's championship football team. Dad was two years behind Alan in school. One of Dad's fondest, and most repeated, high school memories is being flattened in practice day after day trying to tackle Alan, the guy they called 'The Horse.'"

"Your father was an athlete," Doyle said. "Genes that must have helped lead you to being a jock. At UW-Madison on an athletic scholarship, right?"

He paused to say, "That idiot," referring to a Consolidated Printing Express sixteen-wheeler that had just pulled in front of them in the passing lane to begin a ponderous blockage. "It'll take this idiot five miles to ease past that lead truck," Doyle said. "He's going about a mile an hour faster than the right lane truck."

"Calm yourself, Jack. I think some of these long distance truck drivers pull these capers just to amuse themselves, maybe irritate drivers of the cars behind them."

Doyle said, "Well, what do you know? Here beside me am I hearing a governmental voice sympathetic to overworked, Dexedrine-fueled, bored-to-shit truckers?"

Karen finally pulled abreast of, past, then around the Consolidated truck, using her right blinker. The Consolidated driver gave an appreciative two-tap honk for her road courtesy.

Doyle said, "Good driving. Another question. Coming from where you did, I mean from liberal leaning UW-Madison, how'd you wind up joining the Bureau?"

Karen said, "Long story I'll make short. Got my BA degree in social studies, then my law degree from UW. Didn't have to pass a bar exam because in Wisconsin, if you graduate from either UW-Madison or Marquette University in Milwaukee with a law degree, you automatically become a member of the Wisconsin Bar."

"Really? You can make it out of a single law school and go right into practice? I think Chicago plumbers have to meet more licensing requirements than that. Whatever. What'd you do then?"

"I was recruited by a, quote, very prestigious, unquote, Milwaukee law firm, Bowen and Michaels. New hire entry assignments, scut work, did great, got promoted. Two years onto that payroll, I married the man in the firm who was mentoring me."

She paused to accelerate past another commercial truck caravan before saying, "And two years after that, I divorced him. A nice guy, actually. But it just didn't work out."

Doyle turned to look out his window. "Maybe like my sorry matrimonial experiences."

She smiled. "I don't think so, Jack. Not comparable." She paused, looking straight ahead, said "I think my life partner, Cynthia, would agree."

He sat up and turned to look at her. "Cynthia?"

Karen kept her eyes on the road ahead. "Cynthia Sandler. She's a pediatrician at Children's Hospital in Chicago. We've been together for nearly three and a half years."

Doyle said, "Well, I'll be damned." He paused. "On the other hand, maybe I won't be. Just surprised."

"So were my ex and my parents. I guess it just took me longer than a lot of people to discover exactly who I was. I'm just glad it happened. Cynthia and I have a great life together."

Doyle frowned. "What about the Bureau? Do you have to, uh, keep this relationship from them?"

"No, no," Karen laughed. "Times have changed. There's been a sizeable increase in Bureau personnel in both women and ethnic minorities. The 'White Boys' Club' of the past has been markedly broken up. And the Bureau doesn't discriminate against a person's sexual orientation with regard to either hiring or advancement. We have openly lesbian, gay, bisexual employees. Our Sexual Orientation Program was created to address diversity issues, to ensure equal employment opportunity. I've had no trouble along those lines."

Doyle said, "So, just asking, how many of your colleagues know that you're a lesbian? And how about Damon? Does he know?"

"I don't flaunt my lifestyle, Jack. I don't bother keeping track of whether people other than my immediate supervisors are aware of it. Damon? Sure, he knows. I told him more than three years ago."

"And," said Doyle, thinking of Karen's married FBI partner with his very conservative outlook on life, "how did Damon react?"

Karen said, "Like the friend he has been to me ever since we first partnered. My lifestyle has never been an issue between us. In fact," she smiled, "Cynthia and I spend parts of some holidays with Damon and his family."

They rode in silence for several miles before Karen said, "You're pretty quiet there for you, Jack Doyle. Have I shocked you by telling you about Cynthia and me?"

Doyle said, "You should know me better than that by now. I haven't found a whole lot of life to be shocking for a whole lot of years. Not after my oldest brother got killed in the first Gulf War. For me that was the leadoff item in the reality check lineup. What the loss of my brother did to my folks, to me. Then the stuff I dealt with, on the Bureau's behalf I might add, with Rexroth and his scumbag minions. I'm not really surpriseable anymore." He went silent, looking out his window.

"Are your folks living?"

"No. Long gone. Think about it," Doyle said, turning to smile at her, "for years now I've been an orphan. Without receiving any sympathetic treatment."

"There you go, making light again of something serious. Seems to me, Jack, you put in a lot of effort to skirt the border of your emotions."

"C'mon. That sounds like you're quoting psychobabble from some afternoon cable TV sensitivity show. Please."

No response, so Doyle said, "I take that back. Didn't mean to be harsh with you. Karen, I've always respected your professionalism. Talking to you today, I further respect your personhood, too. God bless you. Must have taken some courage to apprise the FB Bureaucrats of your status. More power to you."

She reached over and patted his hand. "You've such a way with words, Jack Doyle. Sometimes, even, with emotions."

He reached down to the car floor to retrieve the Brooklyn Bagel Boys bag. "There's one sesame still in here. Want to split it?"

Chapter Twenty-three

Karen checked the GPS and took a right turn after their ten minutes on U.S. 52 East. "Carmel," she said. "Eighty thousand residents of an affluent suburb selected as, quote, One of the Best Places to Live in America by *CNN Money Magazine,* unquote. That's what our web search came up with."

"Maybe not one of the best places in America for horses to live," Doyle said. "At least not where we're going."

A crowded arterial intersection temporarily halted their conversation. When the light finally went green for them, Doyle said, "I have a fortunately distant cousin, Doris Morton, who grew up someplace around here. Now she lives in downstate Illinois. She sends what's left of our family a Holiday Letter every year. Filled with boring details nobody but Doris gives a shit about. Last year she included before and after photos of her son Bo and his successful acne treatments. Doris, along with her mother and a lot of her friends, are addicted to those televised afternoon mclees. All those unhappy people, screaming at each other, so eager to exhibit their various degrees of unhappiness. I guess that's life, for them. Just not life slices I want to watch."

"Hey, Jack, much of life is messy," Karen said. "Much of it brutally so. But we go on dealing with it, right?" She turned to ask, "How do you deal with it? You've been down several different paths I know of. Probably some I don't know."

Doyle smiled. "Maybe later I'll detail how I deal with life's messy aspects."

Entering the city limits, they passed a green sign declaring the population of Carmel to be 80,110. "Many of them living comfortably," Karen said. "When I Googled Carmel, it said this is a very well-to-do suburb of Indianapolis."

He said, "You've got to turn right up there at the next intersection, onto Spring Mill Road, that's what the sign for Carmel College says. The school must be on the southern edge of town." Karen switched to the right lane and came up behind a black pickup truck bearing a bumper sticker sign reading Hoosier Daddy.

Waiting for the light to change, Doyle said, "To answer your question about life dealings, paths I've gone down, et cetera, I'm going to paraphrase something that I've been told the great jazz saxaphonist John Coltrane once said about his music, or maybe his life. Both of which a lot of people had trouble understanding."

Karen said, "My dad had Coltrane records. Played them all the time. Who told you about what Coltrane said?"

"Guy named Kelly Sill, a terrific jazz bass player I've gotten to know in Chicago. Kelly said some old grouchy guy, probably from the Glen Miller era, once confronted John Coltrane between sets at a New York jazz club and said to him, 'That stuff you're playing? Sounds like scrambled eggs to me, man.' And 'Trane said to him, 'Man, it's *all* scrambled eggs. Depends on how you *scramble* them eggs.'"

"I'll go along with that. This bass player, how do you know him?"

"Kelly's a big racing fan. Sometimes he rides out to Heartland Downs with me. Funny guy. One time we're at this stoplight on Willow Road, waiting for it to change, and there's a big semi next to us. When the light changes, there's a sharp sound from the truck. Its air brakes, I guess. Anyway, I kind of jumped, and said, 'What was *that*?'"

"'E-flat,' Kelly shot right back. Broke me up."

The light changed. They'd moved a block north when a soccer ball hurtled onto the street from between two cars in front of them. Karen stomped the brake just in time to avoid striking its young, towheaded, first oblivious but now startled, pursuer. Doyle could hear the boy's father hollering at him, at them, from the nearby yard. Karen waited while the kid shame-facedly retrieved the ball and ran back to his father. The man hugged the boy with one hand, waving a thank you at their car with the other.

"That should be Ninety-sixth Street ahead of us," Doyle said. "Take a left."

Karen pulled into a slot in the visitors' parking lot behind the main Veterinary School building. "Ten o'clock. Right on time," she said.

In the outer office Kim Budnik, the very attractive reception- ist, informed that Dr. Oettinger was "certainly expecting you. No, my dear, I don't need any identification." When Karen started to return her brown leather wallet to her purse, the woman said, "Wait, wait, I've changed my mind. I'd like to see an FBI badge in person." Karen smilingly obliged and displayed the gold-plated item with its impressive seal. Doyle fidgeted for the few moments the women made small talk about Karen's occupation. "I'd long thought about going into law enforce- ment," Kim Budnik confided. "But here's where I wound up, charting the progress of animals, and actually darned happy to be doing so. Although, I can't say that my parents feel that way about it," she added.

Doyle said, "Why is that?" Kim blushed. "I shouldn't have mentioned that. A few years ago, I was a runner-up Miss Illinois with a degree in drama. My folks believe I should have pursued a career in theater or movies. I didn't share their expectations."

"*Runner-up?*" Doyle said. "The judges must have been blind and deaf."

It was a two-block walk on a gravel pathway to the major barn during which Karen said, "You are so full of crap, Jack."

"Of what do you speak, woman? One of my father's heroes, H.L. Mencken, said men should always wink an eye at homely girls. I do that. I also find it just as much fun to flatter knockouts like that Kim. They never seem to tire of hearing such comments."

Waiting for them at the barn entrance was a stocky, middle-aged man wearing green scrubs and a welcoming smile. "Agent Engel? Mr. Doyle? Glad to see you. I'm Hank Oettinger."

"Our pleasure, Doctor," Karen said.

"Please. Call me Hank. I just completed a small surgical procedure on one of our resident goats. That's why I'm dressed this way. Come into my office and we can talk."

Karen said, "If you don't mind, Hank, we'd like to see the exact stall in the barn where your horse was killed."

He led them past a collection of curious four-footed herbivores and stopped in front of a stall occupied by an old gray mare. "This is Knight's Girl. A retired racehorse we accepted from our donors' list once we lost poor Fullerton Avenue. Luckily for us, there are many horse owners who are interested in supporting our research. A fact that, I am sure, enrages those crazies in that ALWD."

Oettinger showed them the door whose broken lock had been repaired in the wake of the killer's forced entry. "Up there, as you can see, we've installed a closed-circuit camera. Yes, I know, this is kind of like closing the barn door too late. But at least now there are two more cameras that have been placed in this building. Anyway, that's the scene of the crime."

Karen said, "It's not much different from the other ones. According to your college security report, there was no evidence that the attacker had been here?"

"None. And whoever it was must have been quick," Oettinger said, "because our night security patrols are closely spaced and, especially now of course, rigorously maintained. But," he sighed, "as you can see, all these precautions are long after, well, the horse has left the barn."

Karen handed the veterinarian her card, thanking him for his time. Walking back toward the barn office and parking lot, Dr. Oettinger turned to Jack. "Mr. Doyle, I take it you aren't a member of the Bureau. What is your...in what capacity are you here, if I might ask?"

"Ask away," Doyle said. "Crack Assistant would be the answer to that."

Chapter Twenty-four

Ingrid McGuire finally arrived home after a long, draining day at work. Trainer Buck Norman's favorite stable pony had suddenly come down with a bad case of colic. But Ingrid's treatment had saved the old horse. Then, driving home in the dusk, she had received another call from Jack Doyle about the veterinary school horse deaths.

Had she heard anything at all about this matter when at the track?

"No. Sorry, Jack, but no."

"Ingrid, I know you're busy day after day. And you sound worn out as hell right now, and I'm sorry to bother you. But I'm asking that you please try to keep this on your front burner. The FBI agents are getting tremendous pressure to find this criminal. And they keep pressing me. So, I'm just passing on this request again. Okay?"

"I hear you, Jack."

Minutes later, she entered her Palatine townhouse, washed her hands and face, and went to her favorite living room chair. Put her head back. Thought about going to Netflix for a movie. Thought about quickly reviving and driving the two miles to her favorite barbeque restaurant. Thought about those horses now back from pasturing and in their stalls for the night in veterinary school barns, either already feeling the effects of experimental drugs or soon destined to do so. "Criminal," Jack had said, describing someone who obviously had gone against the grain in trying to prevent these practices.

She walked into her kitchen, wineglass in hand, filled it, entered the bathroom and ran tub water. Minutes later, that day's dusty, soiled, work clothes tossed into the hamper, she stepped into the tub and lowered herself into the still rising hot water.

Maybe it was the second glass of wine, something Ingrid rarely resorted to. Maybe it was the tremendously stressful hours she had spent working on Buck Norman's cherished old pony, saved for now but not with many more years in front of her. She lay back, head propped on the tub's back, and closed her eyes, trying to scrub all thoughts of horse from her mind—at least for a while.

Chapter Twenty-five

Parking his four-year-old brown Volvo in the graveled space in front of his white bungalow, he turned off the ignition and sat back in his seat. Anthony Xavier Rourke, wizard accountant of the Shamrock Off-Course Wagering Corporation, felt "bone tired," as his father used to describe the feeling. Difference was that Da made his lifelong living prying peat from the Wicklow hills and selling it to people in need of fuel. He pictured that uneducated, country-strong exemplar of industry home from another long day's work, filthy overalls discarded inside the back door of the cottage, sitting after a hasty scrub-up in fresh clothes with his tea, responding to a claim of "bone tired" with a laugh. "Ya can't get bone tired unless you lift things by the hour."

But there was no denying Rourke was exhausted, both from a terribly busy day at work and from the increasing succession of sleepless nights of the past months.

He locked the car and carried his raincoat and briefcase to the bright blue front door of the cottage that, except for his depressed presence, had been empty for the last seventeen months. Moira's death at age forty-five, twenty-five years into their marriage, the result of tardily detected and then viciously advancing cervical cancer, had sucked the life out of their neat home, and out of him. He hung his suit jacket up in his bedroom closet. Then, as usual, he reached for the nearby doorknob of Moira's closet. It remained full of her clothes and shoes and hats, none of which he had been able to bring himself to discard despite the entreaties of their only child, Bridget. "Da," she repeatedly said, "you must begin to let go. Ma would want you to." Their conversations were via long distance. Bridget had married a fellow Trinity College student, computer whiz Ross Malone, and moved with him to California's Silicon Valley the previous summer. He had not visited the U.S., and Bridget and Ross had returned to Ireland only for Moira's funeral since emigrating.

Rourke inventoried his refrigerator's freezer and took out a Salisbury steak, regarding it with little enthusiasm. Food meant little to him, now. He opened a bottle of merlot, poured a glass, and took it and the bottle out the back door onto the tiny patio that faced the small back garden. In this tranquil, twilight setting, he felt his fatigue combine with frustration and the persistent resentment he could not seem to shake. He drained his wineglass, refilled it, and sat back in the lounge chair, again reviewing the disappointing events of the last few months. His goal was far from being achieved. His fault, really, since he'd employed an aged thug whose criminal skills had evidently seriously eroded. The results were amateurishly unproductive. He needed a true expert. What he knew was called a "hard man." Eighteen minutes later, decision made, he picked up his cell phone and dialed the Dublin number he'd been given.

Chapter Twenty-six

The howl of the daily six a.m. wake-up horn was the first thing that really horrified Harvey Rexroth during his introduction to life at Lexford Federal Prison. As someone who during his days as a free man had thrived on a nocturnal schedule featuring, as he proudly put it, "booze, broads, and bawdy happenings," Rexroth had been accustomed to rising at the stroke of noon. Shaving, leisurely bathing, then slowly moving into the business part of his day. That was the routine whether he was in residence at the Montana ranch founded by his robber baron great-grandfather; his Manhattan penthouse or Bahama estate; or, had been most often the case for most of the year, at Willowdale, his palatial thoroughbred horse farm near Lexington.

Widely acknowledged to be in the upper echelon of America's most brilliantly rapacious commercial leaders, Rexroth had inherited much, and then increased it to much more, primarily through his media empire. It included popular magazines, a chain of newspapers, plus television and radio stations. Among his immense holdings had also been *Racing Journal*, which he had launched in hopes of driving out of business the venerable *Racing Daily*, so-called Bible of thoroughbred racing, thus creating a lucrative monopoly in that field of sports journalism.

The one hundred twenty-five-year-old *Racing Daily* had been justifiably dismissive of Rexroth's efforts. As a power-wielding CEO of his various companies, Rexroth's intelligence, ambition, and ruthlessness had served him well. Those were qualities he'd been born with that were then buffed by the training he received from his late father or that tycoon's able assistants. But daily journalism was a field in which Rexroth had never previously set foot prior to *Racing Journal.* When he did, his feet sank in a swamp of debt and his start-up publication failed concurrently with the last appeal of his fraud and racketeering conviction.

At 6:05, Rexroth exchanged his electric blue silk pajamas for his drab khaki uniform. The inmates were permitted to provide their own night wear. Rexroth's head butler at the Park Avenue residence had shipped three pairs of expensive silk pajamas to his employer, all emblazoned with small, tasteful horse head designs. The irony of this, his involvement with equines having led directly to his imprisonment, was lost on the hard-headed multimillionaire.

His prison accommodations in the Eight-Building also angered him greatly, starting with his earliest Lexford days. How often he thought longingly of his Manhattan bedroom suite, with its circular, king-size bed beneath a widely mirrored ceiling, yards removed from the expansive windows overlooking nearby Central Park. Now, he awakened on a single bed near a simple chair, wall locker, and bulletin board, and next to a small table atop which rested his radio, turned to one of the dozen stations he owned, his favorite actually, the one headlined by bombastic commentator Rance Lamburgh, easily Rexroth's favorite among his thousands of employees.

Next to the radio stood a two-picture frame, the prison allotment. Rexroth's original entries were of two of his coterie of young, gorgeous, near naked female employees skating around on the specially built indoor track at Willowdale Farm. After one glance at those photos on Rexroth's first afternoon in residence, his Unit Counselor called for the immediate removal of these colorful souvenirs of Rexroth's past life. After that slap down, Rexroth left the picture frame empty.

Rexroth cautiously took his time before first visiting the communal bathroom having himself published several harrowing accounts of penal penetration. But he actually never felt uncomfortable there, or while showering, convinced that there was "None of that don't drop the soap and bend over bullshit in this higher-class facility." Like all Lexford inmates, he had until seven thirty to sweep and/or mop his small room. He usually finished these chores before breakfast. Prisoners were allowed ten to twenty minutes for that meal as well as the other two meals served in the large cafeteria during the day. Following his usual intake of syrup-drenched pancakes and three cups of cream-laden coffee, Rexroth visited the prison library to read the day's newspapers. His job hours were twelve thirty to three thirty p.m.

Rexroth and Aldo Caveretta had arrived at Lexford the same week. Like all new arrivals, their first work assignment was in Indoor Maintenance. Coming down a long Administration building corridor from different ends wielding brooms one Monday, backs turned, they had bumped into each other at the midway point. "Watch where you're going," Rexroth shouted, his face turning the color of a hydroponically grown tomato. It was his normal reaction to the unexpected.

Caveretta calmly stood back. "Why, Harvey Rexroth, nice to meet you." He leaned on his broom handle, smiling and composed.

The surprised Rexroth said, "Who the hell are you? How the hell do you know who I am?"

Caveretta frowned as he regarded Rexroth's blood-infused features. "Know who you are? Why, you're a famous sort of fellow. By the way, I'm no doctor, but I'd say, about 180 over 140."

Rexroth said, "*What*?" He stomped his foot, turning his right ankle on the broom's bristle block. "Ouch" was followed by "Damn" succeeded by "What the hell numbers are those? And who are you?"

"Aldo Caveretta, Kansas City," said the tall man. "Those numbers? That's my estimate of what would be your current blood pressure reading." He shook his head. "That temper won't stand you in good stead around here, my friend. You should settle down."

Rexroth, still smarting, said, "I suppose you don't have a temper. And you are like the rest of these losers in here, an 'innocent man wrongfully convicted.'"

"Why don't we finish our work before we earn demerits? We can have a talk today at dinner. I'll look for you." Caveretta turned his back and resumed his sweeping.

Dinner hour at Lexford was four o'clock. Caveretta spotted Rexroth pushing his way into the cafeteria line and smoothly moved to join him. "What's on the menu today?"

"Monday, must be some kind of spaghetti and that awful collection of steamed veggies," Rexroth replied. He shook his head in disgust. "The American taxpayer is not getting his money's worth with this dismal fare."

Caveretta said, "What are you talking about?"

The irritated Rexroth replied, "I am talking about the fact that each one of us here in Lexford, and each person in every other federal prison, costs thirty-six to forty-thousand dollars a year to maintain. Every fed joint serves the *same* lousy meals on the same day. Think of it. Thousands of us forcing down similar crap simultaneously. Talk about Big Government Ripoffs!"

Caveretta thought about suggesting that such punishment was perhaps what prison was for, but instead he reached for a Caesar salad. "I don't agree with you, Rexroth. I don't think the food is all that bad. Burger Day is okay. So is Fried Chicken Day. Tuna Salad Fridays, yes, you're probably right on that. But, my friend, Thursdays, with the baked *ziti*, not bad at all. Not like home, but not bad."

They filled their trays and took a small corner table. Rexroth said, "That's what you call that dago slop on your plate? ZBT? There were kikes in a college fraternity near mine called that. Or, excuse me, is that Italian cuisine?"

Caveretta slowly chewed his mouthful of the heavily sauced pasta before saying, "That attitude you've got, it's no wonder you wound up in here. You arrogant prick. It's called *ziti*. Pass the pepper."

Rexroth's face flushed again. He struggled to remain composed. "Being an arrogant prick in this place would be nothing out of the ordinary. And that includes you."

"Probably does," Caveretta said. "Aren't you going to at least try your *ziti?*"

"No."

"Well, then, hand it over here."

Rexroth scraped the pasta from his dinner plate onto his companion's. "Did they put this stuff on the menu in honor of the wops in here? Excuse me, Italian-Americans?"

"I have no idea. Maybe they were trying to appeal to all *The Sopranos* fans they've locked up. Who cares? I like it. It beats that WASP crap they shove out to us most days."

Rexroth sat back, quiet for a few moments until he said, "There's a good idea for a Rance Lamburgh radio essay. Which over-reaching Big Government son of a bitch, maybe a Study Team of them, determines what we are given to eat? Probably D.C. bureaucrats dining like kings on the taxpayers' dollars."

"I somehow doubt that, Rex. Hand me that salad you don't want."

Rexroth said, "Now that we're both finished with Maintenance Duty, what's next for you?"

Caveretta said, "I'm going to give Italian lessons. Mornings, Monday, Wednesday, Friday. I'm told six guys signed up. I'll probably know some of them. What about you?"

"I registered for classes in leather crafting. Why not, as long as I'm here? I'm getting tired of paying top dollar for my guinea-made, oh pardon me, Italian-made shoes and belts. Maybe I'll learn something useful like how to make them. Belts at least."

This conversation went on during the third week of the shift from Maintenance to Electives for this Lexford class. Talk at the other dining room tables was also about choices to be made from such possible curriculum items as Landscape Design, Computer Graphics, Personal Fitness, Horticulture, and How to Make Stained Glass.

"Now," Rexroth said sternly, "Aldo, I would like…" He paused to look over his shoulder. "I would like a progress report on Our Agreement."

"I'm sure you would, Harvey. But nothing's set yet. I'm going to use some of my phone time tonight. Maybe I'll know more by tomorrow."

Rexroth knew the attorney was referring to his PAC, the personal access code number issued each Lexford inmate for use in making outside phone calls, maximum usage limited to fifteen minutes per day per inmate. The media baron had been using his daily calls to upbraid, upset, browbeat, bully, threaten, and issue directives to the top-ranking managers of his empire. These regularly badgered but well paid executives were used to Rexroth's manic management technique and actually found the PAC phone time limit to be a boon to their health.

"All right. Let's talk tonight," Rexroth said. He walked to the refuse container and slid in most of his tray's remaining contents.

They met in the nearly deserted prison library at seven o'clock. Caveretta pulled a novel from a shelf, Rexroth picked up a copy of one of his company's magazines. They sat across from each other at a small, otherwise deserted table.

"Well?"

Caveretta sighed. "Harvey, were you *ever* equipped with any social graces? To answer your abrupt and, I might say, impolite query, things are in motion."

"Elaborate, Aldo. For fifty grand, I expect more information than that."

"You haven't yet transferred a damn dime to that offshore account number I gave you. Until the entire fee shows up there, you will be getting only minimal information. *Capice?*"

Rexroth leaned forward to whisper, "I'll set the money in motion tomorrow. Just assure me again that this pro you people are providing is good, no I mean *excellent*, at his job."

"You expect a four-color brochure dossier of his achievements? For God's sake, can't you take anything on faith?"

"The last time I did involved that fucking Jack Doyle. And it landed me in here."

Caveretta said, "I'll know more within a day or two. My man in Kansas City assures me the talent he's contracted is the best, the very best available. Details will follow as to the methodology and timing. The people involved see this dealing with you as a great opportunity." *And so do I*, thought Caveretta.

He stood up and replaced the novel on the shelf. "I'll tell you more when I know more, Harvey. Good night."

They didn't speak again until morning exercise hour the next day, Rexroth scurrying to catch up to the long-striding Caveretta who was touring the running track at his usual brisk pace.

"Aldo," said Rexroth, breathing a little heavy after his five-pancake breakfast, "I made the call. The, uh, transfer has been transferred. Did it early this morning."

Caveretta stopped to tie a shoelace. "Good going. Things will now be in motion. Let's take a break, sit down over there."

They went to one of the benches situated along the quarter-mile synthetic track, watching as some of the younger inmates jogged past.

"I'll be anxious to hear any developments."

Caveretta gave him a cold look. "I will report any progress when there *is* any progress. *Capice?*"

Unused to being talked to in a brusque manner, Rexroth sighed. He sat back, turning his broad face up toward the summer morning's sun. "Okay," he said. "I'll back off. But, if you don't mind me asking, why are you in here? I've never known anything about that."

"My godson ratted me out."

The stunned media mogul hesitated before saying, "Uh, how could that be? What happened, Aldo?"

Caveretta sighed. "Fuckin' government wiretaps. I'd been very careful for years. Then I got careless. They caught some damaging stuff. In the net they threw out they caught up my godson, Rudy Randazzo. My oldest sister's first-born! He's always been a weak little son of a bitch. Rudy was on the FBI tapes. They used him. He betrayed me and everything our family stands for. The little weasel plea bargained, and they wound up nailing me for 'interstate racketeering.' I refused to say anything except 'Not guilty,' which the stacked jury did not believe. I was offered the chance to turn on our family, people I've known since we were kids. Naturally, I refused. So, Rex, here I am, on a sunny day in June, next to another convicted criminal. What brought you here?"

Rexroth's plump hand tightened on the plastic bottle of water he was holding. He gritted his teeth as he muttered, "That fuckin' Doyle. The Feebs caught on to a little scheme I was running. It involved some of my heavily insured but badly under-performing stallions. They sent Doyle to infiltrate my operation on my farm in Kentucky. Bastard fooled me good. He's the reason I'm here. That's why I want him dead."

Chapter Twenty-seven

Doyle, irritated because his cell phone buzz was interrupting his morning pushup routine on his condo's bedroom floor, said, "Yeah, Karen. What's up?"

Karen Engel said, "And good morning to you, Jack. Do I hear some huffing and puffing besides the sound of being pissed off?"

"I was at my one-hundred mark in pushups, my dear. That gives me a right to wheeze a bit. Hold on, I've got to grab a towel." There was a pause before he said, "To repeat myself, what's up? Have you captured the horse killer?"

She sighed. "We wish. No, the reason I'm calling is to invite you to Damon's annual Fourth of July cookout. He told me to ask you to come. Also, for you to invite Ingrid McGuire, since she's been trying to help you on this case."

"Why didn't Damon invite me himself instead of having you call?" He really didn't expect an answer. "Ingrid and me? This is pretty short notice considering that the holiday's tomorrow."

Karen said, "Damon asked me to call because he's busy. This is a big deal for him. He shops for days before the party. What's the difference, anyway? I think he's trying to make nice with you for the efforts you've made for us, as disappointing as they've been so far. You're invited."

"'As disappointing as they are.' You've got to get that zinger in?"

She laughed. "Maybe it's a being-from-Kenosha thing."

"Where is this gathering?"

"Damon lives in Skokie. Take Dempster west off the Edens to Crawford, turn right, it's a couple of blocks up on the right side. You'll see a big American flag next to a good-sized Italian flag. He said parking is tough, so he'll hold a spot for you in his driveway. Do you think Ingrid would come? I know Damon would like to meet her."

Doyle said, "I'll give her a call. She's probably already planning to do something with Bobby Bork. He's a racing official she's been going with."

"I'm sure Damon wouldn't mind in the least if Ingrid brought her friend. There's going to be a bunch of people there anyway."

"What time?"

Karen said, "Anytime after two. See you there."

Doyle parked in Tirabassi's driveway. He saw Ingrid and Bork walking around the corner from where they had parked. She was dressed casually in tee-shirt and jeans, the hefty Bork bulging out of a gray short-sleeved sweat shirt and a pair of well worn black Bermuda shorts. As Doyle waited for them, he listened to the sound of excited children's voices and the strains of a recorded Italian opera he could not identify, smelled meat being cooked. He greeted them and the three walked into the crowded backyard together.

Dozens of men and women were seated along the flowered borders of the yard in lawn chairs, or at picnic tables, or standing in groups talking, or watching their kids cavort in the large, above-ground swimming pool. Other youngsters were concentrating on booting soccer balls into a net at the rear of the long yard. A half-dozen of the older boys concentrated on the basketball backboard and hoop on the nearby garage. The music was louder here. "I think that's Pavarotti," Doyle said. "I guess Damon's an opera buff."

"Is that what that racket is?" Bork said. Ingrid, scowling, gave him an elbow nudge. Looking at the vocal and enthusiastic crowd on hand, she said, "This is quite a scene. I had no idea it would be this large of a gathering."

"Neither did I," Doyle said. "Let's say hello."

They sidled their way past a group of males around a half-barrel of beer arguing about the comparative talents of the Cubs and White Sox pitching staffs before approaching the outdoor cooking headquarters at the back of the beige brick ranch house. Visible amid the clouds of smoke emanating from three Weber grills lined up in a row was Damon Tirabassi, apron-clad, sun-glasses steamed, spatula in one hand, Miller Lite in the other, slightly sweating in the afternoon combination of July and cooking heat.

"Mein host," Doyle said. "Happy Fourth."

"Jack. Hi. Thanks for coming." With a slight bow, he said, "And you must be Ingrid. Welcome."

She said, "Thanks for inviting us, Mr. Tirabassi. This is my friend Bobby Bork." They shook hands as the agent said, "Please, make it Damon." A short, stocky, smiling woman appeared at his side balancing two trays of fruits and cheeses. She placed them on one of the long tables nearby that already held huge bowls of salad, plates of Italian cookies, and several sheet cakes. Damon said, "This is my wife Angela." He completed the introductions before again concentrating on the grills he was managing. Doyle said, "Bobby, you want a beer? Ingrid?" Ingrid declined. Bork said loudly, "Then bring me a pair, okay?" Jack gave him a look before picking up one red plastic cup. "Bobby, you want two, get 'em yourself." He went to the end of the line leading to the beer spigot. A little man wearing a "Fergie Jenkins Forever" tee-shirt said, "Hey, man, where do you stand on this? You know, comparing our Chicago teams' pitchers."

"I stand aside."

When Doyle returned to the grilling area, Damon waved him to where a burly, friendly-looking man wearing a white chef's hat and smoking a large cigar was tending to slabs of ribs and seasoned chicken breasts and thighs on two adjacent flat grills. "Jack, meet my brother-in-law, Greg Luongo. My right-hand man at these gatherings. Makes ribs that'll make you beg for more."

Doyle smiled as he watched Tirabassi so relaxed and enjoying himself. He had never envisioned the veteran FBI agent, a man dedicated to by-the-book in all their previous dealings, to be capable of relaxed fun. *I'll be damned*, Doyle thought, *the man actually looks happy.*

Bobby Bork emerged from the half-barrel area, carrying a beer in each hand. Not looking at Doyle, he pointed at the contents of the grill. "Great-looking Italian sausages, Damon. It's Damon, right? What kind are they?"

Damon turned over some of the meat and pushed the rest to the side before placing them in a warming pan. "Both sweet and regular. We get them from my cousin in Melrose Park. Homemade. The best." He looked over Doyle's shoulder to say, "Hey, partner. Happy Fourth."

"And happy holiday to all of you," answered Karen Engel, who was toting a laundry basket filled with packaged sausage buns. Next to her came a short, trim, blue-eyed, blond woman who grinned as she said, "Hello, Angela. And Damon."

Karen introduced "Cynthia, my companion," to Doyle, Ingrid, and Bork. The Tirabassis obviously knew her. They greeted her warmly. Doyle said, "Karen, what's with the bakery goods in the basket?"

"Products of Paeilli's Bakery in my home town, Jack. Cynthia and I drove up to Kenosha this morning to pick them up fresh. They're the best. Wait till you plunk one of those fabulous sausages in one."

With a nod to Karen and Greg Luongo, Doyle said, "Damon, you've got a hell of a good supply chain here."

Damon smiled. "No question about that."

Doyle went to get beers for Karen and Cynthia, refilling his own cup as well. "Cold beer on a hot day," he said as he handed Cynthia her cup, "hard to beat."

"Thanks, Jack." She took a big swallow before saying, "I've heard a lot about you from Karen. I understand you've been a big help to her and Damon on more than one occasion."

"Modesty prevents me from anything more than a subdued acknowledgement."

"Karen also says you can be a major pain in the posterior at certain times," Cynthia smiled.

"Honesty precludes me from arguing with that assessment."

Cynthia looked up at him, starting to laugh, then caught herself.

"What's so amusing?" Doyle said.

"Just the accuracy of Karen's description of you." She thrust her beer cup forward for a toast. Doyle brought his to meet it, carefully avoiding spillage.

Their conversation was interrupted when Karen, next to Damon at the grill, called out, "Jack, could you come here for a minute?"

He excused himself. Cynthia put her beer cup down and trotted over to join the group of youngsters kicking the soccer ball around. The Tirabassi children hailed her arrival, their youngest daughter running up for a quick hug.

"Some big news today, men, "Karen said. "Just got a call saying that a fifty-thousand-dollar reward has been offered for the capture of the vet school horse killer. Or killers."

Doyle said, "Who is putting up that money?"

"A woman named Esther Ness."

"Well, I'll be damned," Doyle said. "She was kind of on my suspect list. How did this come about?"

Karen said, "Ms. Ness called our boss and told him what she wanted to do. He checked her out. I understand she's a horse owner and an heiress. He said she wired the money to the Bureau early this morning. She called from Costa Rica where she's gone to visit friends, she said. I guess she does a lot of traveling. But, Jack, why was she on your list of suspects?"

"I didn't have a strong feeling about Ness. There were just some interesting things about her. An eccentric, super rich, headstrong woman with a great love for horses." Ingrid and Bork joined their little group and Doyle informed them of the new reward offer. "That could help," Ingrid enthused. She was about to say more when Damon began enthusiastically ring-ing a hand-held dinner bell. "Time to *mangiare*, people, come and get it," he shouted. The crowd surged to the serving tables. Doyle politely ushered Karen forward, where she was slightly brushed aside by the impatient Bork who had Ingrid in tow. Ingrid looked back over her shoulder apologetically as she was tugged close to the front of the line.

"Amazing," Doyle said. Karen gave him a quizzical look. "I mean," Doyle continued, "it is amazing to me how that nice woman continues her history of hooking up with jerks."

〉〉〉

Ingrid and Bobby bade their farewells just after six. She was due back at Heartland Downs to check on the condition of trainer Buck Norman's beloved stable pony Irene.

"That was a nice time," she said, as Bork gunned his red Corvette convertible away from the curb. He just nodded, knuckles white as he gripped the steering wheel and barreled toward Dempster.

"What's wrong?" she said.

Bork snarled, "Your friend Doyle, that's what. Guy put me down in front of people there about three times."

Ingrid turned away and looked out her window. "Well," she said softly, "you were kind of rude to him to start off, you know."

"Bullshit. I should have knocked him on his ass." He blasted his horn before zooming around a slow-moving old green Ford station wagon. Behind its wheel was a small, white-haired woman peering worriedly ahead. A large black Labrador was sitting up on the front seat next to her, looking equally concerned.

In the ensuing silence, Ingrid thought about her relationship with her angry companion. There was no doubt that Bobby was loudly opinionated, self-confident nearly to the point of arro-gance. But she enjoyed his company. He was a good-looking guy. For the most part, he had the kind of sense of humor she enjoyed. And he was an experienced and rewarding sexual partner.

Head still turned to the window, she smiled ruefully as she considered Bobby's threat to physically take on Jack Doyle.

Someday she should probably gently let Bobby know about Doyle's amateur boxing career, describe the recent example of his prowess when he so efficiently decked the woman-threatening groom outside the Heartland Downs track kitchen. But she wouldn't go into all that this evening.

Bork accelerated onto the ramp leading to the Edens Expressway. With the Corvette straightened away and pointed north, Ingrid reached over and patted Bobby's knee. He took a deep breath and put his hand over hers. "I'm cool, babe," he said. "Want to rent a movie tonight?"

Chapter Twenty-eight

Back at his condo early that evening, Doyle was a well-fed, well-treated man. Even Damon's parting admonition to "Keep looking, Jack. You know what I mean," couldn't infringe upon his good mood. He had very much enjoyed the holiday at the FBI agent's backyard cookout.

He turned on his television and began a search of cable channels for a movie. This quest was immediately interrupted by one of the numerous commercials for male sexual dysfunctional remedies. He swore at the screen that was showing a succession of goopy-looking baby boomer couples making eyes at each other before an announcer read off the possible dangerous reactions ("Call your doctor if the condition persists for four hours") to the magic remedy. Doyle, to his dismay, had noticed an increasing number of these artificial enactment scenes in recent months. They so irritated him that he had dashed off an e-mail to one of the major manufacturers of this romantic revival elixir, suggesting "*WHY*, I ask you, do you not just show a couple of these couples in simulated copulating? Why fuck around with foreplay?" The pharmaceutical company's reply had thanked him "for your interest."

Venting about these commercials to Moe during one of their recent Fat City workout mornings, Doyle mentioned that he'd heard the pharmaceutical industry was particularly targeting one segment of the middle-aged male population—golfers. "I understand they run ads in all the golf magazines. Why would that be? Why are they pushing this stuff toward guys that play that particular sport?"

Moe grunted from the floor where he was doing sit-ups, "First, let me correct you about golf. It is not a sport. It is a skill."

Stepping to the side of the heavy bag he had been indenting with rapid punches, Doyle said, "What do you mean, 'golf is not a sport'? How do you define a sport?"

"Very simply. A sport is something that causes you to sweat when you're doing it. Golf doesn't. Neither does bowling, billiards, or bridge, for that matter." The little man sprang to his feet, grabbed a towel to wipe his face. "And as to why those ads you're talking about appear in golf magazines, I have a theory."

Doyle smiled. "I'd be shocked if you didn't."

"There was a great golfer back in what my old man's generation called the 'Golden Age of Sport.' They meant Babe Ruth, Man o' War, Bobby Jones in golf, a guy named Tilden in tennis. Besides Jones, the other leading golfer of that era was a guy named Walter Hagen. He had a famous bit of advice for people who are about to putt the ball. Counseling them not to leave their ball short of the cup, he said they should remember the motto 'Never up, never in.'"

Kellman tossed his towel aside and picked up a jump rope. "Wouldn't manufacturers of products to improve a man's sex life advise just that?"

❯❯❯

He turned off the television, picked up his cell phone, and rang Ralph Tenuta. He assumed the trainer would be home from the Heartland races by then. "Ralph, Jack here. Happy Fourth." He could hear a great deal of background noise. "Got a minute?"

Tenuta said, "Bad time, Jack. We've got a house full of noisy grandchildren. Their folks are in a holiday mood, too. Anyway, we're just about to leave here to watch the big fireworks display at Heartland Downs. Can't it wait until tomorrow?"

"Yeah. Sure."

"Look, Jack, I'm running that pretty nice colt for the first time tomorrow afternoon. Fourth race. Mr. Rhinelander, owned by some new clients of mine, Wisconsin people. Remember, I told you about this colt last time you were at the track with me? Why don't you meet me at the barn around three o'clock? You can come with me to the paddock and I'll saddle him, then we'll watch the race from my box. Hey, Jack! This little guy can run! Bring money."

Well aware that the extremely conservative Tenuta very rarely touted one of his starters, Doyle felt a small surge of excitement. "Will do," he said.

"The family is about to leave here without me, Jack. Quick, give me an idea what you want to talk to me about."

Doyle said, "Does the name Esther Ness ring a bell?"

There was a pause.

"A bell?" Tenuta said. "It rings a gong. I'll see you tomorrow."

The next afternoon, Doyle waited in the doorway of Tenuta's Heartland Downs backstretch office while the trainer talked on his phone. He raised an index finger, signaling he'd just be a minute. Doyle was in no hurry. It was a gently warm July afternoon. He had eaten a leisurely late breakfast, ignoring Petros' gibe about "Some pipple, you know, have to get to work like the early worm."

Petros' frequent re-shaping of his second language reminded Doyle of his second ex-wife's loopy Aunt Edith, who had a similar predilection. She was famous in her family for describing various clouds as being "seraphim" or "Stradivarius" or "cunnilingus," labeling books she'd read as "faction" or "non-faction," calling her favorite dill pickles "cashier" rather than kosher. He'd always liked Aunt Edith. She turned out to be a lot nicer to him than her divorce-seeking niece.

As he waited, Doyle glanced around the small office. Not much had changed since his season there working as Tenuta's stable agent. As usual, the place smelled of horses, and equipment for horses, some of which was stored in an old wooden trunk in one corner across from the corner that housed what to Doyle looked like one of the earliest manufactured small refrigerators. The desk was at least as old as its middle-aged owner. Tuxedo, the black-with-white-markings super imperious cat, lay in the middle of the scarred old leather couch, glaring at Doyle. Early in their association, Doyle had remarked to Tenuta that he was "allergic to cats. Not their fur. Their personalities." Tenuta replied, "Tuxedo is a fixture here. Learn to live with her."

His summer with Tenuta had seen Doyle mastering how to prepare daily work schedules for the men and women in Tenuta's employ as grooms and hot walkers; how to enter Tenuta's trainees into races with the Heartland Downs racing secretary for upcoming events; how to occasionally field a call from an owner of a Tenuta trainee, assuring that person that "Ralph will call you back right after training hours." Which was true.

The only new item in this work space was the Toshiba laptop computer Doyle had, with tremendous effort, convinced Tenuta to purchase and learn to use. It had not been easy, but Doyle eventually got the reluctant trainer to the point where he could manage spread sheets of his roster of two dozen employees and the thirty horses they tended almost as well as Doyle.

In the paddock, Doyle waited in front of Mr. Rhinelander's stall as Tenuta chatted with the filly's owners, an older married couple named Burkhardt. The man was calm. Mrs. Burkhardt was fidgeting with her track program, her purse, and her emotions. She said to Doyle, "This is what we think—hope, that is—is our best horse. His first race. I usually only get this nervous and excited before a Packers game."

"I completely understand," Doyle said gently. "Best of luck this afternoon." He followed the Burkhardts and Tenuta into the Heartland clubhouse and up to the trainer's box overlooking the finish line. On their way, Doyle peeled off and went to the windows to bet fifty dollars across the board on Mr. Rhinelander, whose odds were twelve-to-one. When he walked out of the building back toward the box seat area, he felt a welcome, familiar, nervous ripple through his gut. He knew that many bettors in England referred to making a wager as "having a flutter." On the few occasions Doyle made a major bet, he felt that flutter behind his belt.

Out on the track, Mr. Rhinelander warmed up to Tenuta's satisfaction. The trainer lowered his binoculars as the field approached the starting gate far across the Heartland Downs infield. "I see you're riding that apprentice, Ramon Montoya," Doyle said.

"Yeah, he's been doing good for me. Quiet, now. They're all in the gate."

The next minute and ten seconds was packed with unwelcome thrills for the Tenuta party. Through no fault of jockey Montoya, his eager mount was boxed behind horses almost throughout the six-furlong event. First in the middle of the pack, then down toward the rail, and even when the young rider finally attempted to steer Mr. Rhinelander to the outside of the field at the head of the stretch. Every time Montoya made a move away from trouble, more developed. Mr. Rhinelander finally got racing room inside the sixteenth pole and closed powerfully to finish second, beaten just over a neck. As he was slowly ridden back to be unsaddled, Mr. Rhinelander tossed his head. With his binoculars trained on the colt, Tenuta observed, "Look at him flaring his nostrils. He's mad as hell about that outcome. He *knows* he was the best horse."

But the Wisconsites were ecstatic. "Didn't he run just great?" Ms. Burkhardt enthused. "Once he got going, our little fella ran like, well, like Aaron Rodgers getting away from a Chicago Bears pass rush!"

Doyle was disappointed in the race outcome. He took solace, however, in Mr. Rhinelander's place and show prices of $13 and $5.80, respectively. His fifty-dollar across-the-board bet brought back four hundred seventy dollars, giving him a profit of three hundred twenty dollars.

In contrast, Mr. Rhinelander's trainer was equal parts disgusted, disappointed, and encouraged. "Jesus, Jack, what a terrible trip he had," Tenuta said. "Mr. Rhinelander was in everybody's pocket but mine. And he *still* almost got there, God bless him. He's a hard trier. That's what we hope for in a horse."

Jack remained in the box as Tenuta took the Burkhardts back to the barn to see their colt. When the trainer returned a half-hour later, he said, "I hope I can win some races with that colt for those nice people. Now, what do you want to know about Esther Ness?"

"Did you train for her?"

Tenuta said, "Yes. I was one of many men who were very briefly employed by Ms. Esther, the dog food heiress. Her late father, you know, was Ernest Ness. I'm told that people who didn't like him used to refer to him, behind his back of course, as Ernest 'Woof Woof' Ness. Why are you asking?"

"You know I'm trying to help find out who's killing the horses at those vet schools, right?"

"Right."

"Well, Ms. Ness' name came up in connection with that, and I've been trying to get in touch with her for weeks. She's been traveling, her mother told me. Then, yesterday, she calls the FBI and offers a big reward for the capture of the horse killer. I still haven't talked to this woman. I'd like to hear what you know about her. Would she on the up and up with this reward thing? Or could she be blowing smoke?"

Tenuta scratched his head before answering. "Oh, I think Esther's word would be fairly good."

"Just fairly? What, is she a promise-breaker?"

"She broke a promise to me about how long I would be training her horses. Same thing with a bunch of other trainers. She's the most interfering client I have ever had, or heard of, for that matter. Other than that, she seemed to be honest. And very fair. Always paid her training and vet bills right on time."

Doyle said, "When did you have her horses?

"A couple of years ago. I trained for Ms. Esther, as she demanded to be called, for a little under three weeks. A very trying time. That woman could give a meditating monk the twitches. She's demanding, and there's nothing wrong with that, but her demands were goofy. Unreasonable. I was one of eight, that's *eight* mind you, trainers that Esther had just that *one* year!

"Esther about drove me nuts," Tenuta continued. "She'd come to the barn every morning to see every one of the six horses she had with me. I'd have to drop everything else and take her on her little tour. The third or fourth day of that, I said to her, 'Ms. Ness, I don't have time to spend all this time with you every day.'

"She didn't say anything, just gave me a real icy look. Then she just stomped off and got back in her chauffeur-driven limo. On Wednesday of that week, against my better judgment, which I made clear to her, she insisted I run one of her horses in a race I knew the knock-kneed son of a bitch had no business being in. He finished up the track. She was furious and stalked off, wouldn't even look at me. Next morning, she's back at the barn, bright and early, never mentions what had happened the day before. Hey, by now, she's got me shaking my head. What's going on with this woman?

"One of those mornings, she had her chauffeur, a big lug named Hugo, haul in two big bags of what she said was a new product she'd discovered. Some kind of 'organic horse feed,' as she put it. As if the hay and oats I was using weren't organic! She insisted I feed her horses with this. I did. The second day, they all starting shitting in their stalls on a regular basis. Never saw anything like it. They were sicker than hell. I had what was left of her 'new organic feed' thrown away. When I called to tell her that, she hung up on me.

"Next morning, here comes Esther with bottles of some kind of new 'natural liniment.' By now, I had just about had it with her. I told Hugo, 'Take that junk back to your trunk. I'm going to keep using the liniment I've put on my horses for the last twenty-five years.' Esther stalked off after she heard that, too.

"Finally, the following morning, here comes her big Lincoln but with only Hugo the chauffeur in it. He says, 'Ms. Ness sent this for you.' In the envelope is a check for three months' worth of training bills, even though only about three weeks have gone by. He says, 'Ms. Ness said to tell you that Buck Norman will be by this morning so he can transfer her horses from your barn to his barn.' And off goes Hugo."

"Sure enough, an hour later, here comes my pal Buck, guy I've known for years. He's real shame-faced. But he knows *I* know what's going on with this demanding woman. I told him, 'Buck, get ready to suffer. At least you'll be well paid for it.'"

Tenuta paused to signal the waitress who served his box seat section. "I need a drink just thinking about Ms. Esther. You want anything?" Doyle declined. "Bring me a screwdriver please, Jeannie."

Conversation halted as the sixth race concluded in front of them, an exciting photo finish that announcer John Toomey loudly declared "*Too* close to call. We'll have to wait for the photo."

Jeannie returned with Tenuta's drink. He gave her a ten-dollar bill and waved off the change. "Thank you, Mr. Tenuta," she said.

"Nice girl," the trainer said. "Where was I?"

"The amazing Ms. Ness."

"Oh, yeah. Anyway, after Buck Norman had come and gone, she had two or three other trainers work for her. All of them went through pretty much the same torture I did. *None* of them in her opinion could do right by her prized animals. Finally, she fired the last one and folded up her stable.

"What I found out a month or so later is that she gave away all six of the racehorses she owned at that time. She sent three or four of them to a charitable program that assists handicapped people, kids and adults, gets them on horses. Very effective therapy, I'm told.

"The other horses she donated to veterinary schools. It's a tax write-off and a good deal for both parties." Tenuta finished his screwdriver and looked at the tote board where the contentious race's result now appeared. "Dead heat, Jack. Don't see that many of those."

Doyle sat back in his chair, considering all this information. Ms. Ness was obviously very hands-on and caring regarding horses. Hard to imagine her as a suspected horse killer. Not with that background. But, as he knew, people change.

He said, "Ralph, let me ask you this? If your Ms. Ness thought that retired thoroughbred horses at the vet schools weren't being…I don't know, treated right, would she maybe take action?"

Tenuta laughed. "Take action? Jack, Ms. Esther Ness is a candidate to do any damn thing she thinks has to be done. That's the way she's always lived her life as far as I know."

Chapter Twenty-nine

Tony Rourke again rose early after a tossing, turning sleep. Had a hurried light breakfast, and walked the mile to the Cork City train station where he bought a round-trip ticket to Dublin. The seventy-five Euros total cost made no dent in the bankroll he was carrying. It was a large one, for he was certain he was heading for a cash-only arrangement.

During the three-hour rail trip to the nation's capital, Rourke spoke to no one. After arriving, he took a long taxi ride toward one of the city's so-called estate neighborhoods, a rough patch of real estate populated by some of Dublin's poorest citizens.

He'd been very careful with his due diligence after the failed efforts of the first amateurish Cork City hoodlum he'd foolishly employed in his campaign to make Niall Hanratty pay—with his life.

Through a distant cousin of his late wife, a voluble, Dublin-based barrister named Barney McGee, Rourke had heard the names mentioned and dossiers described of several career criminals who'd utilized McGee's counsel in what were, for most of them, disappointing outcomes. McGee was an early-evening drink-infused braggart. There was one name McGee repeated several times, one that stood out. A few surreptitiously successful inquiries, made unwittingly possible by counselor McGee's rather gullible office secretary, produced the very private contact number of this fellow.

He'd heard a raspy, drinker and smoker's voice when the phone was picked up. "I'm calling out of the blue, now," Tony Rourke said nervously. "You don't know me. But you come, well, say, highly recommended for the type of work I need having done. Recommended by a certain barrister. Pay, that is, to have done. Are you with me here now?"

"Ah," said the voice on the other end, "pay. You've hit on a key word there. What particular level of pay is under consideration here?"

"Substantial." Rourke felt a film of sweat developing on his forehead and his mouth turning dry as he persisted. "Yes, substantial."

"The, eh, project under consideration? It's one of shall we say great seriousness?"

"Oh, yes."

On the other end of the line, he could hear muffled exchanges. Then the man at the other end said, "We'll need a meet, now, won't we?"

"Oh, yes."

In less than a minute, the time and place was set and the other man's phone clicked off.

All Tony Rourke could think of at that moment of commitment was, that, yes, he wanted it done. Yes, he'd pay whatever it took. No matter what sort of people he'd need to use, he would go through with it. Yes. He owed it to Moira and himself and, he thought bitterly, Niall Hanratty.

The train station taxi driver asked, "Are you sure, now, this is where you want to be dropped?"

They were driving down Dublin's Stone Street on this gray, mist-laden afternoon. Tenement buildings loomed on each side of the pothole-littered thoroughfare. Looking out the cab window at corporation flats and tenements with bent entry gates, scarred front doors, graffiti-covered sheds, balconies verging on dilapidation, Rourke shivered inside his buttoned-up raincoat at these symbols of despair. "Just drop me here, now," he said, figuring he was quite near his destination.

He tipped the cabbie and stood on the curb until the vehicle had turned the corner and gone out of sight. Then he walked two blocks north, one east, to the address he'd been given on Raglan Road. The mist had turned to a slight drizzle.

Waiting in front of Moynihan's Ould Times Pub was a short, slight man wearing a gray jacket, creased black trousers, scuffed white Nike trainers, and smoking a cigarette that he shielded from the moist air with his cupped left hand. His gray cap was pulled down over his broad forehead. Lively gray eyes appraised the visitor to this bleak setting.

"Sure, then, you're the man from the South?"

Rourke nodded a nervous yes to his little inquisitor, who said, "Right, then." He flicked the cigarette butt into the gutter. "I'm Billy Sheridan. You look just as was described on the phone. C'mon inside here. You must be thirsty after your journey. We'll get you a pint or two."

The dark, dank interior of the pub was sparsely populated at this hour. Although well past his own youth, Rourke saw that he and Sheridan were easily the youngest people present. There was a corner parking area for walkers and canes. Three senior citizens sat silently, empty bar stools separating them, staring into their pints. A fourth old man at the end of the dark bar was reading a newspaper with his nose almost touching the printed page. The bartender did not look up from washing glasses as Sheridan led the way to the rear of the long room. There, at a corner table, sat a thick-bodied, red-haired, blunt-featured man who did not turn away from the television hurling game until they were seated. "Hiya, Billy." He nodded at the visitor.

Rourke's due diligence had led from barrister McGee through Billy Sheridan to this large, brutish fellow. McGee had assured Rourke that the man, known as Crusher Moffett, was "just the sort you'd be needing for what you're after." Crusher's credentials included a lengthy career of strong-arm persuasion on behalf of local loan sharks as well as "a few stints in the nick" for assaults performed solely on his own behalf.

"Crusher, now," Billy Sheridan had said outside on the curb, "is terrible strong. In many circles the very whisper of his name makes men's cheeks pucker. I mean their ass cheeks. When you meet him, regard his huge hands. People say he's so strong he could squeeze your skull till your brains popped out on top." This gory assessment was followed by a chuckle and a disclaimer, "Of course that may just be exaggeration."

Billy Sheridan opened the discourse, introducing the two, then signaled for the visitor to declare what he'd come to Dublin for. "Including pay, now," Sheridan emphasized.

"I want a man killed," Rourke said.

Moffett's small, green eyes concentrated on the visitor. It made for an uneasy feeling, such scrutiny from this thug. But Rourke pressed on, concluding with a sincere, "I hope you'll help me out with this."

Moffett suddenly rose to his feet, his massive thighs bumping the table slightly upward. He walked to the bar.

Rourke, startled, said, "Where's he going?"

"Not to worry," Sheridan answered. "The big lad isn't much for talking. He's thinking about your proposal. Don't rush his process."

Five minutes later, Moffett returned, carrying three pints of Guinness in one huge hand, a trio of short glasses of Jameson's in the other. He distributed them, quickly downed one of the whiskeys, and said to Rourke, "You're on. I need to know the target's daily schedule, his addresses. A recent photo, too. All that information to be mailed to me here at Moynihan's. Don't use my name. Address it to Billy here. You won't have to mark it 'confidential.' Moynihan knows not to open that kind of mail."

Moffett raised a glass of the stout. "Confusion to our enemies," he toasted, then drained his pint. Staring again at the visitor, he said, "I'll need all me money up front." That sum was agreed to. Rourke said, "I don't have all that with me now. But I can get it, yes."

Moffett reached into his jacket pocket for a small notebook. Tore a sheet off and put a stubby pencil to it. "Here's me invoice. If you want this work done before the month's out, send the money here soon."

Moffett stood. He nodded at Sheridan, then extended his right hand to Rourke, who felt his hand dwarfed in the shaking. Moffett said, "I've got one more bit of business to clean up. Then, I'll get right to work on your behalf. But not, of course, before you pay in advance."

Without another word, he turned away and walked down the long bar to the front door. At the end, he slapped the bar with a sound that resounded so that it even aroused the drowsing seniors from their morning contemplations of their half-empty stout glasses. The bartender nodded a good-bye as Moffett opened the door.

Billy Sheridan sat back, relieved. He downed his whiskey and sent some Guinness to follow. "That went all right, now, I'd say."

Rourke took a small sip of his whiskey. Unused to strong spirits, he grimaced before reaching for the glass of stout and taking a tiny nip of that. "What's the address here? And what do I owe you, Billy?"

"Ah, don't trouble yourself with that," Sheridan said. "The Crusher will supply me with a finder's fee. He'd be insulted if I went around him to eke any cash from you. And he's not a man to be insulted."

"Do you have any idea, exactly, how Crusher would carry this out?"

"Oh, he's quite accomplished. Learned all kinds of vicious ways of attack during his Army days. He's a brilliant marksman, I've been told. But no, I wouldn't be about asking him how to conduct his business. Crusher's a pretty private sort of fella. And not a bit keen about being questioned."

Sheridan drained his Guinness glass. Wiping the froth off his upper lip, he said, "Shall I call a taxi for you now?"

The train back to Cork City was crowded, but Rourke took no notice of any of his many fellow passengers. He gazed out at the passing landscape, going over and over in his mind what he had just set in motion. In one sense, he could hardly believe that he had resorted to such a plan. "What would the Sisters think of me now knowing that?" he muttered, drawing a disapproving look from the elderly woman sitting to his left. He ignored her. Said quietly to himself, "But this has to be done."

Chapter Thirty

Trouble came to the unsuspecting Burkhardts of northern Wisconsin in the wake of their sleek brown colt, Mr. Rhinelander, winning for the first time in a most impressive fashion in his second career start. This was on a steaming late July afternoon at Heartland Downs. Thinking about it later, Doyle remembered a famous quote about boxing from the long-deceased writer Heywood Hale Broun, who said that, "Tradition packs a nasty wallop." So, Doyle agreed, did irony.

Performing in a strong field of maidens, including two very high-priced sales purchases, Mr. Rhinelander won by six and a half lengths in eye-opening time for the six furlongs. That victory topped off what Charlie Burkhardt excitedly told Ralph Tenuta was "about the best day a Badger could have." Kicking off the euphoria had been the notification received in that day's mail that the Burkhardts had, after more than four decades on the one hundred-thousand-person waiting list, achieved the prized status of Green Bay Packers season ticket holders. "We applied in 1967 right after we got married," Charlie said. "A long wait, but worth it."

Ralph Tenuta had called Doyle the night before. "Jack, the Burkhardts' good colt goes tomorrow in the sixth. You coming out?"

Doyle had just finished a four-mile run along the lakefront, passing beaches crowded with sweaty Chicagoans seeking relief from the ninety-five-degree heat. He dried his face and head before saying, "I think not, my friend. It's supposed to be another one-hundred-degree scorcher tomorrow. We Irish are a northern race, you know. Can't take heat like that. But, Ralph, thanks for the heads-up. I'll be on the case tomorrow from here."

Next morning Doyle walked to the big Chicago News Stand store in his neighborhood and bought a *Racing Daily.* He perused the past performances as he strolled back to his condo. Mr. Rhinelander's promising second-place finish in his career debut was dutifully noted in the handicappers' comments. But so were mentions made of the two expensive, well-bred first-time starters he would be facing today. His odds were listed at six-to-one. Doyle smiled at that juicy proposition.

After he'd grilled a ham, cheese, and tomato sandwich on his Foreman, Doyle booted up his laptop and went to the Twinspires website. It was an Advanced Deposit Wagering company that enabled him and thousands more across the nation to wager comfortably from their homes or offices. He checked his account. It measured just over six hundred dollars. As he had when he was at Heartland Downs for Mr. Rhinelander's initial outing, he bet fifty dollars to win, place, and show.

The ADW setup had intrigued him from when he first heard of it. Such convenience was both delightful and dangerous. He knew guys who bet with more regularity than they should. One, Stafford Hollis, a successful clothier and racing fanatic, frequently quoted the comment of the old Calumet Farm groom called Slow and Easy who always "put a little money down every damn day, because a man never knows when he'll be walking around lucky." Hollis had admitted to Doyle that his "lucky days" were few and far between. "But, so what?" Hollis said. "It's fun for me to have some action every day. I can afford it." Hollis wound up "affording it" for less than three years during which he developed into a compulsive, inept, and eventually bankrupt gambler.

Doyle treated his finances with much more respect than did the unfortunate Hollis. He'd never considered any form of losing to be "fun." As a result, he was very conservative in his use of Twinspires.

At three, Doyle turned on his television to the HRTV racing channel. It was post time for Heartland Downs' sixth race. His grin widened as he watched Mr. Rhinelander lead all the way and dominate his field, returning $14 to win, $7.20 to place, and $3.60 to show. Deducting his one hundred-fifty-dollar investment, he had profited four hundred-seventy dollars in the exciting course of one minute and nine seconds. "Thank you, Ralph," he murmured. "Thank you Mr. Rhinelander. God bless you Burkhardts!"

Thursday morning Doyle made his bi-weekly trip to the dry cleaners, had his Accord washed and waxed, and visited his man Victor at Jay's Barbershop for a needed trimming. He was driving back to his condo, when his cell phone rang.

"Jack, you ever hear of a guy named Wendell Pilling?"

"And good morning to you, Ralph."

Tenuta sighed. "I don't know if it's good or not. What about my question? This Pilling guy, you know anything about him?"

"Name is familiar. I think I read something about him recently. But I can probably dig up some details. Why are you interested in him?"

"Pilling called the Burkhardts last night and said he wanted to buy Mr. Rhinelander. Offered them a bunch of money."

Doyle said, "Well, what the hell is wrong with that?"

"Two things. These people have no intention of selling. As they put it to me, 'We've never had a horse nearly this good. We want to enjoy him.' They tried to get this across to this Pilling. But he didn't want to hear it. He kept increasing his offering price. Then, he evidently got angry, and rude. After that, maybe a little bit threatening. The guy must be a real jerk. Charlie Burkhardt hung up on him and, kind of disturbed, called me."

Tenuta paused to issue instructions to an exercise rider. Doyle heard him say, "An open gallop of a mile, then breeze him three furlongs. Sorry, Jack," he continued. "I've got a busy morning here. Anyway, would you see what you can find out about Pilling? I don't know how to do something like that. I'd appreciate it. The Burkhardts are concerned."

Doyle said he would.

›››

Wendell Pilling, as Doyle easily discovered with a quick Internet search, was the fellow he'd read about in the newspaper when he was on his plane to Ireland. This famous New Internet Age genius had a kept a very low profile for years. His graduation from Cal-Tech (at age nineteen) plus graduate degrees from Stanford, then MIT, were listed. They were followed by the impressive history of the Silicon Valley dot-com company Pilling had created, launched, and guided into the financial IPO stratosphere, making him a multi-millionaire at age twenty-nine.

There was a photo of this genius, a study in obvious self-satisfaction, taken a year earlier. Pilling was wearing, whether in tribute or not, attire associated with the late, legendary Steve Jobs. Looking at it, Doyle said to himself, "This is one big, homely dude. He must be six feet three or so, maybe three-hundred pounds. He's dressed like Jobs, black shirt, jeans, so on, but it ain't working in this fat man's favor."

According to Pilling's very colorful and well-designed web page, he had been born and raised in Winnetka, a Chicago suburb, and received scholarships at his three university stops after an early high school graduation before "wending his way West to fame and fortune."

"Fame and fortune," Doyle muttered. "A cliché with an eternal shelf life."

There was no e-mail address for Pilling. No place of residence. None of which was surprising to Doyle, who was well aware of the super wealthy's need for privacy. He picked up his cell phone and called Moe Kellman.

"Jack. What's up? I'm about to leave the office."

"You ever hear of a guy named Wendell Pilling?"

Moe said, "Who hasn't? Big shot genius with big bread. He bought a penthouse condo here from a realtor friend of mine last month. Overlooking Lake Shore Drive. Paid big bundles without blinking. My friend is working on steering King Pilling my way so I can outfit him, or his loved ones, in suitable apparel," he chuckled.

"I've never seen the man in person, but I understand numerous pelts would be required to suitably clothe him for our Chicago winters. What I understand, though, is that currently he doesn't have serious companions, of either sex, that he might gift with the outstanding fur items I could make available to him."

"Jesus," Doyle said, "please reserve your sales rhetoric for the suckers swimming upstream toward you. From the photo on Wendell's web page, you'd have to harvest generations of furry creatures on his behalf."

"Jack, I've got to go. I'm already late for my grandson Sean's pre-Bar Mitzvah dinner."

Doyle said, "I suppose you refer to the wonderfully named Sean Berkowitz?"

"You realize, you prick, that these Irish-Jewish names now so unbelievably fashionable pain me deeply. Even when used on such sweet grandchildren as I have."

"Of course I do," Doyle said.

Doyle made three more phone calls of inquiry that were unenlightening except for the last, to a realtor he knew, Sandy Aguirre. Her "farm," as real estate agents' territories were labeled, was Chicago's northern suburbs. But Sandy had access to real estate data banks for the entire Chicagoland area. "Here's what you're looking for, Jack," she e-mailed. "You owe me."

Pilling's penthouse purchase, Doyle read, had actually been reported on the business page of the *Chicago Tribune.* Pilling had shelled out $8.4 million for this ten thousand-square-foot aerie on the ninety-fourth floor of the new Crump Towers with, as the story put it, "its breathtaking, panoramic view of the city and skyline." There were forty-six condominiums in this recently constructed building, prices for them rising commensurately with floor levels.

Pilling, this "wealthy young bachelor," the story continued, "five years earlier had entered the world of top-class dog breeding with a flourish, winding up just two seasons later with a Best-in-Breed champion English mastiff at the famed Westminster Kennel Club Show in New York City. Officially named YeOldeBlimeyBeauty on his pedigree papers, known to his proud owner simply as Big Boy, the dog is housed in a specially made kennel located on the balcony of Pilling's penthouse."

"Great to know Big Boy has a sweeping view of the city skyline," Doyle muttered. He clicked to the next page.

There was a photo of Pilling and the two hundred-pound, three-foot-tall at the bulging shoulder Big Boy, both looming large on the penthouse balcony. Doyle had never given much credence to the claim that owners and their dogs bear notable resemblances. But looking at this photo, he could not miss the similarly sagging jowls of this large white man and his brindle companion.

As the story continued, Pilling explained Big Boy's need for an outdoor residence. "Like some members of his remarkable breed, Big Boy drools a bit. And he has a habit of twisting his head and flipping loose saliva upward. When we first moved in here, he was hitting even my high ceilings with his spit. That's why I moved him outdoors."

"Not content to simply sit back and manage his vast fortune," went on this journalistic love letter, "Pilling has been selling Big Boy's much sought-after breeding services to carefully selected mates. 'The fee is private, but substantial,' Pilling confided.

"I've always been interested in animals," Pilling said. "As a child, I had a white rabbit, several parakeets, and a mongoose. My father was allergic to dogs, so I was prevented from owning one. Now, of course, I can own anything I want."

Chapter Thirty-one

Wiems made Marco Three wait nearly ten minutes. Sitting quietly on his cycle in a dark corner of Shorty and Lammy's large parking lot just before eight that Tuesday night, he'd watched Scaravilli's dark gray MG being received by the valet parker, and its lone occupant hurriedly walk to the entrance. He checked his watch at 8:09, locked the bike and his helmet in the bike's tank bag. Walked casually inside and found Marco at the far end of the long bar, first drink already half-finished, eyes up on the television screen with its first Major League baseball game of the night.

Wiems said, "Marco."

Scaravilli, startled, said, "Hey, man. Didn't see you coming. Listen…" He was interrupted as Wiems tapped Marco's elbow and motioned with his head, saying, "Over there." He led Scaravilli to a small, two-chair table next to the wall. Stefanie, the waitress for the area, walked toward them with an empty drink tray and an order pad, eyebrows up expectantly. Wiems waved her off.

Marco Three protested, "I wanted another drink, man." Wiems silenced him with a look. Said, "You have the money?"

"Yes. Jesus, you don't have to be so impatient."

Wiems sighed. Little did this Outfit scion realize that he was hiring a young man in a hurry. Wiems had carefully observed what he believed to be tremendous yet currently unexploited opportunities in the furiously expanding world of Internet developments. He had ideas that would knock those geeks sideways, ideas for a truly revolutionary computer program that would take advantage of society's raging hunger for self-aggrandizing connections. Working to gain capital for his eventual start-up and envisioned IPO, Wiems had been fortunate enough to connect with two major Kansas City bookmakers he'd heard about at Cartridge Central Range. He'd carefully made himself known to them, one by one. Over the course of a couple of months, he was delighted to discover that each wanted the other dead—by a "new shooter, somebody nobody around here would think about afterwards, you know?"

Wiems assured them that he did. He shot the first bookmaker dead on a dreary early November evening in the driveway of the man's suburban ranch house. Next day, he collected the five thousand dollars he'd been hired with. Eight days after that, acting on behalf of his victim's vengeful sister, he'd murdered the other bookie, the man who'd initially hired him, in similar fashion, on another dark Kansas autumn night, for a slightly larger fee. These two apparently connected events confounded local law authorities. Wiems happily welcomed such synchronicity, it reminding him of his end game dealings with his hated mother and step-father.

He occasionally chided himself for being so slow to discover this killing trade, his avocation really, that he was so remarkably efficient at. But he was quite confident that he could lucratively make up for lost time.

The Kansas City Royals fans in Shorty and Lammy's whooped as their star shortstop homered to left with a man on. Marco Three celebrated along with them, saying to Wiems, "Go Royals! I've got them for a dime tonight."

Marco Three tried to fist-bump his companion, who kept his hands on the table. Wiems said, "The money." Marco Three reached down to grab his briefcase. As he did, he rapidly reviewed what he had come to learn about this imminent transaction.

Some rich desperado in federal prison was paying fifty grand for a hit. Word was that the man doing the hiring of the killer had no problem with the announced price, having declared that the fee "would be cheap at the price to kill that devious son of a bitch who put me here."

Once the prime number had been established, the chopping up of it began. Wiems was promised twenty thousand dollars with half in advance. Marco Jr. and Marco Three were down together for another twenty thousand dollars, with the remaining ten grand reserved for Aldo Caveretta's finder's fee.

Marco Three leaned across the table. "I've got your ten K here. We should do this outside."

"No."

"What do you mean no? That was the deal, man."

Wiems brushed his hand across the table as if he was extinguishing a candle flame. "I'm not arguing about the deal. But I don't want ten now, I want you to give me nine. You'll give me the rest later. That's what I want now. Just nine."

Marco Three took a long look at the young man he'd described to his father as "That crazy but apparently efficient red-haired mother fucker."

"Let me get this straight," Marco Three said slowly. "Our deal is still good, right?"

"Correct."

Marco Three started to slightly perspire in the blue Kenneth Cole plaid shirt he was wearing under his gray Calvin Klein bomber jacket. Looking at the placid yet menacing figure across the table, he thought not for the first time, *What the fuck am I dealing with here?*

Marco Three said, "Do you mind if I ask you why? Why you'd rather not take the full ten grand promised, but knock the payment down to nine? For now, I mean?"

"You know, Marco," Wiems said softly, "I'm under no obligation to explain myself to you. Or anyone else. But I'll make an exception here. I want just the nine K tonight because nine is my lucky number. Has been most of my life."

"Oh."

Wiems leaned forward, elbows on the table. "Do you know what a unique number nine is? I didn't think so. Think about this. If you multiply nine by any natural number, and add up the digits of the result, you will *wind up with the number nine.*"

Marco Three did a couple of quick calculations. First nine times eight, seventy-two, added together came to the number nine. Then he tried six times nine. *Son of a bitch, he's right.* Marco Three laughed for the first time since Wiems' arrival. "I get it. It's your lucky number, why not?" He opened the brown envelope he'd been holding in his lap and took out a hundred hundred-dollar bills. He extracted ten of them and put one back in the envelope. "There," Marco said, extending the envelope across the table. "Nine it is."

"Good." Wiems got up quickly. As he turned to leave he looked back over his shoulder to say, "I'm going to do some research on this project. I'll give you a progress report when I'm done with that."

Marco Three got to his feet. "Wait. I just changed cell phones yesterday. I've got a new number I'll have to give you."

"No need," Wiems said with a smirk. "I obtained that number thirty minutes after you began to use it." He walked out.

Two mornings later, Wiems flew on Southwest Airlines from Kansas City to Chicago. He wore his school clothes, lightweight dark blue windbreaker, long-sleeved checked shirt, pressed khakis atop dark brown Rockport walking shoes. He'd spent the early morning hours using scissors to cut off all of his thick red hair. He spread lather on his head and used a straight razor to denude it. Before each of what he thought of as his "job assignments," Wiems always transformed his appearance this way. He was getting good at spacing contract killings with hair growth and then removal.

Seated in the mid-section of the plane, next to the window on the right side, Wiems avoided conversation with his seat mate, a middle-aged woman who before takeoff had tried twice to engage him. He rebuffed her by plugging his earphones in and pretending to listen to the generic airline music crap. Given the choice, he'd have activated his cell phone and listened to some of the groups he'd put in that device's memory vault. Some of his favorite punk/grunge/garage bands. Meat Rot was currently atop his list, closely followed by Puppy Guts and Dorsal Morsels. He looked forward to the day he could promote these largely ignored artists on his envisioned Internet empire.

At Chicago's Midway Airport, Wiems used a credit card in one of the several aliases he'd created to rent a nondescript two-door brown Kia from National and drove north on Cicero Avenue to the east-bound ramp on the Eisenhower Expressway. He'd used the Internet to find Jack Doyle's address on Chicago's near north side, as well as a reasonably-priced motel located only eighteen blocks west of there.

He had pre-registered, using a different credit card. Upon arrival, he told the clerk to make his "an open registration. One day for sure."

"Thank you, Mr. Vincent."

Shortly after seven o'clock the next morning, Wiems waited patiently for a parking place to open up on Doyle's block a few doors from his condo. He had to circle the block twice. The wait took nearly eleven minutes before a harried-looking junior executive type sprinted out his door and into his Ford Focus before U-turning south toward Chicago's Loop.

Wiems had provisioned himself with two Subway sandwiches, a pair of thirty-two ounce bottles of Mountain Dew, binoculars, dark glasses, ball cap with its brim shielding his forehead, and an empty Mountain Dew bottle for urine if needed.

He maintained the same routine that day and the next two days, observing Doyle coming out of his condo each morning, usually just after seven, stretching, limbering up, then jogging at a brisk pace south for a block before turning east toward the lakefront. Wiems cautiously drove slowly in Doyle's wake before pulling in to a city lot fronting the bicycle, jogging, and walking paths. Doyle returned after some forty-five minutes each time. On the third of these mornings, Wiems watched Doyle jog slowly back to the start while chatting with a pretty young black woman also in exercise clothes. They seemed to know each other. The other two mornings, Doyle had walked directly back to his condo. This routine took an average of forty-six minutes, according to Wiems' careful calculations.

Late in the third day, Wiems returned his rental car to National's north Clark Street office, walked two blocks south to a Hertz outlet, and rented another undistinguished-looking import.

Next morning Wiems followed Doyle's Accord to the Fat City health club. Ninety minutes later, Doyle came out with a short, Jewish-looking man. Doyle walked to a nearby news-stand. Wiems, using his binoculars, saw Doyle emerge opening a copy of *Racing Daily* as he walked to his Accord. That afternoon, Wiems followed five or six car-lengths behind the Accord as it made its way out of the city and north on the Edens Expressway to Willow Road, where Doyle turned left toward Heartland Downs. At the track, Wiems let three cars go ahead of his before he approached the parking lot attendant and paid. He saw Doyle park, then drove to a row three rows back and to the left. He waited for three hours, taking an occasional stroll between the rows, until the races were over. When Doyle came out of the track, Wiems carefully trailed the Accord out of the track parking lot and onto its route back to Chicago.

Seventeen minutes later, going east on Willow Road that preparatory afternoon, Wiems spotted what he thought was the perfect spot, right before an intersection with both north and south turnoffs available. He smiled as his plan coalesced. He was confident his target had no inkling he had been followed.

Reconnaissance concluded, Wiems returned to his motel and checked out. He drove to Midway Airport in plenty of time to turn in his rental car and board a late evening flight to Kansas City. Sitting in the rear row and again in a window seat, he plugged in the earphones to avoid the chatter of the two young girls seated to his left. The one next to him in the middle seat had made a friendly attempt to engage him in conversation before takeoff. He ignored her. She gave him an angry look before turning to her friend and muttering, "What a prick!"

Once the plane was settled in the pilot's announced altitude of choice, Wiems pushed the seat-back button, rested his head, closed his eyes. There was a slight smile on his usually somber face as he reviewed what he'd learned. *Not a piece of cake. But, not all that hard*, Wiems thought, *to kill Jack Doyle.* Then he slept all the way until the uneventful Kansas City landing.

Chapter Thirty-two

Ralph Tenuta looked up from his desk, wondering why the summer sunlight that had been streaming in his Heartland Downs office door was now blocked. He saw a hulking, thirty-ish man who slowly looked around the office interior before settling his eyes on the trainer. The man wore a black turtleneck sweater, black jeans, tinted glasses. In ironic contrast to the size of its owner, Tenuta heard a high-pitched voice say, "Tenuta? Are you Ralph Tenuta?"

The trainer stood up. "Yes. Who wants to know?"

The large man crossed the office threshold, the old floor boards creaking beneath his feet.

"I'm Wendell Pilling. We need to talk."

Without being invited, the visitor walked over to the old, worn brown leather couch. He used one big hand to flip the cat Tuxedo off it and onto the floor before sitting down. She spat out sounds of protest. When the man's wide rump landed, the sound of the creaking couch springs was nearly as loud as the insulted Tuxedo's resentful mewing.

Pilling removed his glasses. His small, brown eyes bored into Tenuta's. "I'm here because of a couple of important phone calls I've made. I don't seem to be getting across to your clients, the Burkhardts, that I intend to buy their horse, Mr. Rhinelander. *I mean buy.* I want you to help me convince them."

Tenuta said, "You got some balls coming in here like this. Talking like this. What I know is that Charlie Burkhardt already made clear to you that he and his wife are *not selling* that colt. Didn't you get the message?"

"I don't pay any attention to messages like that," Pilling said. "I get what I want. Period."

Tenuta said, "Well, not this time. Listen, pal. The Burkhardts have had horses for about fifteen years. They've never had one anywhere close to the ability of Mr. Rhinelander. These people are no spring chickens. Hell, they must be in their early seventies now. They don't need your money. They'd much, much rather enjoy having their horse."

Pilling said with a sneer, "You mean to tell me a quarter of a million dollars, my last offer, doesn't impress them? I find that hard to believe."

"Believe it, pal. They don't want your money."

Tenuta picked up his cell phone. "I've got business to do, Pillars, or Piles, whatever your name is. This meeting is over. Get out."

Paul Albano, longtime assistant trainer to Tenuta, walked into the office carrying his notes of the workouts from that morning. He nearly bumped into Pilling. "Hey, sorry," he said, looking up. "Ralph, you want to enter Mr. Rhinelander for that race Saturday? He worked dynamite this morning. Whew! He can run!"

Pilling took this in with a smirk. He turned back at the door. "Tenuta, tell your clients I'm going to make them one final offer for Mr. Rhinelander."

Exasperated, Tenuta said, "You just don't get it. They will *not* sell. Period."

Pilling shrugged. "There are things that can happen to make people change their minds. You probably have no idea that somebody who really knew how to manipulate the Internet could cause all kind of shit. Credit reports altered. Internet accounts hacked. Identities stolen. Electronic bank deposits and withdrawals shifted and edited. Oh," he smiled, "a talented Internet maestro can do an awful lot. *Tell those stubborn cheeseheads that!*"

Ralph and Paul, standing just outside the office doorway, watched Pilling's big butt disappear into the rear of a white

Lincoln limousine that quickly turned past the nearby electrical horse walker and kicked dust back in its wake.

"Ralph, who the hell was that mad man? What was that all about?"

Tenuta said, "Paul, I guess I'm going to have to do my best to find out." The trainer didn't have to spin through his worn Rolodex to dial Jack Doyle.

Chapter Thirty-three

Moe Kellman had finished his morning workout, showered, shaved, and was putting on his business clothes when Doyle hurried into their corner of the Fit City locker room.

"Jack. Where've you been? You haven't missed a Wednesday here in months."

Doyle said, "I took a run this morning instead. Sometimes I think better zipping along the lakefront than grunting and groaning in here with you."

"What are thinking about? I know you're going to tell me. Make it quick. I'm due to have breakfast with one of the mayor's cousins in about twenty minutes."

It didn't take Doyle long to describe Ralph Tenuta's recent travails involving his loyal Wisconsin clients and Wendell Pilling, the threatening Internet mogul who was refusing to be denied in his quest to buy Mr. Rhinelander.

Moe finished tying his silk tie without looking in the mirror. "Last time when Tenuta was being troubled, we talked to Fifi and he kept his hands off. Told *you* to handle the situation. Which you did. Why would you need Feef's help now?"

"This is different. Me scaring that little Berwyn lunatic who was trying to blackmail Ralph, that was one thing. I don't know if I could pull the same thing with this big shot Pilling. Remember, your pal Fifi Bonadio knew who Ralph was. Their grandfathers came over here from Sicily about the same time. He was kind of sympathetic. That's why I'm bringing him up now. Asking if he could help. He has," Doyle smiled, "certain resources I don't."

Moe put on his tailored tan suit jacket over his beige shirt and adjusted the tan tie and stooped to flick a dust rag across his black Italian-made shoes.

"Jack, you'll have to go see Feef about this. I'll call him for you. I can't go today. One of my five-star spenders is flying in to look at the fall fur lineup. Needs a holiday present for wife number four. Tells me he'd like to keep his total down to a quartet."

Doyle said, "All right. Does Bonadio still live in that luxury stockade in River Forest?"

Moe sighed. "Yes, he does. But I wouldn't be denigrating something belonging to a guy you want a favor from."

Doyle silently agreed, the guy in question being Moe's friend from childhood, Fifi Bonadio, longtime head of the Chicago Outfit.

"He'll know I'm coming, right?"

"I will have paved the way," Moe said. "Just try to be respectful. *Bono fortuna*."

Doyle pointed his Accord westward on the Eisenhower Expressway. The early afternoon traffic was not bad, nothing like it would be in a few hours when the rush began for the city's western suburbs. He knew the way, having previously visited Bonadio after traveling with Moe in Kellman's big Lincoln limousine, retired Chicago Police detective Pete Dunleavy at the wheel. Doyle always felt at ease in the friendly yet somehow fearsome presence of Dunleavy, Kellman's full-time driver and security man. Kind of wished he had Dunleavy along with him today.

He got off at the exit for River Forest and headed north. Two miles later up a quiet street lined with tall oak trees, past expensive looking houses, then nearing what he thought of as Estateville, he turned into the driveway at Bonadio's address. Waited in front of the thick, wide iron gates for someone to emerge from the guard booth on the left side of the driveway.

Within seconds, a young man wearing a security firm uniform and a hip holster displaying a large hand gun hurried to Doyle's lowered window. Before Jack could say anything, the man said, "Go ahead, Mr. Doyle. Vito will meet you at the door." He clicked a remote device on his belt. The gates swung open.

Jack drove slowly the fifty yards or so before parking on the red-bricked driveway fronting the house. There wasn't another vehicle in sight. As he got out of his, the huge mansion's front door opened. "In here, Doyle," waved an old man from the entry. He was wearing a musty-looking black suit and a scowl. Maybe his mid-day nap had been interrupted, Doyle thought. "Should I lock my car in this neighborhood?"

"Very comical," the old man rasped. "In here. He's waiting."

Doyle was led from the front door directly to the rear of the mansion, which he'd read had eighteen rooms, seven bathrooms, a basement bowling alley, an indoor *bocce* court, and, as Doyle was about to see, an Olympic-size outdoor swimming pool. After the long walk down the darkened corridor, lit only by shallow lights illuminating what Doyle thought he recognized as a number of extremely valuable works of art, the old man pushed open doors to the patio. He waved Doyle forward and, without a word, shuffled away back inside.

Emerging from that darkness into the mid-afternoon summer sunlight, Jack paused at the edge of the vast, flower-bordered green lawn that led to another high stone wall at the end of the property. A squadron of Hispanic gardeners was busy on two sides of the yard. Two men dressed in security uniforms patrolled the rear.

"Here, over here," came a gravelly, commanding voice. Doyle turned to his left. Sitting up on a chaise lounge was the Outfit chieftain. Bonadio was wearing a black Speedo swimsuit and dark glasses. His lean, tanned body glistened with sun lotion, drops of which were visible atop the layer of gray hair on his muscular chest. His strong facial features reminded Doyle of the Italian actor Rossano Brazzi, one of his mother's non-secret crushes. Fifi Bonadio was a handsome man, even now in his seventies, even deep in luxury's lap made possible by his iron-fisted control of a profit-producing criminal enterprise.

Bonadio got to his feet and motioned Doyle to join him at the umbrella-shaded glass table close to the pool. He led the way. Doyle slowly followed, eyes riveted on the prone form of the other person present. Her long legs extended from an orange-thonged, marvelously curved butt. She lay facedown. Her dark blond hair in a long ponytail was pulled to the side of her tanned, naked back. Doyle saw there were no loosened top straps, especially when she suddenly turned over, raising her sunglasses to take a brief look at him. Then she lowered the glasses and lay still, arms at her sides, on the lounge. Bonadio smiled watching Doyle attempting not to gawk at this striking sight.

"Doyle, is that a classic set of tits or what?" he heard Bonadio say as his host pulled out a chair from under the round glass table that sat beneath the broad blue umbrella. For a moment Doyle thought that he wished he knew how to say in Italian "How right you are." Bonadio smiled. "That's my young friend Sylvia. If you're wondering," Bonadio said, nodding toward the supine beauty, "those gorgeous bazooms are as real as the air you're breathing."

Doyle sat down across from Bonadio, who punched a remote control device in his right hand. "Guido, bring me a Moretti. Doyle, what do you want?"

"Moretti's good." He sat back in his chair, attempting to look relaxed. Doyle said, "If you don't mind me asking, what happened to those beautiful twins, the Greco sisters, who worked for you on your yacht when I last saw you?"

"They were prime, weren't they?" Bonadio sighed. "Beautiful. Not too bright. And obedient. Everything a man could ask for in a woman. But, I had to let them go."

"Why?"

The Outfit chieftain leaned forward to confide, "I've got a method I use with women. None of this, by the way, has anything to do with my wife, who spends most of her time each year back with her relatives in Calabria." He paused to drain half of the bottle of Moretti. "I have found, over the years, that my good fortune in gambling somehow is tied to the women at my side. This started when Moe Kellman and I were kids betting quarters on Sportsman's Park horse races with a corner bookie on Taylor Street. We were on a real hot streak, when I was going with Rosena Imbo. That was for a couple of weeks. Then, I started losing. After four or five days, I took up with Rosena's younger sister Teresa. Like *that*, my luck changed. I could see there was a pattern there. Every time I've done that over the years since, my luck has gone from bad to good like that," he said, snapping his fingers.

Even beneath the blue umbrella, Doyle was beginning to sweat. His occasional glance toward the nearby Sylvia didn't help him cool off. Every time she shifted positions, he could not avoid noticing. When he did, out of the corner of his eye, he could see Bonadio observing him with amusement. Bonadio snapped his fingers. A waiter scurried tableside carrying another pair of Morettis.

"Let me get this straight," Doyle said, now concentrating on his host instead of the current concubine in residence. "So, that pattern from when you were a kid, changing girls or women in an attempt to change your luck, that's what you've carried forward?"

Bonadio looked away from Doyle and Sylvia toward the rear of the property. He pointed first to the rosebush array on the right side, the two-story greenhouse opposite it across the vast lawn, then toward the grove of native apple and imported olive trees lining the left side. Then he gestured nonchalantly over his shoulder to the mansion looming behind him.

"That method's worked ever since I was a boy on Taylor Street," Bonadio said. "Why change?"

Doyle took a deep breath. He was tempted to suggest to this rich, arrogant prick that decades' worth of corrupt workings by the Outfit he controlled must have contributed as much to Bonadio's wealth as his system of replacing women in his bed for the sake of better luck. He refrained, wondering to himself if the resplendent Sylvia's tenure would exceed that of the Greco twins.

Doyle said, "You're probably wondering why I've asked myself here. It's about some people from Wisconsin who own horses trained by your cousin Ralph Tenuta."

Bonadio sat back and sighed. "Didn't we go through some crap with Ralph Tenuta a year or so ago, Doyle? Some mook was threatening Ralph. You came to me because Moe told you Tenuta's family knew mine. Both our fathers came over from Sicily. And I said I'd help out, even though if I ever saw him I wouldn't know Ralph Tenuta from, who's the guy with the pony on his shirts, Ralph Lauren? And then, as it turned out, that problem went away because Ralph was lucky and that lunatic blew himself up."

"That was then," Doyle said. "This is a different problem."

"So, what do you need from me on this beautiful afternoon?" Bonadio reached into the cigar canister on the table next to him. Extracted what appeared to be a small brown baton. Didn't offer one to Doyle. Took his time clipping the end. Sylvia suddenly sat up on the nearby chaise. "You want I should light for you, Mr. Feef?" she said as she reached for matches. "Naw, sit back, honey. You're gonna give Doyle a heart attack. Or a hard on. Or both. It's okay."

How I despise this guy, Doyle thought. *But I need his help.* "You might counsel Sylvia to adjust that thong. Seems to be sliding up her left thigh," Doyle said.

Bonadio scowled. One of the nearby gardeners seeing this change in his employer's expression hurriedly turned away as Doyle began to describe the worrisome situation involving Tenuta's Wisconsin clients and the demanding Wendell Pilling. Bonadio listened in silence, smoking. Finally, he said, "Only because Moe asked me to help you again," Bonadio sighed, "will I take care of this for you. Within the next two, three days.

"You don't have to mention this to Ralph Tenuta. He probably wouldn't want to know about any favor I do for him. I understand he's straight as they come. He's had a good career and he's got a good reputation to defend. I don't mind helping him out even if he doesn't know about it." Bonadio puffed on the Cuban cigar and sat back, watching the smoke trail upward in the summer breeze. "This will be taken care of."

Bonadio swiveled to the side of the lounge and was on his feet in a second. Doyle watched, impressed, at this swarthy septuagenarian in such nimble action. Figuring their meeting was over, Jack drained his Moretti, look a last, lingering glance at Sylvia, and stood up.

He turned back when he felt Bonadio's right forefinger tapping his shoulder, the Outfit chief's face suddenly right next to his. "I will send some people to talk to this Pilling. That will conclude any and all dealings I have with you, Jack Doyle. *Capice?*"

"Understood. And, well, thanks."

Bonadio nodded his dismissal.

Three strides down the walkway to the mansion's rear entrance, Doyle stopped. Pointing at Sylvia, he said to Bonadio, "I think that left cheek of hers is taking some burn. Better keep an eye on it. Or a hand." Then he hurried out.

Chapter Thirty-four

Crump Towers' arguably richest resident parked his gleaming black Bentley in the building garage's two-vehicle space he owned. He inserted his identification card in the slot at the basement elevator and pressed the button for the ninety-fourth floor. The ultra-quiet car zoomed upward. He smiled to himself as he often did when he thought of the wonderful security system and conveniences this building provided, cost be damned. With his money what did he care?

At his penthouse door, Wendell Pilling stopped, startled. The door was ajar. That had never happened before. First thought that came to his mind was that the daily maid service had carelessly failed to close it after work that morning. He snorted. He'd raise some hell about *that* with management. He pushed the door open and entered the dark foyer. When he hit the light switch next to the door, nothing happened. "What the fuck!"

Wendell stumbled slightly as he moved forward toward the entrance to the huge living room with its deep beige carpet, quartet of brown leather chairs facing the long brown leather sofa, all centered away from the lengthy mahogany dining table with its dozen chairs. Expensive, recently acquired modern paintings adorned the walls. When he flicked the switch for the room's lighting, again nothing happened. "What the fuck?"

Out of the darkness came a measured, low-pitched voice. "Stop repeating yourself, Pilling." A bright beam from the man's large flashlight caused Pilling to cover his eyes. "Who are you?" he yelped. "What's going on here?"

"Follow the moving light" came the voice from the darkness. "Sit down on that big leather couch. Good." The flashlight went off and the room's lights simultaneously came on. In his right hand, the swarthy man facing Pilling motioned with a Ruger LC9 pistol equipped with a suppressor.

Wendell lowered himself slowly and sat, motionless, stunned, attempting to process this unprecedented intrusion. Lino Lucarelli's long, lean face creased in a sardonic smile. "Your building's security system, Wendell? It's *merde*." He glanced at his watch. "You have any idea why I'm here?"

"*What?* What? No, of course I don't," Pilling said, trying to recover from his shock, attempting to work his way up to one of his familiar bluster modes. "This, here, mister," Pilling said loudly, "whatever is going on, is not acceptable." He started to shift forward off the couch. "I'll have the building manager's head for this. I want you out of here *right now*. Why," he sneered, "you weren't even smart enough to wear a mask."

"A mask," Lucarelli laughed. "Like I don't *want* you to remember me, you dumb fuck?"

There was a barely audible pop from his Ruger. The shot plowed into the back cushion of the brown leather couch two inches from Pilling's left arm. Wendell slumped sideways, mouth open, gripping his arm as if he'd been hit by the bullet, his head swiveling as if answers were somewhere in the room back of where this terrifying, authoritative man sat with his legs crossed, relaxed, the coat of his dark-blue suit unbuttoned, light-blue shirt collar open, his weapon still pointed at Wendell. Dark glasses remained propped atop his head of thick, short, graying hair. He smiled, looking at this moment to the shaken multi-millionaire to be kind of a middle-aged but frightening version of the singer Tony Bennett. Pilling shuddered.

"Pay attention, Wendell."

Lucarelli turned around in his chair and said, "DuJuan."

The glass door to the penthouse balcony was yanked open admitting DuJuan Coleman, a man just about Pilling's height, six foot three, and close to his weight. But, unlike Pilling, this very ominous looking African-American was carrying a great deal of that amount in muscle mass. DuJuan on this downtown Chicago Gold Coast assignment was an example of the once tremendously ethnically exclusive Chicago Outfit's need to change tactics and outsource certain assignments. Chicago's notable street gang structure produced many candidates eligible for careers in well paid violence. DuJuan, a former high-ranking officer of Chicago's notorious Blackstone Rangers gang, was toting the large, limp form of Big Boy, which he easily raised up a couple of feet before ceremoniously depositing the dog with a thud in the middle of Pilling's large dining room table.

Wendell screeched, "What have you done to him? Is my dog dead? Oh, you bastards…" He lowered his face into his hands and began to shake as he sobbed loudly. Lucarelli and Coleman grinned at each other.

Lucarelli got up from his chair, placed his weapon in the shoulder holster inside his suit coat. He shook his head as he looked at the blubbering bully wannabe in front of him. "What a sorry sack of shit you are, Pilling." He reached down and slapped Wendell aside the head. "Shut the fuck up. And listen."

To Pilling's relief, he was then advised that Big Boy was not currently a corpse. The dog had been tranquilized with a syringe by DuJuan Coleman after the penthouse entrance had been broached. "Of course," Lucarelli said, "DuJuan was forced to smash his big right fist onto Big Boy's brow in order to begin prep work. That animal will be sleeping for awhile," Lucarelli said. "Actually, DuJuan likes dogs."

Lucarelli gave Pilling another head slap. "If you ever make one more fucking attempt to threaten the owners of that horse, Mr. Rhinelander, if you ever even *call* them again, we'll be back, Wendell. Me and DuJuan, maybe DuJuan's big brother DeLeon. He's the certified bad ass in that family. He *hates* dogs.

"We can walk past any security system that's here," Lucarelli continued. "The people who install security protection here get their own protection—from *my* people. Understand? We can make a visit to you, Wendell, night or day, *any* fucking time we want. So, if you don't completely back off trying to buy that horse, this will happen."

He nodded to DuJuan. Pilling gasped as he saw the powerful black man scoop up the still comatose Big Boy and carry him back out onto the balcony. "Get up," Lucarelli ordered Pilling. "I want you to see, and remember, this."

Out on the balcony, where far below streams of car beams on nearby Lakeshore Drive lit up the Chicago night. Lucarelli signaled DuJuan, who, muscular arms extended, positioned Big Boy three feet outside the patio ledge.

"*No*," Pilling screamed and moved forward. He was banged on the right side of his big head by Lucarelli's pistol. Momentarily stunned, he heard Lucarelli say harshly, "Want to see the doggy drop from here into dog heaven? What say, Wendell?"

Pilling's eyes were riveted on DuJuan, who was extending his canine package slightly farther out over the balcony edge. Even DuJuan's powerful arms were beginning to visibly tremble with the burden he was holding out into the Chicago night.

"*Don't, don't*," Pilling blurted, "please don't. I'll do what you want." Large tears began to mingle with the sweat sheen on his face.

DuJuan briefly extended the somnolent canine another six inches over the balcony edge, eliciting a final Pilling scream. Then, at a signal from Lucarelli, DuJuan brought the dog back in and plopped him onto the patio floor.

"I'll do what you want," Pilling bleated. "I'll do what you want."

Lucarelli gently tapped Pilling on the head with his pistol.

"You fuckin' well better, Wendell. You don't want to see that animal show up in a dead doggie bag. And you deposited right down there on top of him."

Chapter Thirty-five

She parked in a crowded campus lot three blocks away from her destination which was, on this breezy, overcast, July afternoon, the University of Western Iowa's veterinarian school. It was a sprawling complex of plain but functional buildings surrounded by extensive fields of corn.

The signage was very good. She had no trouble finding the broad walkway and registration office for this advertised "One Day Tour for Prospective Students and Their Parents" that she'd discovered on the Internet. Dressed in a long-sleeved, dark blue denim shirt with its sleeves rolled up to the elbows, well-worn jeans, and ball cap brim pulled down nearly to the top of her dark glasses, she melded easily into the crowd of fifty or so. It was primarily a collection of potential vet school enrollees accompanied by their parents, or other relatives, the latter present in advisory and judgmental capacities. Fortunately, sprinkled in the mix, were a few "solos" such as her, scouts on hand at the request of parents who could not attend but wanted information about this relatively new, increasingly well-respected educational facility.

First up that day had been an Information Luncheon in the nearby cafeteria. Many attendees conversed with each other as they moved down the line of "University Garden Produced Food, Compliments of the Agricultural Department," as the brochure stated. She stood alone near the back of the line, avoiding chitchat with the vocal families in front of and behind her. Too nervous to have any appetite, she nevertheless took a small salad and a pear half with low fat cottage cheese. She knew it was best to go through whatever motions were normal in this setting.

A heavyset senior citizen in line in front of her attacked the meat offerings with relish. Surrounding his mound of mashed potatoes with Swedish meatballs, he said to the server behind the counter, "Darling, cover all that up with that great looking gravy, will you?"

The young Latina server slopped a large ladle full of brown liquid on the plate he held out to her. "Hey, mucho gracias," he said loudly. He paused, as if waiting to be congratulated for his language skills. Disappointed, he shuffled forward.

What to her seemed an excruciatingly long lunch period finally neared its end. She swept the remaining contents of her tray into a refuse receptacle and walked out of the cafeteria into the courtyard, breathing deeply of the fresh summer air.

She felt a tug on her sleeve. Looking around, then down, she saw a very short, elderly woman smiling up at her from beneath a large straw hat, one hand atop the handle of a cane. "Hello, sweetie. I'm Irma Milbert from over near Des Moines. I'm here to look at the school my oldest granddaughter wants me to send her to. Could you kind of help me up any steps if there are some when we get to the barn? I'm by myself today, I don't see as well as I used to, and I'm not as spry as I used to be. Wasn't that a real nice lunch spread?"

She and Irma chatted amiably as they moved forward in the line that led them past cattle enclosures, sheep acreage, and horse paddocks, some populated, most empty. As promised in the event brochure, the "large animals would be available for inspection inside the barn where they reside."

She looked at her watch. This was taking longer than she had anticipated, and she began to feel uneasy. She was almost relieved to hear Irma inquire, "What brings you here, sweetie?"

"Well, Irma, I'm looking over the school for my niece Margaux. That's m-a-r-g-a-ux is how they spelled it. She's my older sister's oldest child. Margaux has wanted to be a veterinarian since she was about in sixth or seventh grade. But her family lives in California and they don't have the money right now to spend on too many college visits, especially one this far for them. So, I volunteered to help out."

"That's very sweet of you, dear. Isn't it great that so many girls are now attending veterinary schools?" Irma enthused. "Far different than back in the dark ages when I was in college. That was when almost all the vets and vet students were men." She paused to take a firmer grip on her cane. "I'm sorry. I didn't even ask your name. Or where you are from? Forgive me, please."

Answers to those questions were avoided as the guide holding the barn door open at the top of the stairs began talking and waving them forward. "The tour is about to begin," he said loudly.

"Irma, here, take my arm," she said. Up the steps, with Irma safely in front of her inside the doorway, she tensed. Pulled her ball cap down lower, almost on top of her dark glasses. Felt a rivulet of cold sweat descend her spine as she readied for her first daylight attempt to do what she believed had to be done.

Moments later, inside the large, brightly lit barn, the attendees were assembled in a small staging area and met by two barn tour guides. Wielding a hand-held microphone that sporadically squirted out ear-splitting sounds was a tiny, prominent female member of the vet school faculty, Professor Hilda Janks as her large nameplate declared. She was the picture and sound of enthusiasm. Less so was her tall, thin, male colleague, Assistant Professor Ron Schable, who looked as if he'd rather be palpatating an uncooperative ewe than assisting in this tour project.

She and Irma made their way down the long corridor of penned animals, not talking as they listened to Dr. Janks' description of what they were seeing, what was being done to these "carefully and gently tended animals." How donations to this "valuable exploratory experimental research program" would be "so very, very gratefully accepted."

As they headed toward the large animal section of the barn, she abruptly stepped off to the side and bent to re-tie a shoelace. Irma looked back for a few strides, then began talking to the couple in front of her and walking on.

Down on one knee, she made sure she wasn't being observed and quickly removed the loaded syringe she had taped to her right calf under her jeans leg. She cupped it in her hand as she stood and moved into place at the end of the long line moving past the animals in their pens and stalls and toward the exit.

She lagged behind as Dr. Janks opened the exit door and began ushering people out. Waited until the door had closed behind the last of the other attendees.

She stepped quickly to the web barrier in front of the stall housing the facility's only thoroughbred, a bright gray gelding. The nameplate on the wall identified him as Silver. Some wag had penciled in the question, "Left here by the Lone Ranger?"

As Silver lowered his head and flicked his lips open to receive the peppermint candies in her left hand, she made a deft thrust with the syringe into his neck. He spat out the candies. Shuddered. And dropped to the bedded floor of his stall, rolling over onto his right side.

She reached across the web and dropped the ALWD card on top of Silver's trembling shoulder. Seconds later, the barn door closed behind her and she joined the group that was now surrounding Dr. Janks in the sunlit courtyard.

"Thank you all so much for coming," Dr. Janks said. "If you have any further questions about our program here, feel free to call me or e-mail me. That number and that address are on the brochure you were given."

Dr. Janks paused to look at her watch. "So, I'll say good..." She stopped, mouth open, looking past the group toward the vet school entrance from which young Dr. Schable had just dashed. Not laconic now, his usually pallid face flushed as he ran forward, Schable hollered, "Hilda, we've got a horse down inside. Appears to be dead. It's Silver."

The words "dead horse" ignited a loud group response. Dr. Janks sprinted toward the barn door followed by Schable, his white coat beginning to tangle in his knees. He tripped and fell elbows forward at the foot of the steps. The door had already closed behind little Dr. Janks.

As the news rippled through the group, the babble from these concerned people in the University of Western Iowa vet school courtyard multiplied.

It was easy for her to detach herself from this scene and walk slowly out of the courtyard into the parking lot to her rented car. She was away in a controlled hurry.

Chapter Thirty-six

Every so often, Jack Doyle forced himself to ruminate. It was a mental exercise suggested by his philosophy professor during his senior year at the University of Illinois. "*Ruminate*" was what Jason Marcial advised his students to do at stressful points in their busy lives. Doyle had occasionally followed the good professor's advice in the ensuing years. This July afternoon proved to be one of those times, and rising through the ruminative muck was a question by no means unfamiliar to Jack, it being, "How the fuck do I get myself into these jackpots?"

He'd taken an early evening run along the shore of Lake Michigan, striding out in a punishing pace as he reviewed that afternoon's telephone call from Ireland. "Jack, this is Sheila. Can you talk now?"

He had just tied the laces on his running shoes and was about to leave his condo when the call came. Its content, not entirely unexpected when he considered its source, took less than ten minutes. Minutes in which he'd agreed to do what Sheila wanted. Went along with her insistence on paying his airfare. Agreed to be there as soon as he could book a flight. That proved to be unnecessary. "I've got you on tomorrow's Aer Lingus late afternoon from O'Hare, Jack. Paid in advance. You can print out your boarding pass. You'll be landing in Dublin early the next morning. Well, of course, you know that. You've done it before. I'll be there to meet you." She concluded the conversation with another effusive barrage of gratitude.

When he hit his turn-around point at Waveland Avenue, Doyle slowed to a jog and stepped off the running path to take a seat on one of the broad slabs of concrete bordering the lake. His breathing returned to normal, he lifted the water bottle from his belt pack and drank deeply.

"I'm fuckin' confounded here," he said aloud, startling a pretty feminine sunbather on a slab a few yards to his right. "Sorry," he said. "Thinking aloud."

She flashed him a look of powerful disdain before lowering her head back onto her bunched-up towel.

Doyle's was a conflicted state of mind, a condition he despised. He had listened patiently and sympathetically as Sheila described her increased concern over husband Niall's safety. "There is, Jack, pardon my expression, some serious shite going on here. I'm going to beg you to do something for us," she'd emphasized.

What that "something" involved was Jack's acceptance of an invitation to a Niall Hanratty-sponsored weekend in beautiful Connemara in the west of Ireland.

"We have this gathering once each summer," Sheila said, "inviting Niall's top employees and their wives. All costs paid. A chance to relax and be rewarded for work well done."

Doyle was revving up with a series of questions, but Sheila overrode him.

"I'm sure you're thinking, why you? Well, Jack, because I've got great hopes that you can spend some time with, and talk to, my bull-headed husband and get a grip on what is going on with him! The three so-called accidents so far. A fourth event that had nothing about accident written on it, being that it was very certain intended murder."

"*What?*"

Sheila said, "That's right. Jack, we need you here. We need your help. After your dealings with him in the States, I know he'll listen to you as to what he should be doing. Of that I am sure. He surely won't listen to anyone else."

Doyle hesitated, then started to explain to Sheila Hanratty that he had "a lot on my plate right now. These horse killings at colleges that I'm working on. I feel very obligated to continue that." He paused, and listened to her silence. Imagined her thinking that he was treasuring equine lives over that of her treasured husband. Finally, he said, "All right, Sheila. I'll be coming."

"Oh, Jack, you're a lovely man. Shall I pick you up at the Dublin Airport then?"

Doyle said, "No thanks, Sheila. I'll get another ride if I'm lucky. Please just e-mail the directions to the place we'll be at in Connemara."

Chapter Thirty-seven

"Is this the rising star of Irish journalism?" Jack said.

There was a pause before he heard, "Is this the reigning king of American bullshitters ringing me up now?" They both laughed.

"Nora Sheehan, it's pure delight to hear your voice. Yeah, I apologize for not calling you as often as I promised. But, listen, I have a great proposition for you,"

"God forbid it would involve my walking down the aisle with you, Jack Doyle. Am I right?"

Doyle laughed. "As usual, you are. Not to worry about that. No, I'm calling to invite you to join me on an upcoming, all-expense-paid getaway to the west of Ireland. Connemara. Have you been there?"

"Jack, almost everyone over here who is, or was, into horses at some time made a trek to ride the famous Connemara ponies. I did that when I was twelve with my two later-to-become professional jockey siblings. It was fun at the time, but I'm not interested in a repeat. Plus, I'm very busy with my work."

Doyle said, "Ah, Nora. This would just be a couple of days at a gathering sponsored by Niall Hanratty. He and his wife Sheila will be there and some of his employees. That's how he rewards his best workers each year. I've been invited along this time. When I was asked if I wanted to bring a companion, I thought long and hard. Sinead O'Connor, I learned, was busy. So, what other name but yours would come bold-faced to my mind?"

That did bring a laugh. "I've never met the famous Mr. Hanratty," Nora said. "Maybe I can get a feature story or two out of this. Let me check my calendar." She was back less than a minute later. "Yes, I can do it."

"God love you," Doyle said. "Pack for a couple of days. Could you pick me up at the airport? Dublin, I mean. I'll e-mail the expected arrival time, probably early Thursday your time. Then we can head for Connemara next day if that works for you. I very much look forward to this."

Nora said, "Trained journalist that I am, do you mind me asking what is the actual purpose of your trip? Beside your almost uncontrollable longing to see me, that is?"

"Details when I see you, my dear. Nora, you're the best," he said, drawing another unbelieving laugh from across the Atlantic. "Don't ever let any spaulding say otherwise."

Nora whooshed her breath into the phone. "I can only presume you meant spalpeen, not spaulding. You'll have to start doing a bit of work on your intercontinental compliments. All right, I'll pick you up. When you see an attractive female dressed in a black chauffeur's cap, low cut blouse, short shorts, wearing mesh hose, stiletto heels, and holding a placard that says 'Welcome Back J. Doyle,' you'll find me."

Doyle's Aer Lingus flight landed a bit early that Thursday morning. Having cleared customs, he heard Nora's voice. "Jack, over here."

"Where's your sign? Your chauffeur's outfit?"

Dressed normally, light beige jacket, white blouse, black skirt, Nora said, "I didn't choose to inflame the imaginations of you and the other male passengers so early in the day." They embraced briefly before she said, "Come on. My auto's this way."

They spent a pleasant, restful day at Nora's rental home in Bray reviewing recent news from their respective shores, that night renewing their enthusiastic lovemaking before what Nora declared was "the midnight curfew. We have to rise early tomor-row, dear Jack. I need to do a bit of shopping before we leave." She got out of bed, put on a long white tee-shirt, and went into the bathroom. She was asleep when he returned from the kitchen where he'd gone to pour himself a small nightcap of Jameson's.

Chapter Thirty-eight

They were on the way out of Bray to Highway M4 shortly after noon on Friday, armed with a large thermos of coffee, pair of plastic cups, and half a loaf of sliced soda bread. Their journey to the western edge of Ireland was estimated by Nora to take "between three and a half, maybe four hours."

Nora started out behind her wheel, got them well past Athlone, where Jack took over. The first two hours were marked by long stretches of sunshine flattering the bright, green fields, twice sharply interspersed by quick showers of what Nora said was "lashing rain. It won't last." They chatted about Nora's freelance reporting work which she said was "beginning to pick up quite a bit. At least the decline of our economy seems to have slowed somewhat, so some opportunities are opening up. I'm having a decent year so far."

Doyle asked about Nora's siblings. Both jockeys were also having "good seasons. Brother Kieran is second in the money-won standings. And Mickey ranks sixth in races won. I try to go racing at least once every couple of weeks to watch them. Mickey and I have dinner twice a week."

"Any socialization with 'Clever Kieran'?"

"Only a very occasional phone call. He continues to pretty much go his own way. Like always. Listen, Jack, enough about the Sheehans. What's currently leading your life list?"

Doyle described his efforts, unsuccessful thus far, to find the "mercy horse killer," and the recent developing problem involving Ralph Tenuta and "this rich prick Wendell Pilling, who kept pestering people named Burkhardt, clients of Ralph. But I understand that problem's been solved. Or, so I am reliably told. You ever hear of Pilling?"

"Are you serious? Anybody involved in the computer world knows about that man."

The other side of Galway on R336, heading toward Connemara, Nora warned, "We're out here in the country now, Jack. Keep in mind there are only two roads in Ireland where sheep have the right of way on the road. We happen to be on one of them."

"Sheep in the street, eh? They better hope a New York City cab driver never decides to vacation around here. There'd be mutton chopped onto the pavement."

Nearly four hours after leaving Bray, they arrived late Friday afternoon at Lough Inagh Lodge near the westernmost edge of the island country and overlooking the sprawling lough, or lake. Built in the 1880s as an estate home, it now was a four-star modern "boutique lodge" according to the Internet research Nora had done. Doyle parked around the side of the impressive, two-story structure that sat in isolation with a wonderful view of Ireland's famous Twelve Bens, a range of small mountains. Doyle opened the car windows and they sat quietly before getting out, breathing in the country air, listening to birdsong emanating from nearby trees. Finally, they got their luggage from the boot and went inside to register.

During their drive, Nora had informed Jack that the Lodge contained just "twelve rooms. Breakfast and dinner are served. The food is reputed to be excellent. There's a library and a well-stocked bar."

"Music to my ears," Doyle responded, "especially the latter item."

Walking to the inn's entrance this late afternoon, Nora said, "There is supposed to be excellent fishing in this area. And four golf courses aren't far away."

"There is little attraction in these pastimes for me," Doyle laughed. He told Nora that all but one of the rooms had been reserved by Hanratty for his contingent of employees and, if they chose, their spouses or mates. "You'll like Niall and his wife Sheila," he said. "The only other Shamrock people I know are Barry Hoy and Tony Rourke. Hoy is Niall's bodyguard and driver. Big, tough-looking guy, used to box, very quiet, but friendly. Rourke is older, quiet little fellow, looks like the accountant he is."

Fiona, the friendly clerk at the front desk, signed them in as "guests of Mr. Hanratty." After handing Jack the room key, Fiona asked if they would like "complimentary tea and home-made scones. Standard practice here and available right now," she smiled. They declined. When they looked into the nearby library, the Hanrattys rose to greet them. Doyle introduced Nora. Sheila said, "Oh, Nora Sheehan. I've read many of your stories. How lovely to meet you. Niall, you know who this is?"

Hanratty smiled as he reached for Nora's hand. "Of course I do. The talented writer woman from the family of talented jockeys. My pleasure, Nora." He turned to Jack. "Why don't you two get settled in," Niall said, "then come down and join us for a drink before dinner?"

> > >

Showered and changed out of their traveling clothes, Nora and Jack were prepared for the first social event of the Hanratty weekend, the cocktail reception. Before leaving their large, attractive bedroom with its commodious bath, large flat-screen television, plus a desk on which Nora could position her laptop, they stood at one of the large windows that looked out toward the lough. Dusk was advancing and swirls of fog encircled the tops of the tall pine trees bordering the property. They were silent. Jack reached down and took Nora's hand. It was a stunning view enhanced by the quiet of the advancing evening. They stood for a minute or two before Jack said, "Well, my dear, time to go. Up and at 'em."

>>>

Some of the Shamrock crew at the cocktail reception recognized Nora's name when she was introduced. "Oh, the writer."

"Journalist," she politely corrected. Two of the couples were spurred on by that admission to corner her. Doyle sidled away and came up next to Niall.

"Well, you've done yourself proud here, my man," Jack said. Hanratty smiled briefly. "It hope it all goes well, Jack. These good people of mine deserve a great old time even if it's only for a weekend. And, certainly, my Sheila does."

Before Doyle could respond, he and Hanratty turned toward the sound of a loud voice at the doorway to the reception room. "*Hello,* you Irish," said an overweight, middle-aged man standing next to a small, embarrassed looking woman of about his age. He looked around as if expecting to be recognized, this florid-faced figure with the booming baritone voice. "Are we Yanks invited in?" Without waiting for an answer, he advanced.

"Who the hell is that?" Doyle said.

Hanratty started toward the man, then stopped. "He and his little wife must be the only other guests here. I took eleven of the twelve rooms for our group. Well, I guess I'd better go over and greet what looks to me like an Ugly American. Pardon the expression, Jack."

Jack followed Niall, who shook the man's hand, introduced himself, and didn't have long to wait for a reply from "Dr. Herbert Whitesell. From Ann Arbor, the great state of Michigan. Ann Arbor, the university town. My practice is there. This is my wife, Alice. We're first time in Ireland. Strange little country, isn't it? Not this place, of course," he added, patting Hanratty's arm.

Doyle took a glass of champagne off the waiter's tray for Nora and asked the server for "another Jameson's when you've got the chance." Nora was chatting with Sheila Hanratty near the fireplace that was lit with a small peat fire. He could hear Dr. Whitesell's braying even from yards off. Jack watched as Niall turned away from the Michigan physician and signaled the attentive Fiona to ring the Lough Inagh's little bronze bell marking the end of cocktail hour, the start of dinnertime.

Nora and Jack shared a dinner table with the Hanrattys. Talk was of Irish politics and racing, American racing and politics as well. Jack deferred the few questions about his current FBI-aiding project back home. Overlaying their conversation was the aggravating noise emanating from a nearby two-person table occupied by the irritating Dr. Whitesell and his mousy spouse. Even trying to tune Dr. Whitesell out, Jack could not completely escape the loudmouth's stated views on the vicissitudes of current air travel, the irritating drivers on Irish roads, the disappointing salmon fishing he'd experienced the previous day, and the horrible deficiencies of the current U.S. presidential administration. At one point Jack started to rise and have a word with the doctor, but Nora held his arm. "No, Jack. That's what that idiot is looking for. Attention."

They concentrated on the meal. A starter of filo pastry containing goat cheese preceded a hearty vegetable soup. Broiled salmon surrounded by duchess potatoes and fresh asparagus followed. A lavish cheese plate was offered, as well as a lovely cherry trifle. Nora pronounced the entire meal "brilliant," Doyle and the Hanrattys heartily concurring.

Niall suggested an after-dinner drink in the library, but Jack and Nora declined, "too tired, but thank you." Sheila said "I'm with you on that, come on Niall," and gave them a goodnight wave.

Nora started up the stairs with Jack preparing to follow when he felt Niall tap him on the shoulder. The handsome bookmaker's happy expression from the previous several hours had been replaced by a serious look.

"Jack. Can we go for a walk early tomorrow? We need to talk."

Doyle said, "Sure, Niall. What time?"

"Let's make it seven. I'll meet you out front."

Chapter Thirty-nine

Doyle was up at six, ignoring the effects of jet lag and Friday's long drive through the Irish countryside. He smiled appreciatively at the deeply asleep Nora who lay on the other side of their large, comfortable bed, and looked out one of the large windows. Through the early morning mists, he was able to discern the humpy shapes of the famed Twelve Bens, the renowned range of Irish mountains that in the geography of Montana, say, or Colorado, probably would be dismissed as relative hillocks.

He quickly showered, dressed, quietly closed the suite door behind him, and trotted down the carpeted stairs to the first floor. They creaked a bit, which was not surprising since the impressive building had been constructed as an estate home in the late nineteenth century and not revived and renovated until many years later.

After a quick peek into the dining room, its tables already set for the breakfast crowd, Jack pushed open the heavy front door and paused on the top step to take deep breaths of the cool air. In sweatshirt and pants, he'd started some of his usual early morning, pre-jogging stretches, when he heard a familiar deep voice behind him at the door's entrance.

"Morning to you, Jack. Ready for a bit of a ramble?" Niall said.

"You bet. You look like you're dressed for a long, slow hike. Is that what you have in mind?"

Hanratty zipped up his windproof jacket. He wore a sweater underneath it, corduroy trousers, walking shoes. "I'm not about to trot along beside you. It's a nice, cool morning, as usual in these parts. A brisk walk will do for me. If you feel the need to gallop ahead, just come back to me for a chat, all right?"

Doyle pulled his sweatshirt hood up as the morning mist suddenly shifted into a weak stint of raining. "I just saw the sun a minute ago," he said to Niall as they walked down the drive to the road.

Hanratty laughed. "No surprise there. And this bit of moisture will soon be gone. Jack, you might not be aware of it, but we can have several interesting elements of weather in a single hour here in this grand county. A soft little rain, like this one, which could get you wet enough given enough minutes. Maybe a pounding burst of it. Then a bit of clearing so as to showcase some big, beautiful, fluffy, floating white clouds, followed by a darkening sky, soft rain, and the wind coming into play. It can all happen in the time it takes to run the opening race at the Curragh. But, not today. We're in for a nice, clear sky later on. The sun will make a comeback before too long."

At the roadway, Jack looked right and left. Niall poked his elbow. "Not much need of such caution out here, my friend. You can hear traffic coming for a good distance, autos or the occasional horse-cart Let's go left. There's a path that leads down to the lake."

They made their way past trees and grass still carrying dew, chatting about the previous night's dinner. "A good group, Niall, you have working for you. They were enjoying themselves. And your hospitality, of course," Doyle added, with a mocking bow.

"Most of them were. Though I thought Tony Rourke was kind of quiet, even for him. And Barry didn't appear all that delighted to be there either. Maybe they've been to too many of these gatherings. And then, there was your fellow Yank, Dr. Whitesell, making his presence felt. What an obnoxious arshole, if you don't mind me describing one of your countrymen. Must admit I was glad you were seated slightly closer to him than I was. Some of the guff he was spouting, I would have had to shut that off in a hurry."

Doyle said, "I can offer no defense of Dr. Blowhard."

They came to the end of the wide dirt path and took it to the shore. The dark green waters of Lough Inagh were rippling. Far out they could see three boats of sportsmen with their rods and reels. The sun had begun to probe the dark, heavy-looking western clouds that were retreating. Doyle bent to pick up a skinny flat stone and effortlessly skipped it across the water. "Four jumps with that one," he grinned, looking back at Hanratty, adding, "do people swim in here?"

"Sure. This lake water isn't that terrible cold. Not as bad as the sea near me."

Doyle said, "Is that why you have a swimming pool at your house next to the sea? I really didn't understand the thinking behind that, you know."

"Have you ever tried to backstroke through fifty-two-degree waves, Jack? I didn't think so. That's why I put in my pool. It gives us a nice look at the sea from the water where we'd rather be."

Niall stopped walking, hands on hips, looking out at Lough Inagh. "The waves this morning here are not quite what they were back home last week. When I was almost shot to death."

"*What?*" Doyle stopped and turned to face his host. "Say that again?"

"You heard me right the first time, Jack. And that's what I've brought you out here this morning to tell you about."

Chapter Forty

"I was taking one of my usual early evening strolls on the strand down below my house. Talking on my cell phone. Getting the day's net business figures from Tony Rourke. Leaving a message on Dermott McGrath's answering machine, he's my Kinsale office manager, about next day's schedule. Then, right after I turn off the cell phone, I hear a *crack* sound and feel something zip very close to the right side of my head. I know it's not a feckin' gust of wind. Right off, there's another cracking rifle sound just like the first one. That bullet kicks up sand just in front of my right foot. By now I'm moving. I heard one more shot. No idea where that one landed except it wasn't, thank Jesus, in me.

"I moved damn fast then to the stairs leading up to my house. No shots follow me. I run in and shout to Sheila to get herself and the boys into the basement. I call the Kinsale Garda headquarters and, God bless 'em, they were out there pretty quick."

Doyle said, "The shooter must have been in a boat looking in on you, right?"

"Yes. I'd noticed a small white motor boat maybe a hundred yards off shore that evening. We don't have that many little crafts cruising in my neighborhood, but they're not entirely uncommon. That's why I didn't give this one a second look."

"I'd say you were a mighty lucky man, Niall."

"No argument from me about that. Thankfully, this villain must not have been too strong in the nautical department. The bobbing up and down of the boat must have thrown his aim off enough to save my hide."

Doyle said, "I imagine you gave a description of the boat to the police?"

"Not much of a one. I just saw it was a little white craft. Hell, I was paying it no attention at all until the blasting away at me got underway. I don't even know if there was anyone in it along with the shooter. The Garda had no luck locating anybody else who saw the boat. They used metal detectors to locate two of the three bullets buried in the sand. If they don't locate the shooter and his rifle, those findings won't do them much good."

Doyle bent down for another skinny stone and sent it on its skipping way. He brushed the sand off his hands. "Well, Niall, at least there's one bright element about your recent experience."

"What the hell would that be?"

"At least we know now, without any doubt anymore, that somebody's trying to kill you."

Hanratty's dark look was succeeded by a booming laugh. "Brilliant. That's a great comfort, indeed."

The low, gray Saturday morning clouds suddenly spat out rain pellets that bit into Doyle's uncovered head. By the time he'd pulled up his sweatshirt hood, it was over. Hanratty stood back, amused. "You've just gotten a brief primer in Connemara weather, Jack."

Doyle pointed toward a log that stretched into the grass from the strand. "I want to sit a bit, Niall. I want to ask you again, why does someone want you dead?" Hanratty plunked down, frown back upon his face.

"If I knew that, we wouldn't be here having this early morning discussion. I've no feckin' idea. Other than those letters and cards from harmless looneys, I've not had a threat. You think crazy letter writer 'Tim From Tipperary' could get himself up to wobble about in a little boat firing at me? Hardly."

Hanratty leaned forward, elbows on his knees, face toward the lake. "There's only one man I know of who hates me enough to want to kill me. He just got out of Mountjoy Prison a few months back."

"Mountjoy Prison," Doyle said, shaking his head. "A classic Irish oxymoron. What man are you talking about, Niall?"

"His name is Ciarin Boyle. Ah, yes, he'd be bitter enough to try. But if he decided to do so, I don't doubt that he would succeed and we wouldn't be having this conversation."

A gust of wind off the lake kicked up enough sand to force both men to momentarily shield their faces. "What does this Boyle have against you?"

"He's got a grudge that he believes is righteous. Looking at it from his standpoint, I can see why. Ciarin and his band of merry men attempted one of the great betting coups. It involved a good horse named Gay Futurity that Ciaran owned.

"It all started in August some four years ago. There were a dozen different small race meetings going on around our country. As you know, a race meeting here is not the same length as yours in the U.S. Your meetings run weeks or months. Most of ours go from a day or two to a week or two.

"Ciaran entered Gay Futurity in a hurdle race at little Galway Park, in the very county we're sitting in. It was on Monday of that particular August week, one of our many bank holidays. But neither he nor his cohorts bet Gay Futurity at Galway where he was to run. Instead, they drove to betting shops all over the country, including four of mine. They hoped this carefully timed strike force would go unnoticed by bookmakers. Ciarin himself, of course, didn't put in any of these numerous wagers. He was using what you in the States would call 'beards.' Other men secretly representing him."

"Why are they called 'beards'?"

"Because they are disguising what they're doing. Actually, I believe the term came from the U.S. I read once that Frank James, brother of Jesse, worked as a 'beard' for your famous early twentieth-century gambler Pittsburgh Phil after Frank's brother passed and the bank robbing business dried up. Anyway, Ciarin's plan was clever. He had his beards hook up Gay Futurity in trebles with two other horses in earlier races on that Galway program, two horses that Ciaran secretly owned. They were a pair of no-hopers, for sure. But he never intended to run these long-odds items that day. These multiple bets, as you know, are difficult to win and they pay healthy odds. Ciaran withdrew these other two horses early that afternoon, claiming they had suddenly developed fevers. Which they had. The veterinarian on hand determined that. Of course, there was no way to determine the cause of these convenient infections at the time.

"So, under our rules, *any* of these bets on Gay Futurity in the multiple wagers would become a *single bet* on Gay Futurity after the other two horses were taken out of their races. By going through this enter-and-withdraw charade, Ciaran attempted to hide—for at least until his race was run—the amount bet on Gay Futurity. Oh, this was a well-planned exercise in thievery." Niall shook his head. "You have to give that bold chancer credit."

The two men's heads turned back to the nearby walking path, their attention attracted by a distressingly familiar voice. "Good God, it's that dreadful doctor," Niall said. It was indeed Doctor Whitesell and his wife coming along with the Hoys. Barry and the doctor were in the lead. Whitesell attempted to leave the walking path to approach Hanratty and Doyle. But Hoy clamped one of his large hands on the doctor's arm and maneuvered him back into forward motion. Hoy looked over his shoulder as Whitesell resumed his monologue, mouthing to Hanratty, "You owe me for this, Boss." The foursome were soon out of sight and earshot.

"Good man, your Hoy," Doyle said. "But what about bad man Boyle?"

Niall said, "Well, his good horse Gay Futurity won that race all right. Like a thief in the night. At odds of 10-1 that Mister Boyle had in effect created. Entered in that race on his own, Gay Futurity would have been even money. Boyle was up for a payoff of some three hundred thousand Euros."

"Wow!"

"Wow is right, Jack," Hanratty smiled. "Except it didn't happen. About two hours before that race went off, my man Tony Rourke got a call from his cousin Eddie Kilfoyle, who runs my betting shop in Bray. Eddie said strangers, patrons never before in his shop, had come in and bet heavily on a treble winding up with a horse named Gay Futurity. Two different huge bets in twenty minutes or so. Very, very unusual. Eddie asked if Tony knew anything about these horses.

"No such bets had been made at our Kinsale headquarters. Ciaran was too smart to do that. But Tony started calling around the country to our other shops, then shops of some of our competitors. Sure enough, same result. Out of the blue had come a ton of money on this supposedly longshot treble at this fairly obscure track on a normally very quiet Monday afternoon. But then, of course, when Boyle's first two longshot runners were scratched, it became one huge bet on Gay Futurity.

"And, once we had this attempt at thievery figured out," Hanratty grinned, "we all agreed, all the betting shops across the country, not to pay off Boyle and his men for the Gay Futurity caper. Boyle howled to the heavens before the national Racing and Wagering Board. When they heard the whole story, what they did was ban Boyle from all Irish racetracks for ten years, both as a horse owner and as a patron.

"Ciaran Boyle maintained that his clever taking advantage of odds was a stroke of genius, not a criminal act. The Board disagreed, unanimously, stating that the act warranted his exclusion. On top of that, Boyle was shortly thereafter charged in civil court with several counts of attempted fraud, found guilty, and given a two-year prison sentence. Quite a comedown for that bold fella."

Doyle said, "I don't imagine Mr. Boyle took this well."

"He surely didn't. When he learned that his plan had been discovered by my Tony Rourke, he was furious. With Tony, with me. He came up with several muttered threats of revenge that were duly reported in the press."

Hanratty shrugged. "That's just in the man's nature."

The breeze off Lough Ina picked up, bringing with it a promise of more rain. "We'd better head back," Hanratty said. He got to his feet.

Doyle remained seated on the log, reviewing all that he'd just heard. Finally, he looked up at Hanratty. "So, you're convinced Ciaran Boyle *hasn't* been behind these attempts on your life? What you call the 'automotive mishaps.' The errant rifleman on the little boat off your beach at home?"

"Absolutely, Jack." Hanratty zipped up his jacket and pulled the collar up. "Believe me," he said, "if Ciaran Boyle had been in charge of these events, I wouldn't be talking to you on this soon-to-be-moist morning. I'm telling you all this primarily because of my dear Sheila's urging. She's having dreams about me being cemetery-bound just as I approach my prime.

"My friends in the Garda haven't advanced this matter to their front burner. The leading private security firm I use has done no better in attempting to figure out who has it so mortally in for me. Or why. Sheila considers you to be a very impressive sort off your sleuthing successes in the States." He shrugged again. "I'm inclined to agree with her. If you can help me here, I'd appreciate it."

Looking somewhat embarrassed by even having to make this appeal, the famously tough and independent Hanratty said, "Let's go on back to the Lodge."

Doyle bent down to re-tie his running shoelaces. "I'll see what I can do, Niall. I'm going to take my morning run now. Always a great thinking time for me. See you in an hour or so."

His run was interrupted by a wind-spurred rain that forced him back to the Lodge thirty minutes earlier than he'd planned. That weather continued relentlessly, prompting some of the Hanratty party to leave a day early for home. The dining room that Saturday night for the most part was subdued. Jack and Nora sat with the Hanrattys. Niall said, "The weather channel says this deluge will be over by morning. I hope he's right."

He looked around the half-empty room. "Tony Rourke took off for home before lunch. Barry said he and his wife Maeve were headed tonight for a nearby pub to watch soccer and play darts," Niall said. "At least the Michigan boor has departed."

"Not so," Nora said. "Fiona told me Whitesell had taken to his bed for the night with an illness."

Doyle said, "We can only hope it's laryngitis."

Chapter Forty-one

Nora was already up, dressed for the day, packing her laptop, when Doyle awoke that bright, sunny Sunday morning. She declared herself "wildly hungry for breakfast. And yourself?"

"I am indeed," he yawned. "Give me a couple of minutes. I'm just going to jump in the shower."

"I've never quite understood that expression," Nora said. "Do you mean you're going to take a little run and then a kind of nimble leap in order to get beneath the showerhead? Or be jumping about once you're in there?"

"Hah hah. You're evidently in mid-day form at seven."

Twenty-five minutes later they entered the dining room, which was busy with a lively Sunday morning crowd that included a tour van group. "Ah, shoot," Doyle said to Sheila as they stood at the doorway.

"What's wrong?"

"Only table left open is over in the corner next to the Michigan Mouth. Him and poor Missus Mouse. Oh, well. What the hell! I'm starving. Are you game for placement over there within range of that bloviator?"

They walked through the room waving or saying hello to people they either knew or had recently met. Many cheery faces. Fiona, in her role as a morning server, greeted them with a smile and a choice of tea or coffee. Doyle, hearing the adjacent Dr. Whitesell, said, "Earplugs, Fiona, would be lovely." Fiona smiled sympathetically.

After Fiona had returned with green tea for Nora, orange juice for Jack, she took their orders, granola and fruit, the full Irish fry-up, respectively. Nora said, "So. The inquiring reporter wants to know. What were you and Niall on about out there on your early morning walk yesterday? I didn't want to ask you about it after you came back, sweating and disturbed. So, I went out with the ladies on a shopping group. With the Hanrattys there at dinner last night, I didn't want to bring up the subject. And, after dinner and drinks and that dancing, I never got around to doing so."

"But that, of course, was because you were otherwise occupied," Jack leered. She punched him on the arm. "Don't give me that Groucho Marx jiggling eyebrow act." He reached into the basket of scones, split one, offered her half, and glanced around the room.

"Don't want to talk here now, Nora. Besides," he said, "you'd probably have a hard time hearing me over the sounds of Doctor Buffoon."

After a wink to Nora, Doyle suddenly lurched forward in his chair. He grabbed his white napkin and pretended to cover his mouth. The sound that emerged was a disturbingly loud combination of a cough and a sneeze. Another even longer such utterance shortly followed. Nora looked at him with alarm and started to get to her feet. Even Dr. Whitesell momentarily stopped talking. Doyle took a deep breath, wiped his face with the napkin, and sat back in his chair.

Less than two minutes later, before Jack had apprised Nora of what he was doing, Dr. Whitesell had resumed loudly declaiming his negative views of "Obama Damn Care." Doyle let loose with an even more energetic sneeze/cough combo. This one was loud enough to startle all the nearby tables. He peered up over his napkin at the concerned Nora, laughter in his eyes.

Nora got it. Frowned, sat back, watching Jack take a deep breath and place his napkin back down on the table, giving her another wink. She said quietly, "I presume you're not a victim of choking or allergies, Jack Doyle. What, pray tell, or if you don't mind me saying so, what the hell *is* the meaning of that little performance? Those sounds you produced? I didn't know if you were blowing your nose or choking to death."

"I am glad you asked." He paused to drain his glass of juice. Wiped his mouth again and looked around the room, many of whose occupants regarded him with concern. He nodded toward them reassuringly. Niall and Barry had gotten up from their chairs, but Jack quickly waved a not to-worry hand in their direction and they sat back down. The Michigan physician had thrown his napkin down on the nearby table and left the dining room, Missus Mouse trailing.

"What you heard, Nora, was the sound of WGAF, pronounced woo-guff. I'll explain in a minute."

He offered Nora another scone, which was declined. He buttered his. "It goes back a ways. To be brief, that sound is a verbal acronym. I developed it several years ago for application in the presence of such world-class, boring assholes as Dr. Whitesell. When you hear a person like Whitesell producing a full throated cascade of egomaniacal verbal irritation, you have the opportunity, no, I should say the *obligation,* to respond with a resounding WGAF. Which at least might stop him for a moment or two. Maybe even halt him for more than that. If nothing else, your tipped-off companions will know what that sound stands for."

"Well, Jack, I'm not sure I get it. What *does* that sound mean?"

Doyle leaned across the table to confide, "WGAF, my dear, is the acronym for Who Gives a Fuck? Consider yourself tipped-off."

She was still muffling her laughter as Fiona placed Nora's cereal bowl before her, then served Jack's breakfast. He happily dug into his platter of sausages, rashers of bacon, two fried eggs, black pudding, baked beans, with brown soda bread on the side.

Nora shook her head as she watched him. "A breakfast like that would put me under for the day."

"Aw, it's great. Puts a skip in me step."

An hour later, Jack carried their luggage to Nora's Peugeot. After closing the trunk, he stepped back and admired its still very decent paint job. "All the rain here, they must never have to wash their cars," he said to himself.

The Hanrattys were at the Lodge entrance, accepting thanks from their departing guests, wishing them all "safe home, now." It continued to be a sun-blessed Sunday morning. Dr. Whitesell "and his meek wee woman," Niall told Jack, "left some time ago. Him evidently eager to infect some other corner of our nation."

Nora offered to drive half the way back to Bray. "Fine with me," Doyle said. "I'll leave these rural routes to you. You're probably more capable of weaving your way through the occasional roadway livestock. I enjoy the challenge of your city motoring." There was a dismissive glance and no reply to that. Rummaging through her glove box CD collection, he found another Van Morrison. "I don't know this one," Doyle said. "Mind if I play it?"

"Not at all. But before the music begins, I have this to ask. It's about you here on a return visit to your ancestral home in a matter of mere months if not weeks. Inquiring journalist that I am, I'd like to know why." She deftly turned onto the main highway before turning to smile at him. "I don't believe it's me unknowingly sending out siren songs that lure you back, Jack."

"Don't underestimate yourself. But, to be honest, the nearly overpowering lure of you is not the sole reason."

She said, "I appreciate your candor. So, tell me what's going on here?"

He reached to pat her hand on the steering wheel. "I don't mean to make light of your allure factor, Nora, believe me. Not at all." He stopped talking and gazed out his window at a large pasture dotted with robust, white sheep, an observant black border collie monitoring their pasture parameters.

"Do you think you could put up with me for a few more days, Nora?"

"The room rate will remain the same," she said softly. "But why? I know you're not desperate for my company." She put her right blinker on and angled off the side of the highway to a rest area and pulled the Peugeot to a stop.

"I think I've already had enough driving for this morning. You can drive us home from here. And you can also tell me what you're up to." They got out and exchanged seats.

Doyle sped through five more miles before answering. "Me being here," he said, "all has to do with Niall, his safety. The attempts on his life. Sheila's growing fear for him. Because somebody, identity unknown, seems determined to kill our Niall.

"Right after breakfast at the lodge this morning, Barry Hoy pulled me aside. He said he had some thoughts about who was targeting his boss. Said he couldn't talk there, but asked me to meet him for a drink late this afternoon in Dublin. I said I would. He seems to be as worried about Niall as Sheila is."

"Seems to be? Do I detect a note of doubt?"

"Nah, not really. Hoy strikes me as a reliable sort. He's been Niall's right-hand muscle for a lot of years. Been aboard since the time the company first took flight and seems to be a very loyal employee and friend. He's an ex-boxer," Doyle added.

"Hah! As if that means anything as far as his ethical credentials. The fact that he's laced out punishment and taken the same? Just like you, in your youth?"

"Ah, you journalists. Cynical streaks wider than the highway we're driving." Doyle reached to lower the volume on the Van Morrison CD. "At least you didn't refer to it as my 'distant' youth. But, no, of course I'm not qualifying Barry Hoy for the Morality All-Star Team just because he boxed like I did. But I've spent some time with that fellow, and he seems genuine to me. Niall Hanratty is pretty much a hero and a big brother and benefactor to him. I'm convinced of that. That's why I want to hear what Barry has to say to me."

⟩⟩⟩

Nora was listening to the ten o'clock RTE Radio One news that night when Jack lightly rapped on her front door. "Woo," she said, ushering him into her living room, "did you happen to tumble into a vat of Guinness at the Dublin brewery?"

"Don't be so dismissive, missy. Yeah, I had a few 'arf and

'arfs with Mr. Hoy. That pub I met him in, the breath mint dispenser was empty."

"Did you not eat dinner?"

Doyle said, "This was a business meeting. No time for fooling with menus. Do you happen to have any late night sandwich makings in your larder?"

"Follow me."

After she sliced the bread and cheese and turned on the broiler, and started brewing the tea, Nora said, "Well, how did it go? Was it an enlightening experience with Barry Hoy?"

"Pretty much so. Thanks for making the grilled cheese, by the way. Do you happen to have a tomato to place atop it? Yes, Hoy gave me some information that could prove valuable regarding Niall's mysterious enemy."

Nora handed him a cup of tea, poured her own, and sat down across from him. "What kind of information?"

"Well, you might term what Barry told me is the tip of the iceberg. Now, I need someone to probe under the water into the heart of the iceberg. So to speak."

"Good God, Jack, enough of the foggy talk. I sense there's something here you want from me. Am I right?"

"There is, Nora. In your role as the inquiring journalist, would you be able to find out details about an Irish company's incorporation? Its officers? Major stockholders? Things like that?"

She sipped her tea and sat back, eyebrows raised. "I hope you recognize this as an appraising look."

"How could I miss it?" Doyle said.

"I'm not sure what you're up to. Yet. But to answer your question, yes, it *is* possible for me to undertake that sort of research. If the company is registered here in Ireland, I could access the Companies Registration Office. This can be done online. There'd be a small fee to download the company's filings, which would include the information you mentioned. I could use a credit card to pay for the documents to be sent back to me."

"I'll give you my card number."

"No rush. The Registration Office won't be open for business on a Sunday. And, I leave early tomorrow morning for a conference in Spain, the town of Santiago de Compostella. I've never been there. Supposed to be very interesting. The conference subject is Internet privacy, and I'm covering it for some newspapers in the European Market countries. Once I'm there and set up, and when I get a bit of time, I'll try to get this information for you. Might take a few days. All right?"

"That'd be great. My flight home is tomorrow afternoon. Maybe you could call or e-mail me with what you've come up whenever you come up with it."

"That'll be the plan, then," Nora said, adding, "Are you sure you trust big Barry Hoy?"

Doyle finished the final bite of his sandwich before answering. "As you can see, I am chewing thoughtfully."

"On with it, Jack Doyle. What's your answer?"

"Yes, I trust the faithful Hoy. So far."

Nora was up and off early the next morning for her flight to Spain, giving Doyle a hearty hug at the doorway before hurrying down the steps and walkway to the waiting cab. He waved good-bye, but she didn't see it. She was already on her cell phone as the taxi pulled away.

He showered, packed, and took a brief walk in her quiet Bray neighborhood. Four blocks brought him to a spot with a grand view of the Irish Sea. Its strand was dotted with joggers and dog walkers on this pleasant morning. He wished he had time to join them. But his airport cab was due, as was he due back in Chicago, where two surprises would be forthcoming, one immediate, neither pleasant.

Chapter Forty-two

The publicized notice of the fifty-thousand-dollar reward made her smile. It was being talked about throughout the horse world. "Stop the killer of these valuable, contributing horses" pretty much summed up the outcries. "But what about the crimes being committed against these innocent, unrepresented horses?" she muttered. "What they are being put through in the cause of arrogant science?"

A humidity-ridden August afternoon in southwest Michigan. She'd started early in the morning and curved around the southern border of the great lake that glistened in the sunlight like the bottom of a giant, watery paper clip. Her drive there had been easy. Her research about Washtena College and the routines of its veterinary school indicated promise and possibility.

She stopped at a Dairy Queen drive-in on the outskirts of South Haven for an iced coffee and a grilled chicken sandwich. Kept her ball cap low on her face as she ordered, then paid the teen-aged car hop. Checked her watch. If the vet school's published schedule was accurate, her target should by now be having her late afternoon grazing session in a field farthest away from the school's buildings.

Thirty-two miles later she pulled off the black-topped county highway onto a graveled side road, parked, and picked up her equipment bag. Got out and stood for a moment, breathing in the delightful air of a rural summer, the silence broken only by some treetop bird chattering.

The old black mare was alone in the lush, green pasture, some twenty yards away from the fence. Her head was down, lips working slowly as she nibbled. Flies were nearby and she flicked them away with both her tail and her ears, not looking up.

Standing quietly in the advancing dusk, shadowed by the thick branches of a tall chestnut tree, she whistled softly. Just enough to make the horse's ears come all the way up as she raised her head.

Leaning over the wooden fence, she reached into her kit. Extracted a package of peppermint mints. She confidently crinkled the cellophane wrapper. She'd never known a horse that didn't love peppermint. This one was no exception.

The old mare clopped eagerly toward the fence, head up, ears still pricked, a picture of expectancy. For a moment, the hand holding the syringe trembled. How she disliked doing this. But it had to be done if the message would ever be understood that these innocent, four-legged creatures should never be subjected to physical intrusions, that such treatment no matter how "well intentioned" violated nature's law.

The old mare stopped at the fence. Regarded the visitor, looked away, then looked back. And stepped closer to the outstretched hand.

That hand delivered the candies and its owner smiled at the familiar feeling of soft horse lips on her palm, the grateful snorting sound the horse produced. Her eyes began to tear as she watched the trusting mare's large eyes shift up to her face.

It was with even more reluctance than usual on this sweet-smelling early evening that she gave a final caress to the right side of the old mare's neck, stepped forward, reached across the fence, and plunged the needle into the other side of that neck.

She turned away. Leaned down to pick up the empty cellophane package. Heard the sound of the thousand-pound suddenly dead body hit the grass on the other side of the fence.

Not looking back, she ran, reaching for the keys with her right hand, brushing the tears from her face with her left.

Chapter Forty-three

An overcast August morning. Doyle, restless and unable to sleep soundly, had taken a dawn run along the lakefront. He was back in his condo, showered and dressed before seven, when he decided to drive out to Heartland Downs and watch the workouts with Ralph Tenuta.

It was one of his favorite things to do. Mornings at the racetrack were Doyle's favorite times in that setting. Stands empty but for a dozen clockers, numerous trainers and owners sipping coffee, eyes on the action in front of them. The racing strip with dozens of horses going through a variety of training exercises. The sounds they made, as well as the bright voices of the amazingly physically fit little men and women riding them, darting through the early morning air. Hoofbeats pounding into the loam, equine snorts and whinnies, riders chirping to their mounts or cajoling them, meanwhile exchanging good-natured greetings or barbs. The sounds of a world unto itself.

Ten miles away from Heartland on Willow Road, Doyle picked up his cell phone.

"Have you heard?"

He grimaced as he pulled into the left lane to pass a garishly decorated wide load monstrosity that was wavering back and forth over the center line of his two westbound lanes. In Doyle's experience, any sentence beginning with "Have you heard?" too often meant trouble.

"Heard what, Karen? Assuming that is you."

She said, "Sorry for being so abrupt, Jack. What you evidently have not heard is that another horse has been put to death."

"Aw, damn," Doyle said. "Where and when?"

She supplied the details.

"Whoever the hell is doing this, Jack, it seems he just can't be stopped the way we're operating now."

"How do you know it's a he?"

"You know what I mean," she barked. That's *five* of these horse deaths so far. That's just unacceptable!'

Karen Engel's frustration at the news of the latest killing was palpable. Doyle pulled off to the right at Shermer, drove two blocks, and parked.

"What are you doing, Jack? Did you hear what I said?"

"Karen, I'm attempting to avoid arrest. I just missed being sideswiped by a trailer home bigger than Donald Trump's ego. And on this stretch of Willow, the local cops have been stopping and pulling over cell phone-using drivers like crazy. Court appearances required. Hundred-dollar fines. I heard it on the news. I don't want to be their next victim."

He made a U-turn, parked, and resumed talking to the flustered FBI agent. "I know what you're saying, Karen. But I don't know what I can do about it. Unless somebody somehow spots this villain in action, I think we're screwed."

"I don't know how that is ever going to come about. This killer does his research, does his killing secretly, and leaves nothing but those damned ALWD cards. Damon is pulling his hair out. Our boss is yanking at his few remaining strands. And he's leaning all over us. I don't know what to do."

Doyle said, "Wait a minute." He got out of the Accord and began to pace back and forth next to the car, cell phone in hand. "If you and your FBI forces don't come up with a tip, an informer, I don't see this ever ending. I'll keep asking around. That's the best I can do."

He heard Karen saying, "Damon, I've got Jack on the phone here. Do you want to talk to him?"

Doyle groaned but knew he had to talk to Tirabassi. When he heard the phone transfer, he said, "Is this the voice of justice and truth?"

"You know, Doyle, you make light of so many important things it's almost enough to depress an optimist like me. But I don't want to talk about your effect on your fellow humans. I want to ask you to do something for me. Us."

"I can hardly wait to hear this request."

"I am asking you, Jack, to meet with, and feel out, Esther Ness. Her name keeps coming up in all speculative reports about bleeding heart nutters and their attitudes toward horses. We know this woman has big money. Heck, she put up the fifty grand reward without batting an eye. But she's got layers of lawyers and we don't want to fight our way through them just to be able to talk to her. Maybe you could approach her. You, as a fellow horse person, yadda yadda. What we need to know is if she *could* be, out of some off-the-wall sense of responsibility, financing these horse killings. Or even be carrying them out herself. I know this sounds a little bit out of left field. But we don't have any other irons in this fire. What do you say, Jack?"

"Left field. Irons in the fire. Did the Bureau force you to enroll in a cliché school?"

No answer. Doyle smiled at the thought of Damon seething on the other end. "Damon, my friend, your arm of our government has obviously descended to another new level of desperation. I went along with your request that I poke around in search of information. But, this? Sending me out under a surreptitious Bureau banner to interview a possible suspect? Man, this is new territory. Or, as a graduate of the Bureau Cliché School such as yourself might put it, 'uncharted waters.'"

In the ensuing silence, Doyle felt a tinge of regret. A tinge was usually the most he would allow himself. He recalled the heavy-handed, down-from-the-top pressure he knew was being applied to the Tirabassi-Engel team. A tandem with which he had a shared a frequently aggravating but somehow always rewarding history. These were good people in careers that must seem to them, he thought, to be laden with far more frustration than elation. Doyle liked and admired both agents. Foregoing one more yank on the simmering Tirabassi's emotional chain, Doyle said, "E-mail me Ms. Ness' address. I'll try to see her as soon as I can." He heard Karen Engel say, "Damon, tell him thanks" before the connection ended.

Even before he parked his Accord next to Ralph Tenuta's Heartland Downs barn, Jack knew something serious was up. Ingrid McGuire was there, work clothes on, accompanied by Marla McCarty, Ingrid's summer intern from the University of Illinois' Veterinary School of Medicine. This small, young person was bobbing her head and assiduously taking notes as she listened to Ingrid speak to Tenuta. Marla looked distressed. So did Ingrid and Ralph. Head groom Paul Albano stood off to the side, listening in as he applied saddle soap to the piece of bridle he was holding.

They all looked up as Doyle approached.

Tenuta said, "Jack, hi. As you can see, something's going on here. Let me show you."

The trainer walked down the shedrow to the stall occupied by the Burkhardts' pride and joy, Mr. Rhinelander. This ordinarily energetic two-year-old colt stood stock still in his stall, head dropped, eyes half-closed.

Doyle leaned over the webbing stretched across the stall doorway. "Jesus, Ralph. What's the matter with him? "

Ingrid moved next to Doyle to look more closely into the stall. Her usually cheerful, tanned face was a mask of concern. "The tests came back an hour ago. Mr. Rhinelander has EHV-1. It's a virus that horses get, and it can be a bad one. Two other horses in the next barn over have been similarly diagnosed."

She reached over the webbing in attempt to touch Mr. Rhinelander's head. But the miserable-looking horse dropped his head even lower and backed away a couple of steps.

"He looks terrible," Doyle said. "What is this disease? What do you do about it? I mean, what's the treatment?"

"EHV-1 is a contagious disease among horses," Ingrid said. "The infection makes them uncoordinated, weak. They have trouble standing and urinating and defecating. It can be fatal. It's spread through contact. But it's puzzling as hell, because some horses can be exposed to it and not get it while others do. Unfortunately, Mr. Rhinelander has it."

"How do we deal with this?" Ingrid continued. "There is no one specific method. Treatment could include intravenous fluids, anti-inflammatory drugs, or both. I've got a call in to my old advisor prof at the U. to get his opinion on this. One thing is for sure. Mr. Rhinelander will have to be quarantined. That's mandatory. There is no way to know how the virus is introduced. This stuff spreads by direct horse-to-horse contact, or contaminated hands, or tack equipment. He's got a fever this morning of 105. In most cases, the infected horse will also have nasal discharge, which Mr. Rhinelander has plenty of. And, in most cases, they will go on to recover after a week or ten days or so."

"How many other cases of this are there here at Heartland?" Doyle said.

"There are two in Buck Norman's barn. I heard there was another in the barn beside his. So, four or five so far," Tenuta said. "I heard one of Buck's died."

Ingrid grimaced. "That's true. Happened last night." She reached in to give the lethargic Mr. Rhinelander a final look. "We're going to keep the death toll to one, baby," she said softly. "At least I hope so."

Paul Albano parked Tenuta's truck and horse trailer outside the barn. With Ralph on one side, Ingrid on the other, wide-eyed little Marla bringing up the rear, Mr. Rhinelander was led into the one-horse van.

Doyle said, "Where's he going?"

"He's going into Barn Fifteen, over on the far side of the backstretch," Tenuta replied. "The quarantine barn. According to the new rules just put in by the state veterinarian here, he'll have to stay there for at least two weeks. If he tests negative after that, then he'll be taken out of there and returned to me here."

Mr. Rhinelander balked at the first step of the ramp. Ingrid waved Tenuta off and began talking softly to the nervous, sweating animal, finally leading him gently into the trailer. There was not much room for the two of them, but Ingrid said, "Ralph, I'll ride with him over there." Tenuta closed the trailer door. Albano waited until Marla jumped into the passenger seat next to him, then waved his left hand out the window as he steered the truck out onto the roadway.

Doyle said, "Well, that's a sorry sight. Have you told the Burkhardts about this?"

"Of course, I have, Jack. They're horrified. On their way driving down here from Dairy Land."

"What the hell can they do?"

Tenuta stopped and turned to face Doyle. "There are some people, Jack, that become attached to their horses in a way most other people cannot understand. I'm one of those people. Always have been, ever since I was fourteen and part owner with my cousin Vince of an old riding stable plug called Molly. I loved that old spavined mare and cried when she died a couple of years later.

"Horses can get to you that way, Jack. Look at the effect Mr. Rhinelander's illness has on even such a trained person as Ingrid. You'd think she'd be used to things like that by now."

Tenuta looked at his watch. "The Burkhardts should be here in about ninety minutes. They'll probably set up camp chairs and park outside the quarantine barn. Ridiculous, you think, but I won't stop them. You got time for a coffee at the track kitchen?"

"Naw, but thanks. I've got be somewhere. I'll call you tonight to see how Mr. Rhinelander is doing."

Chapter Forty-four

The smooth, tree-shaded country road wound past pastures dotted with horses of every shade that thoroughbreds come in. Frisky yearlings romped in fields separated by white fences from those occupied by their mothers, who were now occupied parenting this year's foals. Doyle slowed the Accord and crossed a narrow, stone bridge over a slowly flowing creek. The directions he'd been given were precise and accurate. He turned off the highway and onto a long, curving drive that led up to an impressive white mansion. Gables, balconies, shutters, chimneys, tall wide windows. "Tara Midwest," he said to himself.

Doyle parked between a white Rolls-Royce and a red Jeep, both polished and gleaming in the afternoon sunshine. He tossed his car keys on the floor of the Accord, closed its door, and paused to look back and take in the array of flower beds that divided the long, wide, green lawn leading to the entrance.

Up three marble steps to the broad oak door, he was met by a traditionally dressed maid, white pinafore over black outfit, who told him "Ms. Esther" could be found "down at the stables behind this house."

Walking down the gravel drive, Doyle heard a horse nicker nearby. The pleasant odor of new-mown hay hung in the warm summer air. The drive circled around an island of green grass. On each side of it there was a one-story white brick stable with six stalls. Watching him approach from in front of one of the wood-lined stalls was a diminutive woman wearing a white tee-shirt, brown jodhpurs, and dark glasses perched atop her head of auburn curls. She had large, brown eyes widely spaced in a narrow face. Her bare arms were tanned and taut. The long face of a chestnut horse rested on her right shoulder. She was nonchalantly massaging the horse's nose with her left hand.

"Ms. Ness? I'm Jack Doyle. Good afternoon."

She paused before answering, looking him up and down.

"When Pat Caldwell called to tell me you wanted to speak with me, I was at first reluctant. Then I thought, what the hell? I haven't met an interesting man in ages. By the way, how is the 'Voice of Heartland Downs'?"

"Mr. Caldwell is in fine fettle. He sends his regards. As for me, I don't know how interesting you're going to find me. I just need to ask you a few questions. As I think Pat Caldwell told you, I am helping authorities trying to find the person or persons killing thoroughbred horses at vet schools."

He saw her wince at his mention of the dead equines. She composed herself. Giving the obviously pleased horse a final pat, she said, "There's a nice bench around the corner. It sits under a willow and overlooks our creek."

Doyle swatted at a buzzing mosquito near his right ear. "Damn. I'm a target for these damn things. Could we sit inside someplace instead?"

Esther smiled. She had a confident look about her, Doyle thought, that would fend off any impertinent insects. "Let's go to my office."

She strode rapidly slightly in front of him without saying anything. He glanced several times at her face, which seemed to him to be right on that interesting border between pretty and plain. It was an intriguing face, warranting repeated looks. She turned for a stride or two to glance back at him, apparently amused by his interest.

The office was around the back of this barn in a long, wide, obviously added-on extension. An elderly, brown-skinned gardener looked up from his trimming of the thick hedges outside the building's door.

"Buenos tardes, Pedro."

The man doffed his wide-brimmed hat in response and moved to open the door, but Esther waved him off with a smile.

Doyle said, "Dress Pedro in white shirt and pants, he'd look like one of the Mexican peasants in the old movie *Viva Zapata.*"

She pushed open the door and walked in ahead of him. "Pedro is a valued employee, Mr. Doyle. He has been here since my father hired him more than thirty years ago. Still doing the same excellent work on our grounds as he always has. There's nothing 'peasant' about him. His two children are both college graduates."

Doyle considered asking "if Pedro would thank Cesar Chavez for that, or just your beneficent daddy?" but refrained.

The office air conditioner was a model of efficiency. Felt good to Doyle.

Esther sat down behind her large, paper-littered desk and picked up the phone. She began to dial, saying, "I've got to make a quick call. Please relax for a minute, Mr. Doyle."

He used the time to eye the walls covered with photos of his hostess aboard horses in numerous equine competitions. He figured she must have been a young teenager in the early shots of her wearing white shirt, black coat, black helmet, aboard a succession of impressive looking horses. She was advancingly older in other frames, but still poised and sure on different steeds.

This photographic panorama covered three walls of the paneled room. Along the forty-five-foot long fourth wall stretched glass cases packed with trophies. He heard her say, "Great, my darling. I'll meet you there at seven," before she hung up the phone. She sat back in her desk chair, placed her booted feet upon the desk top, and laced her hands across her waist. "Now, then, I know why you're here, Mr. Doyle. It's about those horses dying at vet schools."

"Call me Jack. Did Pat Caldwell mention to you that I was aiding the FBI in this matter?"

"The Voice of Heartland Downs is not my sole source of information, Jack," she said sharply. "I know very well why you are here."

Doyle sat back in his chair and turned to toss his sport coat up toward a nearby coat rack that sported a black porcelain horse head on its top. His coat covered it. "I'll make this quick, Ms. Ness."

He leaned forward in his chair. "I think you, Esther Ness, ex-debutante, current socialite and equestrian and charity ball fixture, might well be involved in these murders of horses you claim to love so well. That's why I'm here."

Esther yanked her boots off the desk and jerked forward in her chair. Her face was flushed beneath its tan. "Murders?" she hissed. "You call those events, those horse deaths, murders?"

She caught herself and sat back in her chair, taking a deep breath. Her confident small smile reappeared. She waited.

"I've never been a champion at semantics," Doyle said. "Some animal dies involuntarily, it's either disease, or accidental death, or murder as far as I'm concerned. Maybe somebody else would term them mercy killings. Maybe even somebody like you.

"I've seen this impressive place of yours," Doyle continued. "I've seen the evidence of your long and continuing involvement with horses. All I'm here for today is to find out if, perhaps, you know something about these 'events' as you term them. Or 'horse fatalities.' Maybe you could point me, and the FBI, in some kind of useful direction looking for the villain. Or villainess."

Other than the tightening of Esther's lips, there was no reaction. He pressed on. "Look, I kind of understand the stated philosophy behind this ALWD movement. Nobody likes to see horses being hurt. But the ones in these vet school studies aren't being harmed by the experimental treatments. They are well cared for animals. They're not suffering. Until, that is, the mysterious killer sneaks up on them."

"Oh, really, Mr. Doyle. That's your view?" She stood up and walked the few steps to a window overlooking the back paddock now occupied by a pair of her showhorses that were calmly grazing. Back turned to him, she took another deep breath. Then she pivoted to face him, brown eyes blazing.

"You don't think that the probing, prodding, of helpless, captive horses is intrusive and against nature? I don't care what they say that the potential useful results of such research could be! It's still something horses should not ever be subjected to. That's my opinion." Doyle saw she was fired up. He waited.

"That doesn't mean I completely countenance the mercy killings," she concluded as she returned to her chair, composure regained.

"You don't 'completely' countenance them? What the hell does that mean?" Doyle snapped. "Do you partially approve of them?"

She sighed. "I would have thought that my putting up a fifty-thousand-dollar reward for the capture of your 'killer' would be enough to show where I stand."

"And where *is* that?"

"I'm primarily on the side of the horse. Always have been. But, no matter how much I abhor these wonderful creatures being treated like helpless lab rats, I do not necessarily agree when ALWD declares the murders to be justified. They *are* attacks on property that does not belong to anyone but the schools to which the horses have been donated, or the owners of the horses who donated them."

Her phone rang. She said, "Just a second, Barb, I'm with someone." Putting the receiver down, she said, "That's all I have to say about this matter, Mr. Doyle. So, if you'll excuse me…"

"So, we're back to *Mr.* Doyle." He stood up and plucked his coat off the top of the rack. "My FBI agent friends might have a few more questions for you, Ms. Ness."

"If they do, they can contact my attorneys. I'm not a fan of such interviews."

Doyle, irritated, said, "Well, the government has lawyers, too."

Esther laughed. "Oh, I'm well aware of that. When my father was involved in a spurious case years ago, his lawyers knocked down the government opposition like, well, like tenpins. You get what you pay for," she added.

Doyle stood up. "I'm going to give you my cell phone number. I'd appreciate it if you'd call me if you happen to get any information about the horse killer. Okay?"

She wrote the number down before saying dismissively, "Couldn't I Twitter you if I hear anything?"

"Esther, I don't look at Twitter. I decided long ago that was a waste of my time. Reading a lot of those messages, it seemed to me they were being written by thirty-five-year-old bachelors who had never made it anywhere. They'd like to beat their dogs, but they don't even have dogs. So they tweet."

Back in his Accord, he sat back in his seat, irritated with himself for being so irritated with this woman. F. Scott Fitzgerald's Daisy Buchanan, he remembered, had a "voice full of money." Ms. Ness' monied voice to him sounded full of confidence, privilege, and invulnerability.

All the natural beauty visible on his drive out of Barrington Hills was lost on Doyle. He didn't like the fact that he had, really, nothing useful to report to Karen and Damon. The reward that Esther Ness, possible suspect, had offered could be for real, or could be a smokescreen.

On Highway 14 going toward the Edens, his phone buzzed. Caller ID showed it was Nora. He said hello, wait a second, and pulled into a 7-11 parking lot. "This is a kick. I don't get many international calls. What's up?"

Nora said, "I can't talk now. But I've sent you an e-mail you should look at as soon as you can. Where are you?"

"Fleeing the boonies. I'll be home in about, oh, forty minutes. Did you get that info I asked for?"

"Heh, heh. Is poteen the water of life? Of course I did. You're dealing with a trained reporter here. Got to go. I'm on assignment as a stringer for the *Irish Times*. Some clerical big shot is going to announce another grand settlement in a series of priestly child abuse cases. They're not doing this in Dublin. I'm on the outskirts of Limerick."

Doyle said, "If an admission of guilt is forthcoming far away from the capital, will it be heard?"

"If *I've* got anything to do about it, and I do, it will. Talk to you tomorrow after you've digested my report about the Shamrock Off-Course Wagering corporate structure. It will give you quite a bit to chew on. In fact, Jack," she giggled, "I would not be at all surprised to see you back here in your ancestral homeland pretty darn quick. Bye."

Chapter Forty-five

Aer Lingus flight 582 approached Cork International Airport poking through a layer of thick, early morning fog that obscured the landscape below.

"Not unusual, you know," remarked Jack Doyle's seatmate, a slim, well-dressed septuagenarian who had introduced himself as Seamus Scanlon soon after their takeoff from O'Hare Airport the night before. Doyle initially feared he was going to be in the seven-hour presence of a too-talkative Irishman. But that was not the case. After a minute or two of introductory chatter, Scanlon plugged in earphones and soon went to sleep. When he awoke an hour later, he yawned, smiled at Jack, and picked up his paperback copy of an Edna O'Brien novel and began to read. Another bit of chat during dinner was the extent of their conversation until now.

"Cork Airport is a bit more than five hundred feet above sea level," Scanlon informed. "Sometimes, like this morning, it's prone to foggy conditions and low cloud ceiling. This can cause delays, like this one. We are circling now, as I'm sure you're aware. If the fog doesn't give us an opening, we'll be diverted to either Shannon or Dublin. That happens every so often."

Doyle said, "You must be a veteran of these weather-related maneuvers. You don't seem too concerned."

"Aw, sure, this has happened to me before," the little Irishman smiled. "It's not what you would term a Big Deal. You learn to live with it." He turned back to his book.

There was the *thunk* of airplane wheels being dropped. "Ah," Scanlon said. "Good. We're going to land here in Cork."

Once the plane was on the tarmac and parked at the gate, Scanlon rose first and opened the overhead bin. "Do you have something up here?"

"It's a dark green carry-on," Doyle said. "Thanks. But I'll get it." Scanlon deftly snatched Doyle's carry-on out of the bin and presented it to him.

Standing in the aisle, they waited while passengers in front of them, many young folks, wrestled down lunks of luggage. Three young women had to be helped retrieving their bulging carry-on cases. Doyle and Scanlon waited patiently.

"You've observed this irritating drill before, I assume," Scanlon said.

"All too frequently," Doyle sighed. "All the time spent struggling with these heavy carry-ons could undoubtedly be better spent awaiting the checked items at the carousel inside."

Scanlon checked his watch as they waited in the aisle. "So, Mr. Doyle, are you here for business or pleasure?"

Doyle smiled as the line finally advanced. "Pleasurable business is what I hope it will be, Mr. Scanlon. Great meeting you."

⟩⟩⟩

The Cork Airport Customs Line for non-European citizens moved more briskly than its Dublin counterpart, Doyle thought. The heavyset, middle-aged woman examining his passport looked up and smiled, "You're back quite quickly now, are you not, Mr. Doyle?"

He leaned forward to peer at her identification badge. "Aw, Maeve, you just can't keep me away from this treasure of a country."

She stamped his passport and pushed it through the slot. "On with you now," she said with a laugh.

⟩⟩⟩

His suitcase retrieved, Doyle bought a bottle of water from the first concession stand he saw. His flight had landed almost thirty minutes prior to the arrival time he'd given Barry Hoy. He found an empty bench near the Arrivals Entrance where Hoy said he would look for him. Ignoring the happy chatter of travelers being enthusiastically greeted in this foyer area, he unpacked his laptop and reviewed once again Nora Sheehan's e-mail.

"Here's the Shamrock information you wanted," she'd written. "Hope it helps. Hope to see you soon."

The detailed report that followed was what had so quickly caused Jack to return to Ireland, seriously fearful for Niall Hanratty's life. The previous failed assaults on the bookmaker had not stimulated in Doyle the level of concern this document had.

Nora's research revealed that Niall's bookmaking empire Papers of Registration had not been changed since the original filing at the inception of the company fifteen years previous.

At Shamrock's inception, Hanratty owned eighty-eight percent of the privately held stock in this now extremely prosperous firm. Two percent had originally been assigned to Barry Hoy "in perpetuity." The remaining ten percent had been designated for Anthony X. Rourke, with a codicil stating that Rourke's percentage would be increased by five percent to be deducted annually from Hanratty's after every one of the company's first five profitable years. Also, as Nora had bold-faced, "Anthony X. Rourke was to be made a partner with ownership in one-third of Shamrock if and when the company recorded ten profitable years in succession. In the case of Niall Hanratty's passing, managing control of Shamrock Corporation would go to A.X. Rourke."

Nora emphasized at the end of her e-mail, "This 'managing control' bit is the stick-out item. That could lead to the 'managing controller' transforming the setup completely. I can't believe this thing is so loosely written. I guess because it was based on a great deal of trust between Hanratty and Rourke. Always, from what I've observed, a mistakenly way of doing business.

"Obviously," Nora concluded, "Niall Hanratty had enormous faith and trust in Tony Rourke when this document was signed. And, vice versa. But the papers were never amended to show that Rourke received his full partnership."

Doyle turned off his computer. Could anything in this document represent a motive for murder? *Sure*, he thought, if *the promise to Rourke of a full partnership was not for some reason kept. A talented man's ambition thwarted? Hell, yes, that could develop into a motive for revenge.*

So lost in thought was Doyle that he turned only an instant before Barry Hoy's hand gripped his shoulder. The big Irishman was grinning. "Must be the jet lag that's slowed you down so, Jack. For a man usually so wary, you caught nary a glimpse of me sneaking up behind you."

They shook, Doyle's right hand nearly disappearing into Hoy's grasp. Neither of these two former boxers was at all interested in macho hand shaking. Too many past busted knuckles involved. "I didn't see you coming, Barry. I was lost in what for me counts as thought."

Hoy snatched up Doyle's bag. "We're over this way."

"I don't know how you ever lost a bout with those huge mitts you've got, Barry," Doyle said as they walked out of the terminal.

Hoy laughed. "Hands of Stone I was called in my early boxing days in Dublin's fight clubs. Like a Hibernian version of the great Panamanian fighter Roberto Duran. And there was at least a bit of truth to that. I could flatten them if I could hit them. What observers failed to add, and I had to take in from painful experience, was that 'Hands of Stone,' in my case, also was found to have 'Chin of Glass.'"

Doyle smiled as he looked at the rueful expression on the big man's face at these recollections. "You've got to laugh a bit, Barry, having a ring career that could be summed up on the slips of paper in a couple of fortune cookies."

They walked to where Hoy said he was parked in a marked area that was being watched over by a youthful airport traffic officer.

Hoy waved at the man. "That's a cousin of mine. I got him the job here."

Settled into the front seat of the black Ford Escort, Doyle buckled up as Hoy sped onto the airport exit ramp.

"I'm not positive that our man is going to be off to Dublin. I think so, but I'm not sure. That's why I want to watch for him up on the E-20. Outside our Kinsale office the other day, I heard him whispering into his cell phone about an afternoon meeting today up there. He mentioned the exact time, and I remembered it. He never noticed my overhearing. He'll have to go out of Cork on this road to get there."

Chapter Forty-six

Hoy pulled off into a rest area eight kilometers north of Cork. He got out and stretched. "C'mon. We can see the highway from over here." They walked to an empty picnic table that sat on a slight ridge overlooking the motorway. Hoy said, "You told me when you phoned me from the States that you'd explain your coming here once you got here. You've been here a half-hour. This would be a good time, am I right?"

Doyle plunked himself down beside the big man on the bench. He thought for a few moments before replying, "Part of it, Barry, was your suspicion that you mentioned to me back at Lough Inagh. The bigger part was the documents I've seen since then about the Shamrock Corporation. They were very informative. And when you told me our man, usually a ten-hour-a-day workaholic, had begun scheduling more and more days off, acting strangely with people he'd worked with for years, I wanted to see what you and I might find out if we worked together. I'm sure you know what I'm getting at, right?"

Hoy nodded. "I do. At first I was kind of torn about bringing you into this, Jack. But Niall has been so grand to me over the years, we've been in and out of so many scrapes together, I just felt that I had to. Even if I told him what my thinking was, what I suspected, he'd just laugh me off. He'd say, as he has many, many times in the past, 'Not to worry. I'll handle this.' I'm not the mental marvel that man is, and I know it, and he knows it.

That's fine. But I figured he wouldn't brush you aside, especially if we had some evidence to present to him.

"When I heard Niall talking to him the other day, and Niall being surprised at our man's request for yet another day off, but not inquiring why, I felt more uneasy. That's why I was glad when you called to say you were coming over here again. Whatever we find out, and it could be nothing at all, you'll be the sort of witness Niall respects. I thank you for flying over on such short notice."

The big man got up to say, "Niall will hardly listen to anyone else on this subject, not even Sheila, much less me. The man can be as stubborn as Corrigan's donkey."

Hoy glanced at his watch. "If what I think is going to happen does happen, it'll be in the next fifty, sixty minutes. According to what I've been able to learn, our man'll be leaving for Dublin during that time. So, we'll wait here." Hoy reached into the back and extracted a thermos. "Would you like some tea, Jack?"

"Thanks, no. Now, what kind of car are we on the watch for?"

Hoy said, "He drives a four-year-old brown Volvo. It's not in his nature to be flashing along past us. He'll be well within the speed limit. We should easily spot him if he comes."

"If we pick him up and follow, he'll know your car, won't he?"

"Sure, and he would, Jack," Hoy smiled. "But we don't have my car. It's a rental."

The morning sun had briefly fought its way through the Cork cloud bank twenty-eight minutes later when Hoy suddenly sat up and snatched the car key out of his jacket pocket. "That was him! Our man's on his way."

It was a time-consuming trip, taking nearly three hours to cover the one hundred sixty miles. They stayed three cars back of the brown Volvo, both of them bored by the inaction. "He drives like an old woman," Hoy said.

On the Dublin outskirts, they encountered heavy traffic, but had no trouble keeping the Volvo in view. "Traffic like this," Hoy said, "is a leftover of the grand Celtic Tiger days. When the money was flowing back then, a lot of it went into Ireland's auto market. Of course, by now, many of those grand vehicles have been repossessed or taken over by the banks. Not all, of course. And, Jaysus, not that one," the normally undemonstrative Hoy shouted, yanking the steering wheel to the right. "Look at it!"

A dark-blue Chevrolet SUV crossed over in front of them, driven by a woman in hair curlers, housecoat, and sunglasses, the two rear seats of the speeding vehicle full of children dressed in junior hurling team uniforms. Steering with her left hand, holding the cell phone to her ear with her right, she signaled a right turn before careening around the next corner to the left, a cacophony of pounded horns in her impervious wake.

"Another menace to society," Hoy grunted. "Our roads are full of them. Did you know that you can *fail* your driver's road test in this country and *still* continue to drive, on a provisional license? Failures at the wheel! Like that woman, probably. As far as I know, we're the only country in the world that allows such nonsense. It's a wonder the curbs aren't littered with casualties."

They trailed the cautiously driven brown Volvo for another fifteen minutes, always three or four cars back. Finally, it pulled up next to the curb on Raglan Road. Hoy slid the Focus into a parking place a half-block back. They watched as Tony Rourke slowly got out, locked the door, looked cautiously about, then walked toward Moynihan's Ould Times Pub. His hat was pulled down and raincoat collar pulled up. He was back outside of the pub within two minutes in the company of a small, cocky looking senior citizen who had his cap on and jacket collar raised against the suddenly arrived drizzle. The little man peered up and down the street before he began talking rapidly to Rourke, occasionally reaching forward to jab fingers into Rourke's chest.

"Jaysus," Hoy said. "That's old Billy Sheridan with him!"

"Who is that?"

"One of the old-time hard men from the IRA's glory days. My Da grew up with him. Billy did his years in Mountjoy, which they say he came to run like it was his front parlor. Once out, the troubles pretty much over by then, he cleverly converted to straight ahead civilian-type crime."

The rain increased. Hoy started the motor and put the wipers on low. He said, "Billy now has a little gang of his own, mostly dimwitted brutes he runs like a chieftain. No patriotic airs there, just bad business for its own sake. High-end burglaries, muscle work for hire, intimidation with leg breaking and extortion. That's what I hear. Billy's a feckin' menace. Always has been no matter what side's he on."

Hoy shook his head. "I cannot feckin' imagine how little, quiet Tony Rourke would have found a way to hook up with the crooked Mr. Sheridan."

Doyle leaned forward to peer through the blurry windshield. Hoy reached over into the glove compartment and took out binoculars. He lowered his driver' side window, leaned out. "Son of a bitch," he growled. Doyle said, "Let me look, Barry." Hoy brushed his hand away. Doyle rolled his window down and poked his head out attempting to get a better view. He felt one of Hoy's large paws yank his collar and himself back into the car. "Sit, now. You don't want to be seen."

The conversation in front of them proceeded, the principals unaware they were being observed. Hoy's hands tightened on the binoculars. "There goes an envelope from Tony's shaky little hand." Doyle could see Sheridan riffling currency with a satisfied look. Hoy said, "I just read Tony's lips, him telling Sheridan, 'Don't fail me again with Mr. Hanratty.'" Hoy threw the binoculars down and erupted out of the car.

Sheridan saw Hoy coming and began to retreat. He whistled a signal. Doyle circled in toward this twosome from the right. The rain had increased and he felt his feet momentarily slip on the wet concrete.

Suddenly seeing their approach, Tony Rourke yelped, "What?" He started to speak as Hoy grabbed his coat collar and snarled, *"You devious gobshite. After all Niall's done for us. For you?"*

Billy Sheridan snapped open a switchblade before sliding toward Hoy, whose head was turned. Doyle caught the little thug square on the chin with a left hook. The knife dropped to the pavement as Sheridan fell face-first next to it. Doyle kicked the knife to the side and turned, hearing a thumping approach. A big, black hooded and jacketed figure had charged up from behind the stunned Rourke aiming for Hoy. Barry kept his right hand grip on the pale-faced Rourke's coat collar. When the advancing attacker was less than a yard away, Hoy pivoted and set his feet and slashed his large left forearm across the man's throat. The man fell to his knees, gurgling, hands scrabbling at his neck.

"Pick up the money envelope, Jack," Hoy barked. He was breathing heavily as he stared down at Rourke's ashen face.

Doyle leaned down to grab the rain-sodden envelope. He could feel the wad of Euros in it. He handed it to Hoy, who had now taken his hand off Rourke, and a deep breath, and then a step back from the Shamrock Off-Course Wagering Corporation's longtime treasurer. The rain was pouring down now, emptying the nearby sidewalks of the handful of startled passersby.

Hoy said, "It makes me sick to look at you, Tony. That you'd be dealing with these feckin' Dublin lowlife criminal bastards trying to get at the man who made you. *Made* you! And himself treasuring yourself all of your years together."

Hoy stopped and slid over to administer a resounding kidney kick to the downed black-garbed attacker who had begun to sit up. Back down he went. Little Billy Sheridan remained with his face pressed onto pavement. "Watch him, Jack." Hoy said. "Tricky little bastard might have another leap in him."

Tony Rourke took a step away from Hoy and then stood still, as if he could somehow remove himself from this reality with the longing look he aimed at the leaden sky above Raglan Road.

Hoy took the pay packet from Doyle and jammed it into Rourke's coat pocket. "Keep this for your upcoming early retirement, you miserable bastard."

Doyle wiped rain off his forehead as he watched Rourke seem to retreat into his wet coat. It was hard for Doyle to picture this timorous little numbers-cruncher as a man bent on having murder committed on his behalf. "Are you going to say anything, Tony?" Doyle said. "Like, this isn't what it seems?"

"*No,*" Rourke said defiantly. "It's *exactly* what it seems.

"Niall was the big man so full of promises," Rourke sneered. "Promises he never fulfilled. He kept putting off my percentage increase, year after year. It was *my* idea to expand the company the way we did. *I* should be running Shamrock. I've known that for years. So did," he stopped and took a deep breath, "my dear Moira. She believed I was being short-changed by Niall. She pleaded with me to do something about it. I was never able to bring myself to do so when she was alive, God help me." Eyes misting, he turned his head and began to slowly walk away. "Finally, I tried to do just that even if it was only in her memory. And then I messed that up, too."

Rourke began to walk away. Hoy started to follow, then stopped. He had a stunned look on his broad face as he said to Jack, "Aw, let him go, the sorry little creature."

Chapter Forty-seven

Four hours later, after he'd left Hoy and Doyle on Raglan Road to shakily traverse the wet highway back to his Cork City home, Tony Rourke unlocked his front door, took off his rain coat, and poured himself a glass of merlot. He drank quickly, poured another. The day-long rain had finally stopped, the heavy gray clouds dissipated. He took his wine out to the small back garden of the home, the area in which he and Moira had shared hundreds of pleasant evening hours. The aluminum-colored sky was gaining a hint of deep orange toward the west. "Should I be surprised," he said to himself, "that I feel so relieved to be found out? I don't know. Just as I seem to know so very little else these days." He put his wineglass down, picked up his notepad, and began to write.

> *Dear Bridget,*
>
> *Years ago, I made the mistake of not acceding to your mother's often repeated request that I "finally stand up to Niall Hanratty" for taking advantage of my talents, that I demand my just due—the partnership he had promised me in Shamrock, the company Niall and I brought from nothing to prosperity. Even though I was making more money than I could ever have imagined, your mother thought that I deserved that title of partner. I was never given it. Despite your mother's insistence, I never brought this up to Niall. I don't know if he intentionally ignored his promise, or simply*

forgot it. But your mother considered my situation to be the result of injustice. After her death, Niall's unfulfilled promise just ate away at me. It changed me in a way that I now very much regret.

Mind you, this campaign of hers to spur me into aggressive action was not constant, by any means. I could always fend her off by saying the "right time had not come." And she would accept that, ignoring what I later came to believe was her disappointed acceptance of my weakness. And it was a weakness.

Remember, Bridget, I admired Niall and was grateful for all he'd enabled me to do. He was always fair about our divisions of profits. So, I always believed he would come through with the promise of a partnership. Really, that was not that important to me. But, it was important to your mother.

I think your mother saw me as too weak to challenge The Man and demand what I had coming. And after she passed, I at first found myself unable to do anything but regret my inaction. But later, in the long, lonely months after that dear woman's passing, the idea of revenge took on a momentum of its own for me. I can't explain how it surged through me. I am ashamed to say it took me over.

So, I began a campaign to wreak revenge on Niall Hanratty. I will admit to you tonight that I wanted him dead! And tried to make it so! I was not thinking wisely. I did it as kind of a warped tribute to your mother, who had been so incensed for years over what she considered the terribly shabby treatment Niall had given me. So I paid for, and put in motion, actions intended to put Niall in a grave. These attempts failed. They were mistakes.

Your mother not being in my life has left me with a life not worth continuing. Starting after that final, terrible hospital day when her poor, sweet, pain-ravaged face was covered with the white sheet and they wheeled her out of that awful room and away from me, I believed that a campaign of revenge against Niall would somehow be carried out in her honor.

And that it would give me something to live for. That this kind of forcefulness would somehow make her proud of me. But that was a ridiculous thought on my part as I have finally come to realize. Your mother would have said just that. My ill-conceived efforts to have Niall Hanratty murdered were doomed from the start. Just as well. Just as well.

I picture you, Bridget, in your fine home and with your grand family in the States. Receiving these words. Feeling horror and shock and, undoubtedly, anger at me. But please, my dear daughter, me saying good-bye to you in this way is as merciful as it could ever be. As much as I love you and your family, this is the truth for me—there is nothing in my life anymore that makes me want to rise to the day.

Love,
Da

Tony Rourke carefully folded the two pages and put them in the envelope addressed to Bridget. He licked the seal. He'd already festooned it with all the necessary postage for America. He carefully placed the envelope beneath the small, bedraggled potted plant on the table next to his chair.

Late sunlight was dwindling, and bustling clouds from the west advanced against the last deep orange layer of light. Rourke picked up the wineglass and took a long swallow, lips twisting in its aftertaste. He'd never been much of a drinking man.

A vivid memory of Niall Hanratty came to him. Some Shamrock Company affair or other, years back. He pictured Niall at the head of the long dinner table, late in a raucous night, calling for collective quiet and quoting "Mark Twain, now, who said beer *corrodes* an Irishman's stomach. Whiskey *polishes* it! Drink up my friends!" Rourke had never agreed with either of those Twain claims.

Rourke reached into his coat pocket and uncapped a tall bottle of morphine tablets, the unused supply from Moira's final days. He placed a handful in his mouth, drank some wine, then another, the last of the wine following. He struggled but managed to keep it all down. And finally took a deep breath and lay his head back on the chair. Within minutes the sun had set.

Rourke's arms lay still on the chair's arms. He felt as if his veins were clogging. "Oh God," he suddenly thought, "did I tell Bridget I loved her? I think I did. But did I ?" He attempted to sit up and reach for his pen, but failed.

Next door neighbor Peter Rafferty found Tony Rourke's dew-covered corpse later that night when, while taking a garbage bag to the bin behind his double garage, he looked across the fence and said, "Hiya, Tony," and was first surprised when he received no reply, then horrified when he discovered why.

Chapter Forty-eight

Less than an hour after their Raglan Road discovery of Tony Rourke's treachery, Barry Hoy stopped his rental car outside Nora's house in Bray to let Jack out before starting his drive back to Kinsale. Their mostly quiet ride together was laden with depression, Hoy saying twice, "I can't believe Tony did that to Niall." Doyle exited the auto and reached back across the passenger seat to shake Hoy's hand and wish him a "safe trip" back. "When are you going to tell Niall about what Rourke has done?"

"As soon as I get back to Kinsale. Thanks, Jack, for bearing witness to this awful development." He pulled away rapidly.

A couple of loud knocks confirmed Nora wasn't home. Doyle found her house key in the very same obvious spot he had advised her not to put it, underneath a front stoop flower plot, and went in, carrying his suitcase. It was early afternoon. He didn't know when Nora would be back. He found the last remaining bottle of Guinness in her refrigerator. Turned on a horse racing channel from England. Lay on the couch and dozed until late in the afternoon when his hostess barged in through her front door he'd left ajar. Jumped up to embrace her and apologize for his surprise entrance and, again, advise her to "hide your damn house key better than that."

Nora blushed. "You're right. And perhaps right now you'll tell me the reason for this surprise return of yours."

"Hey, I started missing you so badly that I..."

She swatted his arm with her purse. "Don't try that brand of blarney on me, boyo," she said with a laugh. "C'mon, now. What's the deal? Sit down and tell me."

"I've had a long, tough day. I'm starving. How about if I fill you in over a few soothing libations and a nice meal?"

They walked to dinner through crowded streets. It was Bray's annual Summerfest Week, an event featuring music, sports, a carnival, dozens of concession booths and arts displays. "The final weekend there'll be probably sixty thousand people or so here," Nora said. "I'm definitely going Saturday night. I want to see Clockwork Noise, one of my favorite new bands. You should hear their violinist, Flo Healy. Outstanding," Nora enthused. "Besides playing like an angel, she's beautiful, too. I believe she's from just over in Dun Laoghaire."

They were lucky to nab a table for two on the second level of Bray's large, popular Martello Restaurant, one with a great view of the Irish Sea. Nora ordered a glass of white wine, Doyle said he'd try "the Hog Head pale ale. A pint, please. We'll look at the menu a bit later."

Nora said, "All right, then. You said earlier you had a quote long, tough day unquote. You want to tell me what that was all about?"

He began to recount his Dublin experience with Barry Hoy and Tony Rourke. What had brought Hoy and him there on Rourke's trail. He had barely reached that point when Nora reached over and grabbed his hand. "Wait. Can I record this?" He shrugged. "Record away," and she reached down into her purse.

His monologue was interrupted only by their expectant waiter, and they quickly ordered their entrees. When Nora had listened to Doyle's complete account of that day's Raglan Road happenings, she turned off her recorder and sat back in her chair. "Whew. That's quite a story. What do you think Niall will do about this, Jack? Any idea?"

"I'm sure Tony Rourke's days at Shamrock are numbered. In single digits. Niall will certainly get rid of him. Will Niall attempt to press charges? I have no idea. I just know that by now," he stopped to look at his watch, "Barry has given Niall a complete account of today's sad happenings in Dublin's fair city. And all that those happenings imply. I'm sure the attacks on Niall are history what with Rourke now exposed. As Barry Hoy said, 'Those Dublin thugs don't favor *pro bono* work.' So, Sheila Hanratty can resume sleeping well at night alongside of her hard-headed husband."

When their entrees arrived, bowls of the house specialty, a rich seafood chowder, Doyle ordered a carafe of white. "Nora, can you put away the tools of your trade now? I've told you all I know. I have no idea," he added, "what you would do with all this information."

Nora tucked her recorder back down into her purse. She flashed him one of her knockout smiles, green eyes aglow above it. She took a sip of wine. "Being the trained reporter that I am, I would say you never feckin' really know, Jack."

Pleased with their meal and each other, they left the restaurant an hour later and, instead of turning up Nora's street, went down long, steep steps to the seaside. The crowds were thick here, too. Nora gripped his arm as they wended their way. "Did you know Sinead O'Connor lives here in Bray?" she said.

"Of course I did. I also know that Katie Taylor, the Olympic women's boxing champ, hails from Bray. I watched a couple of her bouts on television. Outstanding fighter!"

The dusk was gently creeping as they strolled to the water's edge. Young families with children were now heading up the other way, toward the steps and home. Nora suddenly let go of Jack's hand and dashed over to a nearby bench, yanked her sandals off, put her purse atop them. "Watch my stuff here now, will you, Jack?" she shouted, laughing. Then she dashed across the sand into the shallow water, lifting her skirt as she twirled in the surf. A small group of young men passing by gave her an encouraging shout. The little lapping waves seemed to buoy her.

Doyle smiled as he watched, thinking again how much he relished the company of this interesting, interested, and vibrant woman. When she finally pranced back out of the water, he opened his arms to her rapid advance, caught her up, and kissed her. They swayed gently, feet in the sand, ignoring passersby, until they heard an elderly man shout, "Tara, back here quick," and looked up to see an on-charging brown and white spaniel. The dog slid to a stop at their feet, wagging its tail as Doyle bent down to offer the back of his hand to its inquisitive nose. More tail wagging.

Tara's owner tipped his cap to them as he walked her back toward the water. "She's a brilliant swimmer when she's not distracted," he offered back over his shoulder. Nora waved them good-bye.

Climbing up the stairway from the strand to the roadway, Jack said, "This band you like. Clockwork Noise. That you plan to see. Will they be selling CDs of theirs there at the Fest?"

"I'm sure they will."

Doyle and Nora halted at the top of the steps up to look back down at the passive sea and the dozens of strollers now in shadows of the retreating evening sun.

"Good," Doyle said. "So please buy me one of the Clockwork Noise CDs. We can listen to it sometime. If and when I ever come back here," he grinned.

She started striding up the street toward her home, leading him by his hand, looking straight ahead and nodding emphatically as she said, "You'll be back, Jack."

"You have a very confident walk and way about you, Nora Sheehan," Doyle said. She shot him a look over her shoulder.

Doyle stopped her at the beginning of her street that led up to her house. "Nora, you have water there on the bottom of your skirt from your cavorting in the surf. Should we maybe stop here, slip into the shrubbery, and wring the moisture out of it?"

Nora laughed as she grabbed his right hand with her left and yanked him forward. "Follow me. We're not that far from much more comfortable accommodations."

◇◇◇

Doyle shifted in Nora's bed, expecting to feel her hips against his. Gray morning light seeped in through the blinds they had hastily drawn the night before. He sat up when he heard her call, "Jack! Wake up quick! Come in here."

He pulled on his tee-shirt and briefs. She was at her desk, computer open, eyes riveted on the screen and its Flash News Story.

"Good God, woman, it can't be even seven a.m. What's the rush? Did Texas secede from my nation? Don't tell me the Chicago Cubs are again vowing to win their first pennant since 1945!"

The look on Nora's intense face quickly convinced him that whatever had her interest was not to be joked about. She scrolled rapidly to the bottom of the page. Turning to him, she said, "A neighbor found the body of a prominent Cork City businessman last night. An apparent suicide. Oh," she said, hands at her ears, drawn face shaking from side to side, "this is terrible tragic."

"Aw, hell," Doyle said. He backed up a few steps and sat down on the couch. "Tony Rourke, right?" he said softly.

"Yes. 'Anthony X. Rourke, longtime Shamrock Off-Course Wagering Corporation executive,'" she quoted. "'Age fifty-two. Widower. Survived by one daughter. Garda officials have ordered an autopsy to confirm what appears to be a drug overdose.'"

Doyle took a deep breath and got to his feet. He went to the front door and opened it. The remnants of that morning's mists trailed away toward the sea. Nora came up behind him and wrapped her arms around his waist, left cheek buried against his back. He turned around and hugged her.

"What a sorry, resentful, bitter little fellow Tony Rourke must have been," Doyle said. The whole depressing chain of recent events must have felt like it was tightening around his chest. Jack could easily imagine Barry Hoy arguing that "What *we* did in catching him out doesn't make *us* responsible for what Tony did in the end." Which was probably true. But it didn't make Doyle feel all that much better.

Nora relinquished her hug and moved around to face him. "Do you still intend to take your flight in the morning?"

"Yeah. I've got things to do back home. But first I have to talk to Niall."

The Kinsale phone was immediately picked up. "Jack," Hanratty said, "I just heard this terrible news from Barry Hoy who heard it on the radio. Crushing news! First, what Barry had told me yesterday about you and him seeing Tony with that thug in Dublin. Now this. I can hardly believe it."

Doyle heard Hanratty pause to say, "Sheila, leave me now. I'm talking to Jack." There was the rattle of a cup being dropped before Hanratty said, "I can't fathom it, Jack. My good little friend Tony taking his own life. I'm gobsmacked. What could have prompted him to do it?"

"Niall, I can't answer that with any confidence. But I would guess it was an accumulation of things. His beloved wife's death. His depression following that. And," Jack said, "your unfulfilled promise to him."

Hanratty erupted. "What? Are you mad, man? I was paying Tony the exact equivalent of a partner's share. I've *always* been fair with him about the money since we started together years ago as junior clerks in that dinky little betting shop in Bray. I saw the opportunities, and grabbed the main chance, and brought Tony's brilliance for figures right along with me. We did great out of it. We both made gobs of money!"

Hanratty paused before saying, "This is beyond me. After all our years together, and our success, I thought I knew the man. And then he sets out to try and kill me before killing himself!"

"Niall, I don't think what burrowed into Tony Rourke's mind had anything to do with money."

Silence. Then Niall said, "Well, Mr. Chicago psychology expert, what the hell was it about then?"

"I think it was about the fact that you never came through with the partnership in Shamrock that you promised him."

Hanratty said, "Jack, I don't get it. Why would the partnership promise, which I admit I forgot, and never considered to be very important, why would it mean any more to Tony Rourke than the money I was paying him? He was getting an *equal share* with me. What the hell do you mean?"

"What I mean is something you did not understand, my friend," Jack said softly. "With Tony Rourke, his complaint, his smoldering resentment, was probably never about the money. It was about respect. The respect that he thought he'd never gotten from you."

Another brief silence before Niall said, "Whatever it was, Jack, I am terribly sorry about what Tony tried to do to me. And what he did to himself."

It was later that week, when Jack was back in Chicago, that the Internet headline "Exclusive Account of Bookie's Demise" leapt out at him one morning. "Well, of course," he said to himself. "Scoop Sheehan at work."

Chapter Forty-nine

With his summer course work finished, straight A-plus as usual, W.D. Wiems turned his attention to the lucrative task ahead. Heading toward his senior year with a perfect career 4.0 grade point, he had been urged by his University of Kansas counselor to plan for grad school in quest of advanced degrees. He ignored the suggestion, convinced he would know all he needed to know about the intricacies of computers and their advanced programming by the end of his senior year. If he hadn't already.

It was a typical Kansas summer, torrid and potentially cyclone or tornado-ridden, so Wiems looked forward to his Chicago trip and the twenty-thousand-dollar payoff it would produce. Then, he hit a snag.

Through his Internet wizardry, Wiems had gained access several weeks earlier to Jack Doyle's e-mail address and the e-mails that went to and from it. Not much of a challenge for a young man who had already hacked into the supposedly protected inner sanctum computer files of dozens of major financial institutions not to mention several departments of his nation's government. But not much in Jack Doyle's tiny sliver of the Internet world was very informative. Wiems was disappointed to find only very occasional entries, usually just briefly described planned meetings with Doyle's friends, the review of racing results, an occasional exchange with nora@eire.com, and visits to a popular boxing website to which the opinionated Doyle sometimes contributed comments.

"This guy must mainly communicate by phone or snail mail," Wiems disgustedly concluded. "What a throwback."

At the start of the week, when he felt himself primed and ready for action, it pissed him off to access Doyle's e-mail and find the message *I am unable to respond to your e-mails the week beginning today. I will be away.*

Aggravating, but what the hell. Wiems had learned that Doyle's absences were never lengthy. Patience was called for, so patience it would be. Wiems devoted his days to adding to his impressive compendium of underground slasher/porno movie highlights that he intended to package and sell to a select clientele he'd already unearthed on the Internet. Most nights he spent at Cartridge Central sharpening his shooting skills, after which he took lengthy night Harley rides on quiet country roads far outside of Lawrence. These were on primarily empty roadways, their dark borders marked only infrequently by farmhouse lights. The Harley could easily hit ninety miles an hour on these empty stretches. During each ride, Wiems at least once even briefly topped one hundred mph. But most of his time was spent at more moderate speeds, guiding the machine with his right hand on the Harley's steering wheel accelerator control and practicing deadly pistol shooting with his gun hand.

Twice early during that week of Doyle's absence, Wiems rode a couple of hours through the night before ending it with a brief visit to Shorty and Lammy's Saloon where'd had done his initial business with Marco Three. That increasingly impatient employer had stopped phoning Wiems after Wiems finally made clear to Marco "that, if you don't, I'll kill you for nothing. And stay out of Shorty and Lammy's until I tell you. I don't want to be seen with you yet."

"Okay, *okay*. Do it your way. Geez. I leave it to you."

This Thursday night, Wiems took his usual stool at the end of the bar. He put his riding gloves down on the mahogany with a slap. Seats nearby him quickly emptied, one by a bleary-eyed senior citizen named Roscoe who usually drank there after his weekly AA meeting, the other by Sherri, tonight an off-duty Shorty and Lammy waitress he recognized. Randy, the regular night bartender, nodded at Wiems and reached down into the cooler. All three of them knew him.

Wiems drank half of the Corona with one extended gulp before saying, "How'd the Royals do tonight?"

"Led into the eighth. Boom. The bullpen collapsed. What is else is new?"

Wiems finished the Corona. He got off the stool, reached into his jeans, and, as always, left a tip on the bar for Randy. As Randy had told his fellow employees, "Exactly one dollar and fifty cents each damn time! For more than a year now! I've got no fuckin' idea why. I just say thank you and good-bye. Motorcycle Man is one strange cat, I'll tell you that."

Randy took a wet rag to the old, scarred, wooden bar. "That guy, Moto Man," he said to Sherri, "he ever talk to you? Hit on you?"

Sherri grimaced as she sipped her Bailey's and cream. "Are you kidding? I've never seen him even look twice at any woman in here, much less me. Only person he ever talks to is You Know Who."

Randy nodded, not surprised. Motorcycle Man's only conversations he'd observed from afar were with Marco Three. He didn't permit curiosity, ordinarily a good bartender's stock in trade, to factor in here.

Chapter Fifty

The day after the news of Tony Rourke's suicide, another smooth and timely Aer Lingus flight enabled Doyle to get to O'Hare Airport, then his Chicago condo just before eight p.m. He unpacked, fired up the microwave on a pair of frozen beef enchiladas, cracked open a beer, and read his e-mail. There wasn't much. He sent a message to Nora that he was back home safe and sound and copied it to Moe Kellman, Karen Engel, and Ralph Tenuta's wife Rosa. She was in charge of the trainer's at-home communications. He asked her how things were going at the stable. Rosa answered right back. "Jack, glad you're back. Ralph would like you to come to the track tomorrow. He has some very good news to share."

Doyle replied that he would like to, but said he couldn't "make it tomorrow. Tell Ralph I'll see him out there Wednesday afternoon."

In his Kansas apartment, all of these messages were captured and memorized by W.D. Wiems as he continued to access Doyle's computer. Wiems felt himself getting pumped. He quickly packed his small backpack, tucked his Glock .44 in the shoulder holster under his black jacket, and hurried out to his Harley to begin his lengthy trip north. He'd been eagerly looking forward to this new challenge. He was glad to see not a hint of rain clouds in the early evening Kansas sky.

In the years since he had murderously dispatched his despised mother and step-father, Wiems considered himself to be a very lucky young man. And that luck, all of his own making, as far as he was concerned, continued in the course of the next ten and a half hours that saw him cover the five hundred and sixty miles close to his next day's destination: Heartland Downs and the parking lot near Ralph Tenuta's barn to which he had trailed Jack Doyle weeks earlier.

Wiems cycled I-70 from Lawrence to Kansas City where he picked up I-35 to Des Moines. The weather was still clear, the traveling easy. He occasionally amused himself during the long night by veering sharply in front of one of the several hundred trucks he passed. He smiled at every horn blast from each indignant trucker.

He stopped for gas at a Shell station on I-80 just inside the Illinois border. Filled his tank, emptied his bladder, and bought a half-dozen power bars and two bottles of water, paying with a credit card in one of his fake names. That whole stop consumed less than twelve minutes. Three and a half hours later he switched to I-88 near Rock Falls. Took that to I-355N, then I-290 toward Rockford after which he exited onto IL-53 only a few miles from Heartland Downs. He pulled into a Marathon station to buy gas and more water, paying with yet another phony credit card.

Wiems had been on the road for nearly ten hours, the last two driving into the early morning sun. He wasn't tired. He never was on such occasions that involved the thrill of a hunt. But he knew he should rest. He could not permit even a hint of fatigue to compromise his expertise.

Nearing Kirchoff Road in Palatine, he pulled into a forest preserve parking lot that was empty of vehicles this early in the day. He slowly rolled through it and drove his bike gently up over the curb and across the dewy grass where he parked beneath the shade of a towering oak tree. A pair of grackles on a limb overhead loudly protested his arrival. Wiems hurled one of his half-empty water bottles up at them and they flew off, complaining further.

He removed his helmet and folded his jacket and placed it on the grass at the base of the tree for use as a headrest. He tucked the Glock underneath the jacket and lay down, head on the jacket, gloved hands folded across his chest. Wiems was asleep in less than three minutes.

Chapter Fifty-one

Well-rested, ignoring jet lag, Doyle was up early for his morning run. He was surprised at his energy level when he returned to his condo and ripped off one hundred sit-ups followed by one hundred pushups. Breathing heavily as he got up off the floor to go for a bottle of water out of his fridge, Doyle said to himself, "Travel obviously agrees with me."

Showered and dressed, he checked in with Damon Tirabassi. "I can easily tell you're relieved and delighted that I am back on native soil, right?"

"No comment. If you're calling to ask if we've made any progress in the horse killer case, Doyle, the answer is no. Karen is out of the office this morning, trying to track down a lead. After that Ness woman put up the fifty grand reward offer, we've been inundated with calls. And, as always, most of them worthless, just two or three worth following up. Karen is working on those. What are you doing? Now that you're finally back, I mean."

"Do I detect a note of criticism there, Damon? The kind of snide aside you're too often given to? 'Finally back'? Do you think I was on vacation over in Ireland? Bouncing about from Dublin pubs to Connemara pony rides? I had serious business there. Jesus, man! Can you ever be capable of looking past your bureaucratic nose at other people's lives?" He turned off the phone. "What a sorry fucking way to start the day."

◇◇◇

Doyle decided to shake off his irritation with Damon by going out to Heartland Downs that afternoon as he'd promised Rose Tenuta he would do. His mood was immediately improved by the happy vibe he felt after his arrival at Ralph's barn. Ingrid was there standing beside the trainer in front of stall one. Cheerful greetings exchanged, Doyle said, "Is that who I think it is in there?"

"None other than Mr. Rhinelander, Jack. He was released from quarantine this morning, pronounced virus free," Ingrid smiled.

"Ready to go back into training," Ralph added. As Tenuta patted his forehead, the friendly colt nickered in apparent agreement. "We're all glad to have him back, nobody more so than the Burkhardts. Those happy people," Ralph said, "are going to host a celebration kind of cookout here this evening after the races. They're bringing Wisconsin brats, beer, and cheese for my whole staff. Even fried cheese curds, whatever the hell they are. Of course, Ingrid is invited. She did a terrific job treating this horse. And you're invited, too."

Doyle glanced at his watch. It was 4:35. He was feeling the first hint of fatigue from his trip back from Ireland and his Chicago workout. "Naw, I don't think so, Ralph. I'm a little worn out. I'll take a pass on this, but be sure to thank the Burkhardts for me. Ingrid, you have my congratulations."

Ingrid walked with him to the parking lot behind the barn. "Is that right, Jack, that you were back in Ireland? That's what Ralph thought."

"Indeed I was. Some business, some pleasure. It wound up working out pretty well. How about you, Ingrid? Anything new on the horse killer front?" "

"No, I'm afraid not. But at least there hasn't been a killing since that one in Michigan a couple of weeks back. Maybe this campaign is over."

Doyle said, "That, I doubt. Once a fanatic gets going, it's hard to stop him. Or her," he added.

"You're probably right," Ingrid murmured. She opened her truck door and quickly got behind the wheel. "Take care, Jack," she said.

With a wave back at Tenuta, Doyle got into his Accord and drove to the track exit he always used. He nodded at the security officer in the booth who was in charge of opening the doors of the tall wire gate. He turned onto Wilke Road heading for Willow Road just a few miles away. Traffic was beginning to thicken. A huge procession of rain clouds had begun moving west from Lake Michigan. He could see them in the darkening distance to his right. Then it began. Moist pellets started to ding across the Accord's roof. Doyle turned on his radio which, as always, was set on 90.09, the Chicago area's major jazz station. He was just in time to hear emcee Bruce Oscar introduce a cut from "young piano star Aaron Diehl's debut CD." Doyle smiled as he heard the first minute of "Bess, You Is My Woman Now." He caught the light and turned right at Wilke's intersection with Willow, not noticing the black-clad motorcyclist tucked in four cars behind him.

Chapter Fifty-two

Leon Haukedahl, a fifty-seven-year-old veteran of nearly twenty-one years as a long haul trucker, shook his head, blinked, reached into the truck console for his Dexedrine stash in its folded over plastic baggie. Empty. Goddam. He was one tired son of a bitch, a hungry and thirsty one as well. He'd almost not cleared the yellow light at that last intersection, Willow Road and something. He'd turned off the Prime Country station on his SiriusXM radio a half-hour earlier, its songs serving mainly to make him feel more tired than anything else. He loved country music, but country was best heard long after work was done, the miles behind him, a cold brew or two in hand, not while a guy like Leon was struggling to keep in motion and earn some badly needed money by operating far over his legal limit of daily trucker driving hours.

Leon had started his workday right before four in the darkness of a Nebraska morning in North Platte and hauled a truck load of persistently groaning beef cattle six hours to Des Moines, which was supposed to be it for him that day. But at the Des Moines delivery point, he'd been offered an opportunity to hook up an eighteen-wheel oil tanker to his cab and go another 365 miles to Northbrook, Illinois. Some driver hadn't shown up as scheduled. And there was Leon, a prime candidate for overtime, he and his wife as usual struggling to make this month's mortgage payment for their already vastly undervalued tract house on the outskirts of Kankakee, Illinois. It was a property their lender had notified them had gone "under water." Which is where Leon liked to think of putting that smooth talking crook who had led them into this shit deal. Leon didn't even live next to the often flood-swollen Kankakee River!

This was a full tanker of oil riding behind him. Leon hadn't before hauled a load this heavy, his previous trips over the more than two decades of his trucker career involving dry goods, furniture, livestock, sand, street salt, wholesale grocery, and some wide-load trailer homes. This tanker job meant premium pay. He blinked again. Reached down to the small cooler on the floor for a caffeine-infused Mountain Dew. The cooler rattled with those empty cans.

Two blocks from the intersection of Willow and Forest, Leon tightened his grip on the steering wheel as a small, red convertible driven by a ponytailed blond woman wearing sunglasses threatened to cross the center line directly in front of him and veer over into his lane. He blared his big truck horn as he stomped the brake pedal. That shook her up. She dropped her cell phone and momentarily lost control of her steering.

Leon yanked his steering wheel to the right to avoid the convertible. At once, he felt the heavy oil tanker begin to start swinging behind him. He heard one of any trucker's greatest fears, the *bang* sound of a tire blowing as one of the large left tanker tires smashed against the lane median. The tanker and the cab pulling it started to tilt over rapidly to the right side of Willow.

It was getting away from Leon, the whole deal. Panicked now, Leon felt the entire fucking trucking apparatus, cab and tanker, tipping slowly, inexorably, to the right before slamming down sideways and covering almost all of these two lanes. Stunned, lying sideways in his battered cab, head ringing from where it had hit the console beside him, Leon struggled to kick open the driver's door. He smelled the oil that was beginning to spurt from the ruptured tanker. Leon managed to pull himself up and out of the overturned cab. He landed shakily on his feet and, horrified, watched as oil spillage spread across Willow Road East.

Ninety-four seconds earlier, two miles back, W. D. Wiems revved up his Harley Iron 883 and quickly passed the three cars between him and Doyle's Accord. He was smirking behind the plastic tinted shield of his full-face cyclist's helmet. The hunt was not only *on*, it was about to *start*. And *finish*. Closing in on the Accord, Wiems approached what he had chosen to be the killing ground. He moved up to get just behind and to the left of the gray Accord. The closest car in the left lane before him was at least three blocks ahead. Perfect. The rain had even stopped.

Wiems' computer research had led him to conclude that the best way to hit the Target was in the half-mile stretch on Willow Road leading to Elmhurst Road. That intersection would be perfect for his escape. The two miles north on Elmhurst Road could be covered quickly in case anyone had observed him leaving the scene. Then a westward turn onto Dundee Road toward his carefully calculated escape route. Minutes later, a quick change of clothes in the Bixby Forest Preserve from the black jacket into a tan windbreaker with Lake County Bikers emblazoned in red letters on its back. All part of his brilliantly detailed planning. After that, Westward Ho, Kansas City here he comes, ready to collect the rest of his money.

Doyle's Accord was the third car approaching the Willow-Elmhurst Intersection light. Two blocks before it, Doyle glanced in his left mirror. A black-clad and helmeted motorcyclist had pulled out from behind trailing right lane cars, its driver jerking it into the left lane to zoom forward. "Idiot," Doyle said to himself. "Another cycle cowboy."

Wiems figured he had sixty quick yards to go. Beautiful. He reached his left hand into his jacket holster and extracted the Glock. Steered the cycle slightly closer to the Accord's lane. His rearview mirror showed no trailing vehicle within three blocks.

His silenced shots would take just seconds before the Glock went back into his jacket. He mentally congratulated himself on preparing for just this situation where he'd have to control his cycle speed with his right hand and shoot across his body with his left. Deft, was what he had become at that as a result of many nighttime Kansas practice sessions.

Doyle cleared the small rise leading to the upcoming intersection and slowed, leaning slightly forward over the steering wheel, foot poised above the brake pedal. Looked to him like some kind of vehicular chaos a few blocks ahead. Several cars had pulled over to the right shoulder. What the hell was this? Carefully driving forward, Doyle could see that his two lanes were blocked by an overturned tanker, its oil a thick menace spreading across the roadway. What the hell?

"Concentrate. Concentrate." Wiems' mantra. Tunnel vision aimed only at the Target's Accord. Wiems sped closer to Doyle's car, then braked sharply to keep his Target in focus. For a second, he looked in the driver's window at Doyle's startled face and smiled. He pointed the Glock at Doyle's head. Doyle, too occupied in slamming on his brakes to avoid the mess ahead, didn't turn and see Wiems.

Wiems pulled the Glock's trigger just as his bike's front tire crossed the border of the oil spill. *Shit.* He'd missed the driver's window, his two rapid shots shattering Doyle's left rear passenger window.

Doyle's head snapped forward. He quickly grabbed its left side that had been laced with tiny glass fragments. Sudden pain, sudden panic as he felt the Accord skid across the black liquid layer covering the roadway.

W. D. Wiems, fighting his Harley's slow slide, cried out "Shit" when he saw his first shots had not stopped the Target. *Concentrate.* Once again momentarily able to again pull alongside the Accord's driver's side window, Wiems grinned as he saw the wide-eyed Doyle stare out at him and at his Glock. Eyes riveted on Doyle, Wiems slowed the Harley with his right hand and steadied his gun hand. *Concentrate.*

Wiems did not look ahead east on Willow. Never had the chance to factor in the extent of the slick pool of oil emanating from Leon Haukedahl's overturned tanker. The spreading black pool that had now captured Wiems' Harley's tires. He snapped off another two desperate shots as the Harley surfed the oil slick. Both went over the roof of the Accord.

Doyle didn't hear those shots, just as he hadn't heard the silenced shots that had pierced his backseat window behind him. But he could see a helmeted man on a black cycle first next to him on his left, then in front, pistol waving in the air in his gloved hand as he fought for control of his bike.

"What the fuck is this?" Doyle shouted.

Wiems cursed and dropped the Glock to use both hands as he struggled to control the cycle. He'd never missed a Target before. But he had missed this one. Hadn't nailed the twenty-thousand-dollar prize. He fought to wrench up the Harley's front wheel. No go. He felt his right leg scraping across the concrete road, his jeans tearing as well as the skin underneath. He had no control of the bike. Could do nothing, now, to stop his twenty-eight-foot skid directly toward the tanker's large steel back frame.

The Harley smashed into the bottom of the steel frame head on. As his bike slid underneath it, Wiems tried to duck. No luck. His plastic visor shattered on impact, a sharp piece of it going directly into his right eye and three inches farther into his brain.

With traffic now completely blocked on both sides of Willow, Doyle got out of his car and stood on the shoulder, shaken. His head hurt. He began to slowly walk forward toward the tanker and the mangled cycle and its rider whose feet protruded from beneath the tanker's rear section. In only minutes, a stream of Cook County Sheriff's Department vehicles roared up followed by two ambulances. Doyle waved down the second patrol car. Sergeant Wayne Monroe got out and hurried to him.

"My name is Jack Doyle. That crazy cyclist underneath that tanker up there tried to *kill* me. Look, here, at my car. He took some shots that blew out my window before he hit that oil slick. Last I saw of him the son of a bitch was heading straight into the back of that tanker."

Sergeant Monroe said, "That's the report we got. A motorist west-bound saw the cycle rider pointing a pistol at a gray car. Yours, obviously. You know any reason why that happened?"

Doyle plucked a few more tiny pieces of glass from the back of his head. "No, officer, I do not."

An excited Sheriff's deputy trotted up to them from where the tanker lay. "Cycle guy's dead and gone, Sergeant," he said. "You wouldn't want to look at what happened to that poor bastard," he added, shaking his head. "Even one of the veteran paramedics took a look and threw up."

"Any ID on the dead man?" Monroe said.

"Yeah, a license anyway. A young guy named Wiems. From Lawrence, Kansas."

Sergeant Monroe turned to Doyle. "That name mean anything to you?"

"Only in welcome memorium," Doyle spat. "Bastard tried to kill me."

〉〉〉

Nearly two hours later, after leaving the Sheriff's Department, Doyle parked in the garage beneath his condo building. A helpful maintenance man at the Sheriff's Palatine headquarters had helped him vacuum the glass out of the Accord and tape a temporary plastic covering over the empty window frame. This was done after he'd given his statement to Sergeant Monroe and an un-introduced female deputy in charge of the tape recorder.

He felt drained, puzzled, very relieved, and horrified by his nearly fatal Willow Road experience. Finally back in his condo Doyle showered, dressed, poured himself a large Jameson's on the rocks and he picked up his phone.

"Moe, it's me. You and Leah want to have dinner tonight? I know this is short notice. But could you two make it to Dino's at seven?"

"Okay, Jack. Short notice but, okay, fine with us. Something on your mind?"

"Oh, yeah, Moesy. Oh, yeah. Some bastard I never heard of tried to kill me late this afternoon."

Chapter Fifty-three

"You've had a setback," Aldo Caveretta said softly as he and Harvey Rexroth began their early morning walking tour of the Lexford Prison recreation yard. It was one of the two days per week that the inmates were allowed to have a full hour each of such outdoor exercise. The two wore their yellow, hooded rain jackets against the drizzle of this late summer day. More than half of the usual contingent of a.m. exercisers had opted to remain inside.

Rexroth stopped in his tracks. He grabbed Caveretta's elbow. "Setback?" he howled. "What do you mean, setback?" Rexroth's broad face reddened and spittle formed at the edges of his large mouth.

Caveretta angrily shook off Rexroth's grip. "Keep it *down*, Harvey. There's hardly anybody out here now. Still, in this joint, everybody listens to what everybody says if they can. Always looking for an angle. Information is currency here, my friend. You should know that. So, for godsakes, keep it down."

Rexroth snorted in disgust but resumed walking slowly aside the lanky lawyer who, after another dozen yards, stopped, looked behind them, then whispered, "Our hit man didn't make the hit. Not only did he not make it, he got himself killed in the process. An ugly death, I'm told."

Rexroth's big jaw dropped. He stood in stunned silence for a few moments that preceded an explosive response. "You mean that cocksucker Doyle is still alive? Your killer got killed! What the..." He interrupted his tirade to spit angrily onto the rubberized track. Two joggers sidestepped him as they passed, looking back in disgust.

His large chest pushing against the front of his jumpsuit, Rexroth said, "Okay. First question. Do I get my fifty thousand back? Second question. Can you find somebody more capable out there who can take on this job and kill this fucking Doyle with my fifty grand rebate? Honest to God, I thought your people were supposed to be good at this!" Rexroth's voice had risen in the course of these questions. Caveretta looked cautiously front and back before saying, "I'll see what I can do."

The drizzle now was replaced by an increasingly steady rain. Caveretta waited as his infuriated companion resumed his stomping, and frothing, and arm-waving. Another two fellow inmates strode rapidly past, looking inquisitive. Aldo waved them off. "No problem," he said to them.

It took another three minutes for the imperious media mogul to finish acting out. *Like the spoiled rich bastard he is*, Caveretta thought. *I can't take any more of this super jerk. And I won't.* By the time their morning exercise was over, Caveretta had mentally charted his course. Back inside their building, he walked away from the still complaining Rexroth and went to arrange for the phone call he would be allowed later that day. He passed up lunch. When it was time for his call, Caveretta dialed the private number in Kansas City of attorney Paul Trombino. A first cousin on his mother's side, Trombino had unsuccessfully defended Caveretta in the federal trial that saw him winding up in Lexford, eating primarily mediocre-at-best food and dealing with dickheads like Rexroth.

Aldo, ever the realist, had never held his conviction against attorney Trombino, since he had been found guilty primarily as a result of the damning testimony provided by traitorous nephew Rudy Randazzo. Little Rudy, his sister Angela's firstborn, Aldo's only godson, who grew up to be an Outfit button man, and who had been federally entrapped so that the little shit ratted out Uncle Aldo before disappearing into the Witness Protection Program. Such betrayal by a relative would never stop stinging.

Aldo could picture himself thirty-two years earlier holding the blanketed infant Rudy over the Holy Rosary Church baptismal font, thinking to himself at the time *this kid is so ugly the obstetrician shouldn't have slapped him to start breathing, he should have slapped his mother for producing him.* Aldo had come to often deeply regret during his tedious Lexford Prison days that he hadn't "accidentally" dropped and drowned little Rudy in the baptismal water. He wouldn't be here in with Rexroth, this human boil of irritation, had he done so.

During his Lexford Prison phone call that day, Caveretta spoke to Trombino both in Italian and the coded English with which both men were very familiar. Even though Trombino was at first incredulous as he considered Aldo's plan, and by no means certain it would work, he of course went along. An agreement was reached. Trombino could not refuse to carry out this plan since cousin Caveretta's imprisonment had already lowered his grade in the extremely significant Scaravilli Family rating system. Any further decline was devoutly to be avoided.

"Aldo," Trombino finally said, "I will get started on this right away."

"*Prego.*" Caveretta inhaled, deeply relieved after he hung up the phone and walked back toward his cell, smiling to himself and thinking, not for the first time, about the wonderful variety of ways in which the mills of justice could be manipulated to grind.

Chapter Fifty-four

Karen Engel and Damon Tirabassi walked out of their supervisor's office in the FBI's downtown Chicago headquarters. There was a spring in their steps despite the muggy August air.

Their regular reporting meeting had not begun on a high note. They had to listen to a nine-minute, possibly scripted, oration from their boss about "the pressing need to find this dangerous, crazy, criminal horse killer. Not yesterday, mind you, the day before!"

They were familiar with this career bureaucrat's foibles and fantasies, most of them fed by his career spent behind a desk, far removed from the agency's real work. All they could do was listen, nod, and vow to "retriple" their efforts.

Preparing to leave his office, they'd been startled to receive what the Director considered just "an ancillary piece of information." It was that which had them smiling as they waited for the elevator.

"What do you think, Damon? Should we tell Jack about this?" She and her partner were among seven people waiting for the elevator. The other five pricked up their ears at the possibility of overhearing something of use.

Damon frowned at her. "*Sotto voce*. We'll talk in the car."

They made quick purchases at the sandwich shop on the other side of Dearborn Street before walking to their car in the nearby underground garage. Once inside, doors closed, air conditioner cranked, Karen postponed opening her veggie wrap to say again, "What about letting Jack know?"

Damon took a large bite out of his Italian beef sandwich before answering. "I don't see any reason not to. Doyle probably needs a bit of a morale boost after the attempt on his life on Willow Road. He might even like to get an idea as to why that happened." Damon frowned. "I told that server hot peppers, not sweet. Oh, well. Anyway, I'm glad the Harley shooter missed. Doyle's never been a personal favorite person of mine, but…"

"Oh, *really*," Karen laughed.

Damon said, "You know how I feel about him. A major pain in the posterior, but not somebody I'd like to lose."

"I do know. Let me call him."

Doyle was in Ralph Tenuta's box at Heartland Downs. He'd hardly slept two nights earlier even after his dinner with Moe and Leah. He hadn't had too much sleep last night, either. Too many questions on his mind. Some son of a bitch attempting to kill him on his way home from the racetrack? What the fuck was that about?

He picked up his cell phone. "Hey, Karen."

"Good to hear your voice, Jack. In fact, good to know you are still around to have one."

The horses were coming onto the track for the afternoon's first race. He didn't spot any bettable items among them. "Thanks, Karen. Obviously, I'm quite happy to have survived the attempt to erase me from life's entries. I'm out here sitting in Ralph Tenuta's box trying to shake off the aftereffects."

"Yes, and Jack, all kidding aside, we're happy you're still alive."

Doyle said, "Have you heard anything from the Sheriff's Department about this jerk who was firing at me from his Harley?"

"Sergeant Monroe asked the Bureau for help and we gave it. So far, we know your attempted killer was from Kansas, was going to school there at the university. Social loner. Premier student. Supposedly interested mainly in computers, cycles, and guns."

Doyle said, "It's that last part that interests me."

Karen handed the phone to Damon, who had finished his Italian beef, wiped his chin, and burped with quiet satisfaction.

"Jack, it's me."

"I recognize your dulcet tones."

"Jack, I'm ignoring all of your usual sarcasm past this point. What you might want to know is the preliminary investigation has tied this Wiems to the Kansas City Outfit."

Doyle got to his feet as the field of thoroughbreds charged across the first-race finish line. "The *Outfit?*"

"That is correct, Jack. What I am going to tell you now is something you may never, ever tell anybody you got from me. Okay?"

Jack said, "Damon, you know my word is good. What's the deal here?"

"FBI wiretaps conducted in Lexford Prison yesterday have your old enemy Harvey Rexroth arranging to have you killed. He was working through a fellow inmate, a lawyer belonging to the Kansas City Outfit. The lawyer, I can't tell you his name, decided to lessen *his* Lexford sentence by turning over to the government Rexroth's plans to kill you. The incarcerated lawyer wore a wire. He got Rexroth on tape promising to pay to get you killed. This earned the lawyer a reduction of his Lexford time by fourteen months. Great deal for him.

"But," Damon said, "Rexroth, trapped on tape caught ordering a fifty-thousand dollar hit on you, will get his stay in Lexford extended another five years for conspiracy to commit murder."

Doyle sat back down in his box seat. "Rexroth? That crazy fucker? Man oh man. But wait. Who did the hiring of the guy who took those shots at me on Willow Road?"

"The imprisoned lawyer says he never knew the identity of the killer hired by Kansas City people," Damon answered. "He claims complete ignorance of that. Well, of course, he'd have to. And maybe that's actually true. The Outfit top guys always use as many cutouts as they can. But we've learned that the cyclist was a young man named Wiems. Student at the University of Kansas. Some kind of a computer phenom, according to his school records. Parents both deceased. And no criminal record whatsoever."

"The bastard's got one now," Doyle said. "I hope they inscribe it on his headstone. Thanks for the information, Damon." He hung up.

Chapter Fifty-five

Next morning Doyle was in conversation on his cell phone when he heard the click of an incoming call. But he delayed picking it up as he talked with Ralph Tenuta about Mr. Rhinelander, the once ailing, now almost completely recovered colt. Finished with Tenuta, he clicked on his answering machine and was surprised to hear the normally placid Damon Tirabassi almost frothing during his message. "Jack, I think we've caught a break on the horse killer case. Call me sooner than ASAP. *Wait!* Call me before that."

Pleased by Tenuta's report on Mr. Rhinelander's progress, Jack hoped Tirabassi would provide more good news on this rainy, late August evening. He quickly phoned the FBI agent.

"I am returning my government's call," he said solemnly.

Tirabassi grunted. "No time for your idea of comedy, Jack. Hold it. I'm going to put this on speaker phone for Karen. We're in my office."

Karen said, "Here's the situation, Jack. We got a tip earlier this afternoon from Rockland College, up close to the Illinois-Wisconsin state line. Ever heard of it?"

"Barely. Didn't they have a good Division Three football team a couple of years ago?"

"Yes, they did. And one of the linemen on their current team, a kid, or a young man I should say, Randy Meier, contacted our office today. He's working as a night watchman at Rockland's veterinary school in the Large Animal Division to help pay his tuition."

Doyle's lifted his one working eyebrow, the left one having been rendered immobile years before in the bloody course of his final Golden Gloves bout. "Aha."

"Randy Meier said that last night, during his four–to–ten shift, he was patrolling the school grounds. Evidently on these summer nights, the staff there turns the horses they are in charge of out in a paddock. Randy knew all about the other vet school killings and about the fifty thousand reward. So he came to attention when he saw a dark pickup truck pull up on the far side of the paddock on the road that runs along there. It parked, lights out, even the interior light off. Somebody got out of the passenger door and walked over to the fence. A young gelding named Saint Lester, a recent contribution to the school program, was standing in the middle of the paddock. But he started to move toward this figure.

"According to Randy Meier, it looked suspicious to him why the person was calling Saint Lester over to him. Or her. He couldn't see clearly. The figure had on dark clothes including a dark sweatshirt and hoodie. Just about when Randy thought about hopping the fence to go see who this was, he heard a couple of cars loudly, rapidly, approaching from the east. Coming on the road near the paddock area. Their horns were blowing, they had music pumping out, raising hell. I guess this is not uncommon for the American youth living in that area. Anyway, once the two noisy cars had passed, Randy saw that the person who'd been summoning the horse had ducked back into the truck and started to quickly pull away in the opposite direction of the speeding kids. He wondered to himself, as he put it, 'Who the hell could that be out there talking to Saint Lester like that?' Then he remembered the other vet school horse killings and the advertised reward. So he called us."

Doyle said, "This was last night?"

"Correct," Karen said. "And coming right from the sort of out-of-the way veterinary research facility that you wouldn't think would draw any nocturnal visitors. Unless they were there for a purpose."

"Look," Doyle said, "I'm not much for tossing wet blankets about. But what makes you think this was an appearance by the horse killer? Shoot, it could have been some old coot on his way home from a country tavern stopping to take a leak and say 'hello, nice horsie.'"

Damon said, "Randy Meier in his months on his shift there had never seen anything like this happen before. We think it might be our killer. Interrupted by happenstance and some joy riders on that rural patch. But maybe planning to return."

"Did your Junior G. Man get a description of the truck? A license number?"

"No," Karen said. "It was too dark, and it all happened too quickly."

Doyle shrugged. "So, what are you going to do with this sketchy info?"

"We're going to stake out Rockland College starting tonight. Remember, we haven't had the hint of a lead in this case since the first of these killings. Finally, we've got something to take action on. Maybe we are grabbing at straws," Karen said. "But we've got nothing else to grab at. Do you want to come with us?"

Chapter Fifty-six

The agents collected Jack early that evening outside his condo. He came out carrying a small portable cooler. "Hi, folks. I've provisioned us with a few necessities. Bottled water, some nice Italian subs from my favorite deli around the corner, a thermos of caffeinated coffee, and a can of bug spray." He put the cooler next to him on the backseat.

Damon drove. Dealing with the rush hour traffic, it took them nearly two hours to reach Rockland College where they met their eager informant Randy Meier outside the Large Animal Barn. He was a strong-looking young man, biceps bulging in his cut-off Rockland Athletic Department tee-shirt. He told them where to park and walked them to where he suggested they set up observation posts around the perimeter of the paddock. The only horse in that enclosure was Saint Lester. The tall gray gelding paid them no attention.

"I have to bring Saint Lester back into his stall in the barn right before it gets dark," Meier told them.

Karen said, "Just do what you usually do, Randy. Follow your ordinary routine."

Damon had quickly made a small sketch of the paddock area in his notebook. The first tentative drops of rain splotched it. He'd marked positions in the trees for each of the three of them. "Randy, don't come out to take that horse in for a couple of hours, okay? Just wait in the building and keep your eyes open."

"Yes, sir." Randy jogged away.

"Ah, Damon, sir," Doyle said, "perhaps I should position myself back in the car. Next to the cooler. Guarding the sandwiches and coffee."

Tirabassi didn't bother to reply. He walked to where he had planned to be. Karen said, "C'mon, Jack. Let's get this done."

Shortly after eight-thirty, the rain clouds let loose lightly. Doyle was belly-down on a plastic sheet partly under a dripping blackberry bush, some thirty yards from Karen to his left, Damon to his right. He'd used his cell phone to check his e-mail, the Cubs score (another heart-breaking loss in the ninth inning), the day's racing results from Heartland Downs. Then the rain picked up and there was the sound of distant thunder. "Oh, *great*," he muttered. He pulled his ball cap farther down on his head. Felt raindrops starting to hit his jacket.

At nine thirty, the three of them watched as Randy, wearing a yellow rain poncho, came out from the barn, put a lead rope on Saint Lester's halter, and led him back. Doyle and the agents stood up, stretched, and left their hiding places.

"What now, Damon?" Doyle said.

"I'm thinking that the person Randy saw reconnoitering here yesterday afternoon may well come back. Not for a paddock kill, like that last one over in Michigan, but maybe sneaking into the Large Animal Barn. We know that's been done before. I say we wait here for a couple of hours. Somebody's been here that Randy saw. I got a feeling about this. I think we should stick here. What do you think Karen?"

"As long as we're out here, why not? Jack, you okay with this?"

"What if I weren't? I haven't seen any cabs going by here."

Damon said, "Let's get out of this rain." A few minutes later, Randy Meier joined them in Damon's car, seated in the backseat with Jack. "My shift is through now," he said, "but if it's okay with you I'll hang around for awhile." Doyle offered him the last of the sandwiches, which was gratefully received and rapidly consumed. Between bites, Randy said, "Harry Schwartz, the old guard who replaces me, is already in the barn, probably asleep in the little office. Like usual about this time."

Karen said, "Randy, you didn't tell him we were going to be here tonight, right?"

"No, no." He grinned. "If you think old Harry might be involved, and I can't even imagine that, I didn't give him any heads up. Just like you told me not to do."

Damon turned to look into the backseat, nodding in approval.

It was almost ten when Randy said, "If you don't mind, I've got to bail. And…"

Doyle poked him in the ribs. "Bail. Oh, my young friend, not a word to be using in the presence of law enforcement personnel."

Meier grinned, but Damon snarled, "Cut the humor, Doyle. Go on, Randy. You can leave. Thanks for your help."

"It's just that I've got to be in the football team's weight room at six tomorrow morning."

Karen said, "Understood, Randy. If we get anything out of this, we'll surely let you know."

"Even about, like, that possible reward?"

Damon grunted, "Yes, son, even about that."

Doyle grinned his approval. "Randy, keep your eye on the prize. So long."

"Thanks for your help, Randy," Karen said. "Good luck with your football season."

As Meier opened his door he said, "Can I suggest something? Pull your car over there in that real dark tree-covered spot next to the back fence. You'll be able to see both the north and south barn entrances from there. Even through this rain."

Damon got out and shook the young man's hand. Back behind the wheel, he slowly drove to the spot Meier had recommended.

The rain persisted. Doyle dozed off a couple of times as the hours went by, always to awaken and see the agents intently peering at the barn. Just after one-thirty, Karen suddenly sat forward. "*Did you see that?*"

"See what?" Doyle said.

"Looked like a flash of light on the north side the barn."

"Saw it," Damon said. "Let's go. Karen, take the south door. You've got one of the keys Randy gave us. Jack, come with me to the north door. I've got the key to that one."

Chapter Fifty-seven

Karen entered the barn first from the south side. Opening that door, she startled the napping guard Harry Schwartz who almost fell off his chair. She flashed him her badge. "Quiet," she whispered. "Everything's all right. Just stay right here." She didn't look back as the old fellow struggled to his feet.

Damon keyed open the barn's north door. He hesitated for a moment and pulled out his Glock 22 before entering. Jack yanked his arm. "What are you doing with that weapon? You think some armed maniac is in there?"

Damon brushed aside Doyle's hand. "Standard procedure, Doyle. Bureau's rules in situations like this. Shut up. Let's go in quietly." Damon carefully stepped inside, Jack at his back. Some thirty yards from them down the concrete corridor that led between stalls they saw a slim figure clad in jeans and jeans jacket and dark ball cap pulled down low standing directly in front of Saint Lester's stall.

"Hold it right there," Damon shouted as he ran forward. The invader jumped back from Saint Lester, dropping a syringe onto the concrete floor. Karen sprinted forward from the south door, the old guard Harry stumbling along behind her.

Doyle put his hand on Damon's pistol arm and the agent lowered the weapon as they neared Saint Lester's stall with his visitor before it. Jack stepped forward. He saw a frightened, familiar face.

Well, I'll be damned, Jack thought.

"Well, hello, Esther Ness," he said.

Chapter Fifty-eight

Esther Ness slumped to her knees, head down in her gloved hands. Karen ran up to join them, stopped, and said, "Jack, who is that?"

"None other than Ms. Esther Ness, well-known heiress and animal rights activist."

Karen turned to the half-awake and completely bewildered guard standing behind her. "Harry, please take a break for awhile. Go outside. It's stopped raining. We'll handle this." Harry shuffled away.

Esther finally looked up at her three captors and stopped her brief sobbing. Her face was streaked with tears, but her eyes were defiant. "I'm not sorry about what I did," she said, looking directly at each of them. "You'll never understand that."

Doyle stepped forward, took Esther by her elbows, and gently lifted her to her feet. She shook off his hands.

Damon holstered his Glock. He took latex gloves from his jacket pocket, bent down, and picked up the syringe Esther had dropped. Karen handed him a baggie. Jack watched Esther, head down, trembling, suddenly deflated, being led by Karen to the office at the south end of the barn. He shook his head as if to clear out the conflicting thoughts he had, the joy of discovery, tempered by his surprise at the person discovered. "I never figured Esther for this," Jack said to Damon. "Thought that even if she was involved in this campaign, she'd be too smart to be hands-on."

Jack noticed the broken window on the right wall that allowed Esther to gain entrance to the barn. A trio of observant Holsteins watched him walk past, then residents of a two-sheep pen on one side, a pair of curious Kinder goats on the left. Back at the other end of the barn, as rain now pounded down on the resonating roof, Saint Lester let out a series of loud whinnies as Doyle passed him.

Chapter Fifty-nine

Esther was placed in a chair in front of the guard's desk, Damon seated behind the desk, Karen and Jack on the sides. Damon said, "It was you all along and you all alone, wasn't it? All five previous horse-killing crimes. Will you admit to them here and now? Now that we've caught you trying to add another one to your list?"

Esther sat up straight, eyes blazing. "*You* consider them crimes. I do not. I love horses. Throughout my whole life, they've been what I've gone to in order get relaxation, peace of mind, no matter what was happening to me otherwise." She paused, took a deep breath. "Horses have given me *so* much! But what is being done to defenseless horses in places like this, in these so-called research facilities, *that's* what I consider to be crimes. That's what I wanted to stop!"

"Well, Ms. Ness," Damon said, "that's not what the law says."

There was a rap at the office door. Karen opened it. Harry the guard stood there, hat in hand, with a question. "Can I get off duty now?" Karen nodded before ushering him back out the door. Watching them leave, Doyle said, "With that lazy old dolt on duty, I'm surprised rustlers haven't come in here and emptied the place."

Damon assumed command. "Ms. Ness, stay right where you are. I am going to consult with my colleagues." He motioned Karen and Doyle to follow him out into the corridor.

"Doyle," Damon said angrily, "did you suspect this woman was the killer? I'd like to know right now!"

"Oh, Damon, c'mon, man, loosen that knot in your government shorts. I'll say, yeah, the *thought* of her being involved crossed my mind a couple of times. Tell you the truth, I was more worried about discovering Ingrid McGuire as the perp. A couple of times, when I looked back on it, I thought Ingrid seemed to know maybe a little too much about the killings before we talked about them. I mean, in advance of me saying anything. But I was just plain wrong about Ingrid being involved. For which, may I add, I am grateful."

Doyle walked off a couple of yards toward the mean-looking Kinder goat who produced a loud warning bleat. "Calm down, old fella," Doyle said, patting the animal's broad black nose.

Harry Schwartz suddenly reappeared in the doorway. "I forgot to take my sandwich," the old guard said. "Can I get it from the office?" Damon said, "Go ahead. Don't say anything to the person in there." Schwartz quickly emerged from the office, carrying a grease-stained brown bag. He said, "Don't forget to leave the lights on low like I usually do. "Fine, sir. Thanks for your assistance," Damon said.

Chapter Sixty

They sat in silence for a couple of minutes, Damon writing in his notebook, Karen texting their Bureau office, Jack taking deep breaths. Esther had her head down, hands covering her ears. Doyle thought she appeared to have lost weight since he'd seen her at her farm weeks before. Perhaps her ill-advised campaign had taken that kind of toll on her.

Damon finally said, "You're in a serious jam here, Ms. Ness. Karen, go ahead." Karen read the Miranda rights. Esther listened, then looked up. She said softly, "I have feared this day for months. Even after I became determined to go forward after the first horse death. Obsessed with thinking about all the other horses held captive in these vet schools that needed me."

"Esther," Jack said, "you've got me buffaloed here. Didn't *you* donate a couple of your own horses to these schools? Isn't that right?"

"I made a foolish mistake when I did that. I thought it would be a good, a useful thing. But when I went to visit the horses I'd donated, and saw how they were subjected to these research projects, these indignities, I was repelled. I attempted to retrieve them from those schools. I found that could not be done without a long legal battle because I had signed over ownership to the schools involved."

She paused to look at her three captors, one by one, before saying, "I realized I could not quickly retrieve them, so I decided to put my horses out of their miserable existences. And later," she said forcefully, "others like them. I have no regrets that I did so."

Karen said, "Ms. Ness, surely you must have been aware you were breaking laws."

"*Yes*, laws that cried out to be broken. But as I went along, it got harder and harder for me. I knew I was being hunted. Jack Doyle inadvertently kept me informed about the investigation's progress when he questioned me at my farm. Or lack of progress at that point. But I was aware of the great efforts that were being put into it. And," she said, looking directly at Doyle, "guilt was eating away at me. I knew how determined you were to find me."

Doyle thought about saying to the agents, "That's what I do for you, throw fear into the hearts of wrongdoers," but decided not to.

"And the pressure kept building," Esther said. "I started having nightmares about being caught and sent to prison. So, I made an attempt to throw anyone off my trail. That's why I offered the reward. That was an attempt to divert any possible attention from me. Still, I could feel the pressure building.

"That is why I finally decided that after this one, Saint Lester, I would stop. Permanently. I just couldn't live any longer with that growing pressure." She hesitated before adding, "You probably don't believe me. I wouldn't blame you if you didn't. But I swear to God that's how I felt. I was never going to do it again."

Damon said, "Ms. Ness, we're going to have to take you downtown now. You can call a lawyer now, or in the car, or when we get to our office. Up to you."

Doyle held open the north barn door for this somber group. The rain had finally stopped, and this part of rural Illinois smelled refreshingly clean beneath the star-strewn sky. Karen reached up to flick away a few mosquitoes that were advancing, and Esther Ness nodded a thank you. "You can sit in the front seat with me, Ms. Ness. No handcuffs, just the seatbelt if you would. Let's go."

Jack said, "So, Damon, what'll happen with Ness?"

"How would I know, Jack? She hasn't been even booked yet. Arraignment is the next step, then a bail hearing."

Jack said, "Okay, how about an educated guess. Would this woman be facing prison time?"

"Jack, I don't know what's coming for Ness. I got enough to deal with tonight, wrapping up this arrest."

Chapter Sixty-one

Less than five days later, Esther Ness' fate had been decided. Jack had just returned to his condo from his morning run when he heard his cell phone.

"Karen. What's up?"

"Damon and I want to buy you breakfast. Can you meet us at Petros' in a half-hour?"

"I will not refuse such government largesse," Doyle said. "I'll just wonder about it. You must have an update on Heiress Esther. See you there."

Walking into the restaurant, Doyle saw the agents in the back booth. Darla the waitress said hello, adding that "Petros says to tell you and your friends back there that breakfast is on him today. It's, I don't know, some kind of Greek holiday."

"Well, I'll be damned. Darla, tell Smelly I'll highlight this date on my calendar for his only known generous gesture as long as I've been coming in here." He said good morning to the agents and sat down in the booth across from them. "You have something to report?" The looks on their faces caused him to groan. "Okay," he said "Let's have it."

Damon said, "Jack, this is the way these things go, like it or not. Ms. Millionaire Ness' team of expensive lawyers had several long sessions with a team of federal prosecutors. The result? She agreed to plead guilty to two counts of 'victimless' crime."

"*Victimless?*" Jack said. "*Two counts?* How about those horses besides hers she killed? I can't fucking believe this!"

Karen said, "Jack, that is just the way it worked out. What can I tell you? With Ness' plea bargain, the government avoids the expense of a trial and, in the case of this wealthy woman, probably an appeal if she were to lose the first round. So, Esther goes to federal prison for six months, pays a fifty-thousand-dollar fine, agrees to do five hundred hours of community service upon being freed."

"Well, hell," Doyle said. "That must be some all-star team of lawyers she's got." He leaned back in his seat and turned to look out the window. "The fucking power of money," he said bitterly. "There are black teenagers from Chicago's west side in Joliet Prison for *five years* for selling crack to the wrong carload of eagerly buying white kids from Winnetka and Wilmette. And here's Esther, who caused anguish and expense at all these vet schools, and she sashays into a federal country club?"

Damon said, "I don't like it either, Jack. But that's the way it goes." He got up. Karen followed. Jack sat still for a couple of minutes.

"They say 'money talks and bullshit walks'? Naw," Doyle said, sliding out of his side of the booth, "bullshit and money go hand-in-fucking hand."

It was a sunny morning, one hardly reflective of Doyle's mood as he said good-bye to the agents on the sidewalk outside Petros'. He shook Damon's hand, kissed Karen's cheek. "I know you two did your best. Nothing you could do to change this outcome. What the hell…"

They parted, but Jack stopped walking and turned back. "Hey, Karen! Damon! One question," Jack shouted. "What federal country club is Esther Ness headed for?"

Damon said, "What we heard, Jack, is that Ness is scheduled for that new women's prison in West Virginia."

"Well, too bad," Doyle said. "Too bad they don't have coed prisons. They could have sent Esther up there to Lexford in Wisconsin so she could join forces with Rexroth, that bastard. Both arrogant. Wealthy. Made for each other."

Karen walked up and gave Jack a hug, startling both Jack and the nosey Petros who was peering out his restaurant's front window.

"The system grinds on, and we try to do better, but most often we can't, Jack." She backed off, smiling at him now. "We do our best. Take care now."

He watched as Damon and Karen drove south down Clark Street toward the Loop. It was starting to heat up on this typical Chicago late summer day. He nodded at the inquisitive Petros, went to his car, and drove to Fit City.

In the health club's locker room, Doyle quickly changed into his workout clothes. He put on his gloves and warmed up on the light bag for five minutes, rapping it back and forth in a rhythm he always tried to approximate with that of the jazz drummers in the bebop classics he loved.

Then he slid over to attack the heavy bag. Head down, raining left hooks followed by thumping right crosses, moving his feet left-right, then right-left around the swaying canvas target. He pounded away for nine minutes before stepping back, arms at his sides, breathing heavily, sweat drenched, feeling not a *whole* lot better. But some.

Epilogue

At Moe's invitation, Jack joined him in front row third-base Wrigley Field box seats on a beautiful September afternoon. "I buy these seats every year to use for clients," Moe had said on the phone. "Most of them don't want to accept them anymore for this lousy Cubs team. Meet me on the Addison side around one. We'll catch up."

The old ballpark was barely a third-full in this final month of one of the Cubs' all-time worst seasons. The team was right on pace to lose one hundred games. The announced crowd of some eleven thousand in a facility that often held more than thirty-five thousand was, as usual, comprised primarily of white women and men who were spending more time drinking high-priced beer, flirting, or talking on cell phones than observing the ineptitude of the home team. Most of the few African-Americans or Latinos present were in baseball or vendor uniforms.

Moe said, "My secretary told me this morning that Cub tickets for today's game were selling on e-Bay for a *buck*. These seats we're in cost $142 a pop per game. The average price this year here at Wrigley was $44 for a ticket. Talk about fleecing sheep!"

The Cubs were now owned by members of a wealthy family whose ardently tax-foe patriarch had designated millions of dollars trying to defeat Barack Obama in the presidential election. All this, while attempting to wring tax breaks from the city of Chicago for the renovation of the aged, iconic ball yard. That attempt had failed. Consequently, the new owners raised prices ten percent for the privilege of watching their sparse talent perform depressingly.

Today's Cubs lineup included two players with batting averages falling below the so-called Mendoza Line, infamously named for a major league player whose batting average never topped .200 thus creating the sorry statistical plateau that memorializes him.

Doyle bought beers. He said, "I notice they haven't lowered the concession prices to mirror the quality of the product on the field. My Uncle Owen told me this is the worst Cubs team he's ever seen during all his years as a fan. He fell into that trap as a kid in 1943. Got encouraged when they made the World Series in 1945. He's been waiting for a repeat ever since."

The second inning ended with the Cubs down 3-0. "All we can do here this afternoon, Moesy, is catch a little sun, drink a few beers, and relax."

"Good idea. You've had an interesting summer, Jack. Being the target of an attempt on your life financed by your old enemy Rexroth. Back and forth to Ireland helping to protect Niall Hanratty. Working to stop that rich jerk Pilling from threatening those Burkhardts, the horse owners. And helping nab Esther Ness. Wasn't there a reward offered for the horse killer? Fifty thousand? What happened with that?"

"There was a lot of back and forth about that. Then Esther Ness, who actually put up the money, maybe having tried to distance herself from any suspicion in the investigation, declared it should go to the young man who gave us the tip that led to her apprehension! The guy who helped catch her! Nice young man named Randy Meier, who is back playing football out there for Rockland College, where Esther's criminal campaign came to an end. I don't know if Esther was acting out of guilt, or a sense of responsibility. Who cares? She's got the money to spare."

They got to their feet for the seventh inning stretch. In keeping with recent Wrigley Field tradition, "Take Me Out to the Ballgame" was being rousingly led from the broadcast booth by another in the succession of second- or third-rate celebrities eager to undertake this duty, most of whose voices were almost as far off-key as the Cubs were from first-place.

Two innings later Wrigley Field was alive with cheers. The Cubs had come from behind to win 6-5 with a ninth inning rally. At game's end, the players dashed from the field and dugout to join in a joyous piling-on near home plate. The now diminished crowd roared approvingly when the Cubs finally left the field, arms raised triumphantly.

Doyle said, "Can you believe this, Moe? These guys are actually *celebrating* as they approach the end of one of the worst seasons in Chicago baseball history! They should be scurrying off to the locker room, hanging their heads, covering their faces!"

"Jack, Jack, look around you. These people here are ecstatic. Those five drunks sitting over to the left of us are still hollering 'Cubs win! Cubs win!' It's an amazing slice of Cub mania."

Doyle said, "These saps are like my uncle Owen. What they're doing should be interpreted as a cry for help. Let's get our asses out of this cathedral of the delusional."

On their way to the exit, Moe stopped, looking back at the diamond. "When I was a kid, Fifi Bonadio and I used to sneak into this ballpark. I'm talking years ago. Back then, when the game was over, fans could leave the stands and walk across the diamond to the exit on the right field side under the El tracks. I would always stop on the mound. Stand there on the rubber, wind up, pretend I was pitching for the Cubs. It was a huge thrill for a kid like me. I'll never forget it. They don't let people do that anymore."

"The Cubs might have used your pitching talents in recent years."

Moe said, "Ha ha."

Out on Addison, they wended their way through the souvenir sellers of Cubs tee-shirts, hats, and caps, all doing a brisk business. Moe's driver Pete Dunleavy was standing next to the double-parked Lincoln, chatting with a Chicago Police patrolman. Moe waved at Dunleavy before saying, "Jack, have you ever considered giving up on the Cubs? Becoming a White Sox fan?"

"Not for a second," Doyle said.

To receive a free catalog of Poisoned Pen Press titles, please contact us in one of the following ways:

Phone: 1-800-421-3976
Facsimile: 1-480-949-1707
Email: info@poisonedpenpress.com
Website: www.poisonedpenpress.com

Poisoned Pen Press
6962 E. First Ave. Ste 103
Scottsdale, AZ 85251

CPSIA information can be obtained at www.ICGtesting.com
Printed in the USA
BVOW04*1259081114

373687BV00003B/3/P

9 781464 202742